Also by Sara Cate

Highest Bidder

SARA CATE

sourcebooks
casablanca

Published by Sourcebooks Casablanca, an imprint of Sourcebooks
P.O. Box 4410, Naperville, Illinois 60567-4410
(630) 961-3900
sourcebooks.com

Originally self-published in 2023 by Sara Cate.

Cataloging-in-Publication Data is on file with the Library of Congress.

Printed and bound in the United States of America.
LSC 10 9 8 7 6 5 4 3 2 1

For all the daddy's girls

Author's Note

Warning: This contains spoilers for the first four books in the series.

Welcome back to Salacious Players' Club!

It's been a while since we've stepped foot in the club, so here's a quick refresher on what's been happening with your favorite kinky characters.

Highest Bidder picks up two years after the beginning of *Praise*. Charlotte is now Mrs. Grant, and her ex-beau, Beau, is now in Phoenix, running a club of his own with his new Madame, Maggie.

Our favorite throuple, Drake, Isabel, and Hunter, are now the proud parents of twin girls and almost ready to start trying for a third.

Garrett and Mia are happily married after a fall wedding at the lake last year.

Things have been quiet around the club lately, leading the wealthiest member to find a little trouble of his own...

Trigger Warning

Dear Reader,

As always, this story will have some intense themes I'd like you to be aware of before embarking on this journey with the characters. There is a heavy emphasis on grief, parental loss, as well as child loss. There is also healing, recovery, and remembrance. Rest assured that I would never write the sad parts without the happy parts. Grief and joy coexist.

Much love, my readers.

Enjoy.

Love,
Sara

Prologue

Ronan
Nine years ago

From: Emerson Grant
To: Ronan Kade
Subject: Investment Opportunity

Ronan,

I'm looking to start a new company, and I'd love to meet with you regarding an investment opportunity. I can give you more information during our meeting, but I have reason to believe this would be a fitting addition to your corporate shareholding portfolio, for financial and personal reasons.

Please call me at your earliest convenience.

Hope you're doing well, friend.

I look forward to hearing from you soon.

Emerson Grant

"RONAN, ARE YOU LISTENING TO ME?"

I glance up from my computer screen to see Shannon standing

teary-eyed in the doorway, watching me with anguish on her face. Fuck, I didn't even see her walk in. What an asshole I am.

Just a few moments ago, she tried to tell me it was over between us and rather than facing the truth, I escaped to my office. I told her I needed a moment to think. Instead, I started checking emails, as if anything in my inbox could erase the pain of losing yet another woman I love.

Quickly, I click the monitor off and rise from my seat.

"I'm sorry," I reply as I cross the room to stand in front of her.

"See?" she mumbles, taking my hands in hers. "We'd never make it. You're obsessed with your work and I'm obsessed with you. I have a daughter to look after, Ronan, and she deserves my attention more."

"Bring her to Briar Point." I reply with a desperate plea. "Let me take care of you both. I promise I'll work less."

She squeezes her eyes closed, a tear slipping through and running over her beautiful cheek. I wipe it away, pulling her against my body, wanting to shut out the world and just hold her.

It's been so long since I've loved a woman this much and fallen in such a short amount of time. Shannon came out from Indiana to Briar Point six weeks ago to settle a real estate deal, and we met on a whim. Her two-week trip tripled as we fell hard and fast for each other. But we knew this affair would have to end eventually.

Not even my last wife could steal the heart out of my chest the way Shannon does. But Shannon isn't like the other women I've been with. She doesn't care about the money or the security. All she truly wants is to be by my side, and the best I can give her is a sliver of my time.

I'm a fool.

"I can't," she whispers against my chest. "I need to go home. It's bad enough I've been gone all summer. But Daisy deserves a normal life and a mother who puts her first."

"You know this makes me love you more," I mumble, tilting her face up so I can gaze down at her. Even with her bloodshot blue eyes and blotches of pink on her pale white cheeks from crying, she's still breathtaking. Her love is written across her features, love for me and for her daughter—she's a woman being torn in two.

Unable to hold back, I gather her tightly in my arms, squeezing her against me as if I can avoid the truth: that this whirlwind of a summer must come to an end and when Shannon leaves for good, I'll be alone again.

Anguish and desperation are building inside me, and I feel the need to make it right. To fix it. To throw money at the pain in hopes that it somehow disappears. Gently, I pull away. "Let me give you something."

She shakes her head with her eyes shut tight. "No, Ronan. Please. I don't want your money."

"I can't stand the thought of you wanting or needing anything, Shannon. Please," I plead.

She opens her eyes, tears still streaming as she forces a sad smile onto her face. She takes my hands in hers again, squeezing tight, and the words that come out of her mouth obliterate me. "No, Ronan. I love you for free."

I'm frozen in place, staring down at what I know is the last real love I'll feel in this lifetime. What kind of fool lets something like this go? But what match am I for her daughter? I know the weight of that love. The willingness to sacrifice whatever it takes. A love so rich you'd willingly drown in it.

With that, I get an idea.

"Then, let me give *her* something," I say in desperation.

"Ronan…"

I'm already moving to my desk, grabbing my checkbook from the top drawer. "Please, Shannon. If you won't take it for yourself, take it for her. So I know you understand that she is just as important to me as you are. So she never has to want for anything. So she knows she's worth it. Do this for your daughter, Shannon." I look up at her with a pleading expression. "I know a parent's love."

There's a hint of sympathy in her eyes as she takes the check from my fingers, her gaze slowly trailing down to the number written on the paper. When they go wide, I know she's about to argue.

"It's too much—"

"I'll have my financial advisor call you. He can put it into an account for her, so it accrues interest. By the time she starts college, you won't have to pay a dime. You'll be able to relax, knowing she's taken care of."

When her eyes drift back up toward mine, I see the softness in her expression. In the next breath, she's in my arms again. I'm breathing in the scent of her shampoo and memorizing the way she fits in my arms, tucked just under my chin.

I mumble into her hair, "You were never just a fling to me. You know that, right?"

When she nods, I hear the tiny yelp of a sob escape her lips. I want to try and convince her to stay again. I wish I had the guts to throw all of this away for her. Sell the company and my properties, give away all of my money, just to give her and her daughter the normal lives they deserve.

But I'm too afraid that my pain will seep back in and ruin it all. Without work to bury myself in, what is left of me?

Shannon and her daughter deserve better.

"Let me drive you to the airport," I whisper, but she shakes her head.

"No. I can't stand to drag this out any more than it already is. I have to go, Ronan."

When she pulls herself out of my arms, it feels like another stab to the chest. Another loss. Another woman slipping through my fingers. It's like living that same tragic day over and over and over again.

I can't watch her leave.

Instead, I turn and face the window overlooking the city below, then hear the sound of the front door closing, like the ring of a gunshot that nearly kills me.

Just like that, she's gone.

And I'm alone.

The pain is sharp and unyielding, so instead of feeling it, I sit down at my desk and turn the monitor back on, the email from Emerson still open on the screen.

Without another thought, I click Reply.

From: Ronan Kade
To: Emerson Grant
Subject: Re: Investment Opportunity

Emerson,

Let's meet at your earliest convenience. I'm very interested in hearing about your new company, and my schedule is wide-open.

Sincerely,
Ronan Kade

Rule #1: Put your money where your mouth is.

Daisy

"THE PRETTY BLOND WITH THE BIG EYELASHES," I CALL, DROPPING my drink tray on the bar and catching Geo's attention as he pours a pint of beer. His eyes squint as he surveys the crowd of people near the stage.

"You think so?" he replies with a laugh.

"Yes, I do. I've figured him out. He never bids on the first girls, and he's had a thing for blonds over thirty lately," I say with confidence, loading martinis onto my drink tray.

With a shrug, he nods. "I'm going with the Shibari instructor."

"Shibari instructor?" I reply with astonishment. "No way. She's much too dominant for him."

"Maybe he wants to change things up."

"Geo, the man is fifty-six. I doubt he wants to change anything up at this point."

As he sets another espresso martini on my tray, he gives me a smug expression. "You have a lot to learn around here, Daisy."

I've been working at Salacious for the past three months, and I have to admit—I did not see drink server at a sex club at twenty-one on my vision board when I was growing up. It just sort of…happened. And although I haven't explored much, I have to confess, this place is not what I expected. Granted, I haven't peeked behind any black curtains, but all that matters to me is that the owners are kind, the management is fair, and I make enough to live off of.

It's not like some sleazy strip club or gross members' lounge. No one tries to grab my ass or catcall me as I walk by. The owners do a pretty good job of making sure things stay respectful.

And it provides some of the best people watching on the planet. When I was a kid, my mother would sometimes take me to the mall and we'd get ice cream and just watch the shoppers go by, making up ridiculous stories about them for fun. Well, now I do that in a sex club, and it's a hundred times better.

On a good night, I can string together a few song lyrics out of a single shift of people watching, humming the made-up tune as I work.

Making auction night bets with the sexy, dark-haired bartender has been a fun perk of the job too. Geo and I start every Thursday night by checking out the guys and girls that are signed up to get onstage. Then we make our wagers for which one is most likely to garner the highest bids from the club's wealthiest member.

So far, I'm undefeated.

Shaking my head at Geo, I carry the tray full of drinks over to the high-top table, placing them on the surface with a polite smile.

On my way back, I catch sight of Mr. Kade himself, the richest member of them all, strutting in through the front entrance toward his regular spot at the back. You can't miss him with that head full of silver hair and exquisite style. I may not be into older guys, but I understand how a man like him is so popular with the women here.

He's in tight black pants and a white shirt with the top two buttons undone. His eyes don't shift much as he walks. I've noticed that about him. A normal person would scan the room as they enter, but not him. He just waltzes straight to his table, glancing back at Geo and giving him a curt wave as if to signal his need for a drink.

I must be staring at him for a moment too long because Geo notices.

"You sure have been watching Mr. Kade a lot." Geo shoots me a wink as he starts on Ronan's bourbon neat.

I screw up my face at his insinuation that my interest in Ronan Kade is anything sexual. "Not like that."

He laughs. "What? You're not into older guys?"

I lean closer. "No, and neither are any of those girls. We all know they're only into him for the diamonds and breast implants."

As soon as the words leave my lips, sounding harsher than I like, I wince. That didn't sound like me at all. I'm not that girl.

Then again, I haven't recognized myself in a while.

My eyes cast downward as I chew on my lip, my fingers moving to fiddle with my mother's clover charm necklace hanging around my neck.

The truth is that I do watch Ronan a lot.

"Ronan's not like that," Geo replies with a chuckle. "Believe it or not."

"If you say so," I reply, faking a smile. "I just can't imagine any straight male billionaire on earth that wouldn't use his riches to entice beautiful, young women into his bed."

"Sounds to me like you need to see for yourself."

If only Geo knew the truth. I'm not scrutinizing Ronan out of judgment. And it's not out of romantic interest either. It's out of pure curiosity…well, that and to solve a little mystery of my own.

"Still betting on the busty blond?" Geo asks as he places the bourbon on the tray. I glance over at the beautiful woman currently greeting Ronan with a simmering smile. There's something about the way he's giving her his attention tonight that's making me think he's about to go big. I can't say how I know, but it's just a feeling.

"One hundred percent," I reply.

Geo chuckles to himself. "Are you willing to put your money where your mouth is?"

I furrow my brow at him. "Very funny. You know I don't have any money."

With that, I take the bourbon neat over to where Ronan is sitting. The blond walks away just as I arrive.

"Evening, Mr. Kade," I say sweetly, without making eye contact, as I set his drink down in front of him.

"Thank you, Daisy," he replies, using my name like he knows me, which he doesn't.

Like every other night when I serve him his drinks, I let my eyes cascade over him for just a moment, noticing the gentle crow's feet around his eyes and the salt-and-pepper coloration of his hair. Then I stare at his face, really taking in his expression. He seems a little less cordial tonight, his eyes fixed on the stage. He looks determined, as if he's ready for the auction to start already.

When I return to the bar, I'm feeling a little more confident than before. "Okay…what are we playing for tonight?" I ask Geo.

He chuckles. "You sound confident."

I glance back over at Ronan. He's still staring at the stage. He's definitely in the mood to win tonight. I bet he's had a rough day at work and doesn't want to bother with flirting or having to get a date the regular way, so he's playing to win.

"Loser has to mop," he replies, while wiping down the bar.

"That's it?"

"Have something better in mind?"

"Winner gets to pick the bar tomorrow night, and the loser has to buy the first round."

He screws up his face in anguish. "You're going to pick the piano bar down the street, aren't you?"

With one sweet smile from me, he has his answer. Geo immediately rolls his eyes. "Ugh, fine."

I beam triumphantly, already looking forward to the cheesy Billy Joel covers.

Then, his expression shifts into something contemplative. After cleaning the glass in his hand, he shelves it and looks up at me. "Actually, I have a better deal."

"Oh yeah? What is it?"

"Okay, if he wins the blond, I'll take you to that piano bar. But if he doesn't pick the blond, then I win, and you have to get up there."

He nods toward the stage, and I spin around to see what he's referring to. The auction is just about to start, but there aren't any girls onstage yet. The crowd of bidders is growing, though, like it usually does on Thursday nights.

"What? Onstage?"

"On the auction block, Daisy."

My face falls. He's not serious. "Me?"

"Yes, you."

I lean over the bar to get closer to him. "Are you crazy, Geo? I'm not getting up there!"

"Why not, Miss Judgmental? I think it might be good for you to gain some perspective."

"I'm not judgmental," I argue. "I was just kidding. There's no way I can get on that stage."

"So, no deal, then?" he asks in a mocking tone.

I glance at the stage, then back at my friend. Then I let my eyes trail over to Ronan, who's already almost done with his bourbon, which he normally takes longer to drink.

At this point, it's not even about wanting to go to that piano bar. It's more a matter of pride. I've never lost a bet where Ronan Kade is concerned and I don't plan on it now. With this past year being one bad decision after another, I need this win. If for nothing else than to prove to myself that I know a good call when I see one.

I won't end up on that auction block. I'll be singing "Piano Man" twenty-four hours from now.

"Fine," I snap. "Deal." I thrust out my hand and Geo grins wickedly as he shakes it.

Then, I turn on my heel and belt out, "Sing us a song, you're the piano man," as I carry another tray of drinks out to the floor. Geo laughs loudly behind me, and I catch Ronan's curious gaze as I go. I square my shoulders and try to look more confident than I feel. Inside, I'm shaking because I can't help but wonder if I just made one dangerous deal.

Rule #2: Avoid being predictable.

Ronan

THE LITTLE REMAINING BOURBON IN MY GLASS SWIRLS SLOWLY AS I turn it, the soft yet smoky aroma hitting my nose as I watch the crowd bustle around me. It's a lively night at the club, as auction nights often are. The ostentatious show of wealth, the promise of sex, the potential of what one winning bid might bring. It's easily my favorite night at Salacious.

I almost didn't come in tonight. It's been a hell of a day. I couldn't sleep last night, couldn't focus on work today, and couldn't muster the energy or the desire for sex if I tried.

Of course, death anniversaries will do that to you, though. They're like evil little reminders dwelling on your calendar, not to be celebrated but impossible to ignore. Even after twenty-eight years.

I toss back the remaining sip in my glass just as the waitress passes by.

"Another, Mr. Kade?" she asks with an innocent-looking smile.

"Yes, please, Daisy."

With a gentle nod of her head, she takes my empty glass and walks away. This girl showed up at the club after the holidays, and I find her strangely intriguing. She's young and far too angelic-looking to be a drink server at a sex club.

I have a keen enough eye to notice the way I intrigue her too. The way her gaze always seems to find its way to me, especially on Thursday nights. To her, I'm an enigma, someone to gawk at, to marvel, to internally question, but never to approach or speak to.

I get this reaction with a lot of people—mostly people who think I'm nothing more than a callous CEO or an arrogant Dom. And maybe that's true, but I know how much I like to be surprised by the people I meet. I only wish the same opportunity was afforded to me.

Just as Daisy brings back my bourbon, this one heavily poured, I direct a curious brow in her direction.

"Happy bidding," she croons with a sugary grin.

"Thanks," I mutter before bringing the drink to my lips. No point in telling her I *won't* be doing any bidding tonight.

Just then, the auction starts with a few familiar faces, men and women who grace the stage nearly every week. I know from experience that many of them will make every penny paid for their time worth it. Not that sex is mandatory in this situation. They're simply offering up an hour, whether it be for drinks at the bar or in a private—*or less than private*—room.

It's the eager and audacious attitudes toward sex that I appreciate anyway, which means I haven't won the time of any willing participants that I didn't enjoy.

When the beautiful woman with shoulder-length blond curls takes the stage, looking a little more nervous than the others, I wish I were in the mood to entertain company tonight. She looks like the kind of woman who could hold a good conversation— before we fuck like animals, naturally.

There are two men at the back of the room volleying their

bids back and forth, and I'm pleased to see her date going for over ten grand. She looks quite pleased with herself too.

Just as the bidding gets heated, I feel Daisy saddle up to my side. I do a double take, at first, wondering if she's already here to refill my glass, but then I notice she's wearing an anxious expression.

"Aren't you going to bid on her?"

My brows pinch together as I gaze up at her in confusion. What on earth is Daisy so worried about?

"Is there some reason I should?" I ask skeptically.

Daisy has her bottom lip pinched between her teeth and she's rubbing her fingers anxiously over the silver charm of her necklace.

"No reason," she stammers. "Just curious. She...seems like your type, is all."

This time my eyes widen as I completely turn my body in her direction. "She seems like *my type*? Do tell, what exactly is my type, Daisy?"

Now, I'm amused. This is by far the most words Daisy has ever uttered to me, and I can't help but wonder if the woman currently onstage has put the young waitress up to this, doing her best to coax my bidding hand.

The auction proceeds while I'm staring at Daisy in curiosity. She looks almost pale as she watches the auctioneer—who's really just the resident emcee that Garrett has hired to run these events. I'm still waiting for Daisy's response to my question as the announcer calls out, "Sold to the man in the back for fifteen thousand!"

Daisy's eyes are wide as saucers now, and before I can ask what the hell is going on, she scurries off like a frightened field mouse.

Meanwhile, the blond is beaming down at the gentleman who walks up to the stage and takes her sweetly by the hand, leading her to the empty chair next to his. She looks pleased with how that turned out, and I smile to myself as I bring the bourbon to my lips, realizing that the club seems to have done its trick tonight. For the first time today, I'm not in pain, and it's a welcome relief.

But as the next player takes the stage, this time a handsome sub, who I've heard likes a lot of pain, I realize I can't get my mind off of Daisy. Standing from my seat as the bidding begins, I find Geo at the bar.

"Hey, where did Daisy go?" I ask.

Geo is pouring a glass of wine as his cheeks stretch into a toothy grin. "My guess would be halfway to Sacramento by now."

"What?"

He laughs as he sets down the drink in front of the waiting woman. "She lost a bet and she's probably hiding so I don't make her pay up."

My brows pinch together as I stroke my hand over my beard. "Did this bet happen to have anything to do with me?"

Geo's smile grows more mischievous. "Maybe."

With a shake of my head, I level a stern glare at him before returning to my seat. This explains Daisy's peculiar behavior. I'm sure if I were working every auction night at the club, I'd find ways to make it interesting too.

When Eden takes the stage a few minutes later, I catch sight of Daisy nearly spilling a tray of martinis due to the shake in her hands. I don't know what her wager was, but by the looks of it, she's not too eager to settle up.

The bidding war for Eden goes down between a lot of patrons, as it usually does. It doesn't take long before half of them are priced out and she's standing onstage proudly, while a man and a woman go to war for her, costing them somewhere in the six digits. For most of these people, that's equivalent to twenty bucks in their bank accounts, but as I watch my best and oldest friend see just how badly these people want to spend one sexy, fuck-filled hour with her, it makes me really fucking happy.

She deserves this.

The woman ends up on top—with the bids, I mean. And

Eden wears an enthusiastic expression as she slinks off the stage and nearly drags the woman toward the stairs.

And I figure my night is over. Not a total loss for an evening at the club. I could have spent the last two hours of my night in much worse ways, so I toss back the rest of my drink and start to rise.

But that's where the night takes a turn.

Just after the announcer starts to thank everyone for coming and declares an end to the auction, a voice bellows from the bar.

"Actually, we have one more!"

The announcer smiles at Geo from the stage. "Is our bartender joining us on the auction block tonight?" he says excitedly.

Geo snickers. "Oh, not me." Then, I watch as he points directly at Daisy, and every pair of eyes in the room shift, landing on her. "Our drink server Daisy will be auctioning off a one-hour date for tonight!"

The emcee looks straight at her. "Daisy? What a treat. Would you care to join us onstage?"

Her smile is forced as she meanders awkwardly up to the stage. I have to pinch my bottom lip between my teeth to keep from smiling like an idiot as I watch her take her place, front and center.

This answers my question. Daisy lost a bet, and it's time for her to pay up.

When she's standing under the lights, highlighting her nearly white-blond hair and petite stature, I find myself suddenly admiring her for the first time.

She's a cute little thing. Long wavy blond hair that she always keeps braided down one side. Stunning sky-blue eyes and a button nose. But she's young—*too young*.

Not that I have a problem dating women younger than me. I'm at the tail end of fifty-six. I don't have a preference either way, but a woman as young as Daisy wouldn't be interested in a man of my years, at least not for the right reasons.

I've learned that lesson the hard way.

She's standing in the middle of the stage next to the emcee in her tight little server skirt and black top with red heels. She's holding her hands clasped together in front of her, looking way out of her comfort zone. I almost feel bad for her.

After an awkward introduction and some goading from Geo at the bar, they start the bidding, and I have every intention of only being a spectator. A couple people I know end up getting it going.

I find myself scrutinizing the people placing bids—low bids, if you ask me. One is a lawyer in his thirties, another, a younger guy I've spotted in the voyeur hall a lot, and then a new guy I've never seen here before. I shift in my seat.

I trust Emerson and the rest of the team to vet their members harshly, but there's something about seeing a new face at the club that gives me pause. He looks like something the stock market spit out. Cocky expression. Cheap suit. Big attitude. And I can't help myself.

"Fifteen," I call. I figure it's my fault she's up there in the first place. The least I can do is save her from the misery of having to spend an hour with one of these guys.

Daisy's eyes land on my face with her eyes wide as saucers.

"Ronan Kade bids fifteen thousand," the announcer exclaims. "Do we have a challenger? Can I get sixteen?"

"Twenty," the new guy returns. The other two stay silent.

My spine stiffens when I watch his eyes cascade over Daisy. He's sure as hell not looking at her face. And something about him just gives me a bad feeling.

"Twenty-five," I say with certainty.

This time, the kid in the suit turns to glare at me, adjusting the tie around his neck, clearly uncomfortable. As our eyes meet, I watch the fight in his expression die. He's not going to outbid me, and he knows it. So it's all a matter of how much he's willing to risk and how badly he wants to get this fear-stricken girl alone.

But I promise, I'm ready to gamble more.

Pressing my shoulders back, I wait for his next bid.

"Do I hear twenty-six from the young gentleman up front?"

He swallows, then turns toward the stage. Daisy is starting to look a little green as she waits for the next move. Hesitantly, he raises a hand.

"Twenty-six!"

All eyes are on me as I nod to the announcer. "Thirty."

Daisy bites her lip.

My competitor laughs, looking cocky.

"Forty thousand," he calls out, trying to appear brave.

"Fifty," I say, without even blinking.

The young guy comes back with another bid, and another, and another. I outbid each one until he nervously stammers, "Seventy-five."

"One hundred thousand dollars," I proclaim, my fingers thrumming against the leather of the chair.

There are stirrings of surprise in the crowd. Daisy's already pale skin takes on a new shade of porcelain, like the keys of a shiny new piano.

"One hundred, going once...going twice..."

Her eyes dance back and forth between me and the young guy.

"One hundred thousand to Ronan Kade!" the emcee announces, and Daisy looks about ready to faint.

I watch the young guy's jaw click as he clenches it in frustration. The crowd cheers, staring at me in fascination as Daisy makes her way down from the stage, meekly walking in my direction, but then pauses when she reaches me.

I stand, putting out a hand, in which she places her delicate fingers. Her eyes don't leave my face as she gazes at me with intrigue. Within moments, the crowd disperses and loses interest. So it's now just me and a nervous-looking waitress.

"Are you all right?" I ask. There's a tremble in her hand.

"Yeah," she replies unconvincingly. Then she starts to shuffle her feet, looking around at the busy room.

"I have to finish my shift, but if you plan on sticking around for a while…" she says as her eyes cascade toward the bar.

A part of me wants to consider taking the date. I could escort her upstairs to my private room, get to know her a little better, maybe prove to her that I'm not, in fact, too old, too rich, or too boring. But something holds me back. That old voice in my head that sees her as potential for heartbreak more than anything else.

So I touch her gently on the arm. "Actually, Daisy. Do you mind if I get a rain check on that date?"

Her mouth forms a small O as she turns to gaze up at me. "Of course."

"I look forward to it," I reply with a smirk, although I have no intention of cashing in on that rain check. "Have a lovely evening, Daisy."

"Um…good night, Ronan."

With that, I walk toward the exit alone and find my driver out front waiting for me. As I climb into the back seat, I realize that I never found out what exactly Daisy wagered when she lost that bet. But I make it a point to ask her another time. The last thing I want to be is predictable.

Rule #3: Those who live in run-down vans shouldn't judge others.

Daisy

MY BREATH COMES OUT IN FOGGY PUFFS AS I SCROLL THROUGH various apps on my phone. There are three layers of socks on my feet, but no matter how much I rub them together, they still have a chill that goes down to the bone. My tiny little space heater does a nice job of heating up the van, but it smells like burnt hair and I'm too scared to sleep with it on, so I'm curled up under three blankets instead. I wish I could sleep, but I can't shake the nip in the air.

Plus, I'm too busy reliving my strange encounter with Ronan Kade. I've barely spoken ten whole words to the man in the past three months, even though I see him nearly every night.

Then, tonight, he randomly bids a hundred grand on a date with me...that he doesn't cash in on.

Why?

I mean, maybe he did actually want a rain check? Maybe he wasn't in the mood or wasn't feeling well. So then why bid at all? None of it makes sense. Even Geo was thrown off by Ronan's behavior.

In some weird way, I feel like I've earned some bragging rights from this. For just a few minutes up on that stage, I had the attention of the richest man in Briar Point. And yes, I looked him up online. He's worth 1.5 billion dollars.

He's not just rich—he's *filthy* rich.

And he bid on me in an auction. I probably shouldn't feel special. I've watched him do the same with dozens of girls, but it still felt nice.

I mean…I didn't really want the date anyway. If Ronan Kade were about thirty years younger, I would have been all over it. I've seen pics of him in his twenties. He was seriously gorgeous, but no matter how well he's aged, it doesn't change the fact that there are three and a half decades between us. He's still handsome…but I just can't seem to convince my sex drive to see him as anything other than a dashing silver fox.

Suddenly, I find myself laughing out loud like a crazy person. Because here I am…sleeping in my van and judging a billion-dollar man for not being young enough for me.

Daisy…you're an idiot.

If I were smart, I would have thrown myself at that man. I had the perfect opportunity to do just that, but I blew it.

A smart girl would have used tonight to get close to him. Perhaps even slept with him to get the answers I want. I mean… sleeping with Ronan Kade is hardly a sacrifice. I'm sure plenty of women do it for free.

But I'm not all that smart, or sexy, or cunning.

The truth of the matter is that I have a savings account with over a million dollars in it, issued to me nine years ago by a man named Ronan Kade, who before three months ago, I had never met.

So yeah, I might be willing to trade sex for that information if it came down to it.

All I know is that when my mother passed away three years ago, there was a folder in her files with some lengthy paperwork and a high-yield savings account in a bank in Briar Point, California, listing me as the beneficiary.

My mother, as amazing as she was, failed to tell me the reason this complete stranger left me with enough money and compounding interest to get me through college. And I won't touch it until I know why.

Which is why I have gone to great, slightly unhinged lengths to figure it out—including some minor stalking, moving across the country, getting a job where I know he goes, and slowly studying him over the course of three months.

Is it the most deranged thing I've ever done? By far.

Do I have anything better to do with my time? Sadly, no.

Until I figure all of this out, I'm not using that money for music school or a fresh start. I need to know why it's there before I touch it.

After placing my phone on the shelf next to my bed, I roll onto my opposite side. The thought of my mother feels like picking at a wound that refuses to heal, so I attempt to brush the thought away. This always seems to happen. It's like a cruel game of six degrees of separation. Thinking about work makes me think of Ronan, which makes me think of the account, which makes me think of my mother, which immediately makes me think of her grisly and torturous death.

It seems every thought leads to this point eventually.

I have a hard enough time sleeping as it is. Once I get going, thinking about her in that bed, sunken, pale, and struggling to breathe her last breath, it's all downhill from there. And I know sleep will never come.

There I go again...my brain replaying the whole thing, even though I explicitly begged it not to.

I was eighteen when my mother died—which is a terrible age to lose a parent, not that any of them are all that great. But being thrust into adulthood, both literally and figuratively, is bad enough on its own, but carrying the weight of grief on top of that is completely unfair.

I had nothing when my mother died. In the figurative sense, I mean.

So I coasted for three years in a home that reeked of her absence, and soon that home turned into a prison. Until one day late last year, I was going through her paperwork in search of something the insurance company wanted, but instead of finding it, I found a bank statement from when I was twelve with the name of a man I had never heard of before.

To say I became obsessed would be an understatement. My life revolved around this mystery and still does.

There were a few things I ruled out immediately.

First, I asked my dad if he knew a Ronan Kade in Briar Point, and he said no.

Second, and this one is a relief, Ronan and I are not in any way related. He's not my long-lost grandfather or secret daddy. Thanks to my dad's strong biological genes, I look just like him, so that's a saving grace I didn't ever think I needed.

And Ronan is old but not old enough to be my grandfather, so that's ruled out.

My first observation was that Ronan Kade didn't know me. I worked at the club, my name tag in full view, and not once did he say, "Hey, aren't you that kid I gave a million dollars to almost a decade ago?"

Not once.

So whatever the reason, I'm clearly a mystery to him as much as he is to me.

Which leads me to my last two theories.

One, that I won some random Ronan Kade lottery for a hefty sum that neither of my parents chose to tell me about. Doubtful.

Or two...it has to do with my mother.

My parents split when I was twelve, and that first summer, as a child of divorce, I spent it with my dad. My mom went on a work trip to Briar Point. This much I was able to find out thanks to social media, but that's all I have. I know she was here and from what I can tell, she stayed longer than she was supposed to.

Did my mother have an affair with Ronan Kade?

This seemingly impossible scenario still doesn't quite explain why he would leave me so much money. And yes, I admit, I could just ask him, but I don't think I'm ready to know the answer to that question just yet. It's like a vault I'm too afraid to open.

So here I sit in a renovated camper van I purchased with the money I got from selling the house, and I call it freedom.

Freedom from that house with all of its memories.

Freedom from all the empty spaces my mother should be filling but isn't.

Freedom from the suffocating weight of disappointment, mostly in myself.

I could have driven this van anywhere. Woken up on the beach or at the base of a mountain range. Instead, I drove straight to Briar Point because I knew he was here. I got a job at Salacious because I stalked him just enough to know he'd be there. Now, I'm sleeping in public parks and, on occasion, Geo's couch, until I get the answers I need to move on—or the guts to ask those questions.

And as for the money, until I know why it's there, I'm not touching it.

I call it freedom, but even I know that's a lie. I simply traded one prison for another.

I'm supposed to be writing my own songs. I'm supposed to be filling my book with deep and thoughtful lyrics, in search of life's purpose.

None of it is really going as planned.

My phone lights up from the cluttered shelf next to my uncomfortable foam bed. Turning over, I grab it and read a text from Geo.

> Do you realize that you lost your bet and then won a date with Ronan Kade?
> Who gets that lucky?

I roll my eyes at his message. With a chuckle, I reply.

There's no date. I doubt he'll ever talk to me again.
Besides, he's way too old for me.
Age is just a number.
Yeah, and fifty-six is a big number.
I'm not sure my dad would be too fond of me bringing home
a guy older than him!
LOL
I would love to see the look on his face.
Please invite me when you do.
It's not happening. I'm not going on that date.
Sure.
You know you get a cut of that money, right?

I sit up so fast, I knock my head on the shelf over my bed. "Ouch, fuck!" I squeal, holding my forehead as I read his text again.

What?! How much?
Twenty percent.

"Holy shit!"
Quick, what's twenty percent of a hundred thousand?
"Ten percent is...ten thousand...oh my God. Twenty thousand dollars?"

You're freaking out, aren't you?
Are you saying I'm going to get twenty thousand dollars on
my next check?
Yep.
OMG. Geo!
When is the next auction night?
Easy, Pretty Woman.
I am nothing like Julia Roberts. She relied on a rich man to
save her. I think I just saved myself.
With money from a rich man.

Semantics.
I hope you're not **parked anywhere dangerous** tonight.
The couch is open **if you don't want to be homeless.**
Is your boy toy there?
Not tonight. He's **working.**
*You mean with his **girlfriend**?*
You're being mean **tonight. The money** has changed you.

I giggle to myself. The pit of anxiety in my stomach is gone, and it's been replaced with excitement. I can't believe I just made twenty thousand dollars.

Thanks, Geo, but I'm good tonight. Parked down by the beach, in that family campground. I'll stay over tomorrow night. Promise.
Okay, babe. I'm **glad to hear that. You need** to take care of yourself. Get some **sleep. Night.**
Night.

When I put the **phone back on** the shelf, I feel a little bad again. I lied about **staying at the family** campground. I'm in a city parking lot downtown, **close to the club.** For some reason, I think that if I lie about **how great my life is,** then I'm somehow manipulating it to be better, **but it's not. It's** still the same disappointing mess it's always been.

Rule #4: You can't kidnap young women living in their vans— even with good intentions.

Ronan

"THANK YOU, AGATHA. IT WAS DELICIOUS," I SAY, SETTING MY fork on the plate and leaning back in my chair as my housekeeper comes over to clear it from the table.

"I'm glad you liked it, Mr. Kade." When she scoops up my plate and silverware, I catch a glimpse of her watch and grimace at the reminder that it's well after midnight.

"I really wish you wouldn't insist on staying so late. I'm perfectly capable of heating up my own dinner."

She laughs on her way to the kitchen. "Oh, I like the late hours. The boys are all grown and out of the house. It gets lonely there by myself."

"Make sure Tyson walks you to your car."

"Of course, Mr. Kade."

She cleans the dishes in the sink, the gentle sound of her ministrations calming my nerves as I swirl the bourbon in my glass and stare out the giant window overlooking the city. When she leaves, it will be too quiet.

I think she must know that I find comfort in hearing her work because she busies herself for longer than she needs to, wiping down counters, sweeping the floor, preparing my morning coffee so it will start brewing by seven.

"See you tomorrow, Mr. Kade," she calls from the entryway.

"Night, Agatha. Drive safe, please."

"I will. I promise."

I hear the sound of her keys as she picks them up off the center table by the door.

"Oh, Mr. Kade," she calls toward me, and I turn to her expectantly. "Eric wanted me to remind you about his benefit for the organization tomorrow."

"At the harbor?" I ask.

"Yes, sir."

"Perfect. Tell him I'll be there."

"Thank you so much, Mr. Kade." With that, I hear her shuffling out with her coat and bags, always trying to juggle so much at once.

When the door closes, the apartment is bathed in silence.

It's deafening.

There's something weird about silence, as if it holds me hostage. It won't let me move. Won't let me put on music or the TV. And it certainly won't let me sleep. Instead, it forces me to be alone with my thoughts. Cruel, cruel silence.

But at least tonight, my thoughts are filled with a sweet face. Round, blue eyes and blushing red cheeks. I can't get the nervous look Daisy wore up on that stage out of my head.

After I left the club, I came straight home. Agatha was here, my meal prepared and waiting for me. And she can tell me she waited up for me because she doesn't like the silence, but I know the real reason. Agatha knows what today is. She was waiting for me to get home because there is no one else to.

It's kind, but I wish it weren't my widowed housekeeper.

I should have taken Daisy on a date. It makes me feel pathetic to admit it, but I should have. Even if for no other reason than one night of company.

One night that could potentially become a month or a year. Until it starts to feel like she loves the luxury I provide a little too much. Then it will inevitably end—painfully.

But hope, that stubborn fungus that seems to grow wherever it can, has me thinking that maybe it wouldn't.

No, stop. Don't go down that road.

I suppose I should get some sleep, but I can't seem to force my mind to quiet enough to relax, so I don't even bother trying. Instead, I grab my phone off the table and my jacket off the hook as I head toward the front door. After stepping into the empty elevator, I press the main floor button instead of the garage. Sometimes I go for drives at night to relax, but other nights, I enjoy a quiet stroll around the city. Tonight is one of those kinds of nights.

The cold air bites at my neck, so I button my jacket as I pass through the door of the lobby. It seems we have one last cold snap before spring quickly becomes summer.

"Need me to call you a ride, Mr. Kade?" the doorman asks.

"No thanks, Tyson. Going to enjoy a midnight stroll instead."

"Enjoy, sir."

It's quiet, but not the same quiet as my apartment. In there, it's loneliness, but out here, the sounds are like a melody—peaceful and harmonic. Cars driving by, crosswalk signals, music in the distance.

The streets are relatively safe in this part of town. Upscale apartments and boutique-style businesses line the streets.

A few blocks down, there's a bar. The distant sound of voices echo through the empty streets. It's a comforting sign of life, night owls having their fun while the rest of the world is sleeping. I've always loved the nightlife—not that I go to bars like that anymore.

In my younger days, I would. After my world fell apart, I took comfort in binge drinking and casual sex to distract me and blur reality, so I didn't have to feel the excruciating things I didn't want to feel.

That was all before I discovered the lifestyle, which sort of happened by accident. I was in my thirties, wasting my life away on a vicious cycle of money and sex, when I started sleeping with a woman who had a taste for being tied up and submitting her body to me. That was when I discovered that I, too, had certain tastes—a taste for pleasure and domination.

So I started to seek out more women who had similar cravings.

Soon, it became less about sex and numbing the pain and more about focusing my attention on something that actually made me feel useful and needed. I found my purpose again.

Then, nine years ago, the Salacious app launched and for the first time in nearly twenty years, I had a semblance of a family again. Friends, like Emerson and Eden, didn't make me feel so different for what I liked in the bedroom. They gave me a place to truly be myself, without judgment or ridicule. I had almost forgotten how fulfilling a family like that could be.

Deep in contemplation, I continue my walk. Instead of staying straight and heading toward the bar, I turn to the left, approaching a city park after a couple more blocks. Across the street is a gas station that stays open late. The owner's name is Sherie, and her husband died last May, so I try to stop in more often to see how things are going.

Sherie is behind the counter when I walk in, the doorbell chiming and alerting her of my presence. She looks up from her book and smiles at me with a warm greeting.

"Ronan," she says with a tilt of her head. "Out late again?"

"Can't sleep," I reply groggily.

"You can never sleep."

"It's true. How are you holding up here?" I take a quick look around the store. It's in good shape. Nothing that seems to be in dire need of repair.

"Everything is good. Business is great this time of year," she says. "But I'm not ready for spring break. It'll be so busy."

With a chuckle, I nod. "I'm sure it will. You'll let me know if there's anything I can—"

The door opens behind me, and I turn to see who's coming in so late. I do a double take before I recognize the thick blond braid draped over her shoulder and those round, blue eyes staring up at me like a deer in headlights.

"Ronan?" she shrieks, standing frozen in the doorway.

My brow furrows as I turn toward Daisy. I glance behind her, waiting for a boyfriend or husband, hoping that she's not walking into a downtown gas station alone at 2 a.m.

But there's no one. Not even a car parked out front.

"Daisy?" I ask, confounded to see her here at this hour.

"What are you doing in a gas station?" she asks incredulously.

I glance down at my watch. "It's two in the morning. Are you here alone?"

"Um…" she stammers. "I need hot water for my tea, and Sherie lets me have it for free."

I spin around and stare at Sherie with confusion, then back at Daisy. "Making tea in the middle of the night?"

"It's chamomile. It helps me sleep—wait, why am I explaining this to you? I can go wherever I want," she adds with her head held high.

My jaw clenches, and I force myself to breathe before snapping at her for being so naive. "Why can't you make hot water at home?"

Daisy's eyes dance back and forth between me and Sherie. Then she composes herself, shoulders back, as if she's forcing herself to be strong. "None of your business."

It's almost cute the way she says that with her soft, breathy, high-pitched voice. Or at least it would be cute if it wasn't so goddamn frustrating.

She brushes past me and walks directly to the coffee station, grabbing a large cup and filling it with steaming hot water, then covering it with a plastic lid and holding it to her chest as if to steal its warmth.

I watch in silence, trying to piece together this random turn of events. I mean, I like when people surprise me, but this girl is throwing me off at every turn.

"Night, Sherie," she says. Then she turns her serious eyes on me, glowering at me as she says, "Night, Ronan." With that, she marches out the front door without another word, leaving me staring at Sherie with far more questions than answers.

Daisy is right. It's none of my business. But since when has that ever stopped me?

Sherie shrugs at me and I know she's not about to disclose any of the girl's secrets. So I turn toward the door and watch Daisy crossing the dark parking lot toward the street, alone.

What the fuck?

My feet move on their own. I'm practically chasing her out the door and across the parking lot. She's huddled in a thick sweatshirt and a pair of tight black leggings that leave very little to the imagination when it comes to the shape of her ass.

I'm at a loss for words as she strides alone toward the city park. She can't be going there, can she? She's getting dangerously close to a shifty-looking white van parked under a giant oak tree. What on earth is this girl up to?

"Daisy," I call from across the street. She turns toward me just as she reaches the white van. Her expression is tense, lips pressed together and shoulders raised up as if she's nervous.

"What?" she replies, sounding exhausted.

"What the fuck are you doing?"

"Good night, Ronan. Just go home." With an exasperated sigh, her shoulders sag away from her ears, and I can't believe what I'm seeing when she pulls open the sliding door of the van and climbs into the back.

It's open long enough for me to make out a small platform bed piled with heavy blankets. The fight in me dissipates. She can't really be living in there, can she? Does Emerson know about this? He'd never let his employees struggle like that.

I cross the street in a hurry. When I reach the van, I bang on the window.

"Daisy, open up," I bark.

"I said good night, Ronan," she calls from inside.

"Get out of the fucking van," I bellow, my teeth clenched. I thought I could keep my cool, but I guess I was wrong. Apparently, I'm incapable of remaining calm at the moment. I'm too appalled, and to be honest, more than a little fired up.

A moment later, the door slides open and she's staring at me with an angry expression. "Who do you think you are?" she argues. "You think because you're a man, you can just boss me around?"

"Are you sleeping in your van?" I ask, ignoring her antagonizing question.

She leans closer, those baby blue eyes piercing me with anger. "It's. None. Of. Your. Business," she snaps, punctuating each word.

I've lost control. It's long gone. I act on impulse as I snatch her by the waist and hoist her over my shoulder, turning as if I mean to carry her home like this.

"What are you doing?" she screams.

Clearly, this won't work. I'll be thrown in jail within minutes if I try to abduct this flailing young woman and bring her to my apartment. I drop her onto the ground, so she's standing just in front of me.

Get your head together, Ronan. What the fuck is wrong with you?

When she rears back her hand to slap me, I grab her by the wrist before she makes contact.

"You're fucking crazy if you think I'm going to let you sleep out here."

"I'm not homeless," she replies. "Lots of people live in their vans. It's like…a mobile home. I've got a bed. And I'm safe."

"You think walking around at night, letting people see you get into that van, is safe? A man could easily break the windows and hurt you." I'm seething at this point.

"The only one bothering me is you," she replies coldly, letting her eyes slide over to where my hand is still holding her wrist.

Am I overreacting? Am I wrong for wanting to stop this girl from sleeping in a van on one of the downtown streets?

Daisy is no one to me. Why should I care what she does?

I should walk away right now.

Except I can't.

There is something holding me to this spot, keeping me tethered to her and this situation.

You can't fix everything, my wife used to tell me. And she was right, but it would never fucking stop me from trying.

"I have plenty of room at my place. You can even park your van in the garage to keep it safe."

She practically flinches, staring at me as if I've offended her. "Are you crazy? I can't go with you."

"Yes, you can, and you are," I reply impatiently.

"Are you going to throw me over your shoulder again?" Her mouth is set in a straight line and it's kind of cute how confidently she's arguing with me—like she'd actually win.

My jaw clenches and I fight the urge to do exactly that. It would make me feel better, but it would only piss her off and I could never get her to stay. Instead, I lean in and look her in the eye. She seems a bit surprised by my proximity, her eyes going wide and the tension in her shoulders melting away.

"Daisy, I'm just trying to help you, okay? Let me help you."

Her lips part as she struggles to find her response. "I...don't need your help."

"You don't have to need it. Take it anyway."

I watch her gaze dance back and forth between my eyes before she finally forces herself to swallow and I see the fight die in her.

"This park is no place for a woman to sleep alone. I couldn't rest knowing you're out here. So just come with me tonight."

Her brows are pinched together when she asks, "What do you want...in return?"

"Nothing," I reply without hesitation.

"You don't need to lure young women to your apartment to get laid, do you?"

I laugh a little at that. "Not really."

With that, she lets out a heavy exhale. I notice her glance behind me at her van before sending me a quick nod. "Fine. If it'll make you feel better, I'll go."

"Thank you," I reply.

"You always get what you want, don't you?" she asks as she moves toward her van, sliding the door closed and then facing me with a stern expression.

For a moment, I wonder if it's some sort of twist of fate that brought us together twice in one night. If there was something more powerful at play when I left my apartment to walk the streets, without knowing she'd be walking them too.

I don't bother letting my eyes drink in the long, slender shape of her legs or the stubborn expression on her face. I refuse to get attached to the idea that Daisy and I are anything more than acquaintances because I know better. She's right. I don't have to do much to get women into my bed, but I'm dreaming if I think I can get one like her to stay.

Getting my heart broken is painful enough. But getting mine broken by a woman like Daisy might kill me.

So I lie. And with a smile, I nod. "Yes, I do."

Rule #5: Some opportunities are too good to pass up.

Daisy

Well, this is an interesting turn of events. I'm in an elevator in my pajamas with Ronan Kade in the middle of the night, about to sleep in his apartment, like some sort of vagrant he found on the streets. Which…technically, I am.

I can't decide if I'm incredibly lucky or incredibly stupid.

We stand in silence until the elevator chimes and the doors open. Then we're in a foyer area, and he strides across the small space, using a key to open the heavy door. As we step through, my jaw nearly hits the floor. It's an expansive space that leads to floor-to-ceiling windows overlooking the city and the bay beyond. The kitchen is bigger than my entire van, and the living room has a TV that's surely taller than I am.

He walks into the room, his shoes clicking against the marble floor. But I'm standing by the door in silence, wondering how I went from shivering under three blankets an hour ago, to now standing in a penthouse suite in the city.

"Come in, Daisy," he calls, his deep, authoritative voice echoing through the room.

I quickly follow him, but I can't stop looking around.

"Agatha will be here in the morning. She will make breakfast and get you anything you need."

I pause. "Who's Agatha?"

"Agatha is my housekeeper," he answers matter-of-factly.

He leads me down a long hallway with rooms on each side. The one straight ahead appears to be an office with another large window, where the night sky is shimmering through the glass. My eyes linger on the office, knowing that it must contain a lot of important information.

"This is the guest bedroom," he says, opening a tall door that leads into a massive bedroom. As I step in, he clicks on the light for me. The bedding is a crisp white with more pillows than necessary. "There's an en suite bathroom here too. Help yourself to whatever you need."

As I spin around to see the bathroom, I come face-to-face with Ronan. His chestnut-brown eyes stare down at me expectantly.

"Why were you walking in the middle of the night?" I ask.

His jaw clenches. "I like to go for walks when I can't sleep."

"At two in the morning? Aren't you afraid of getting mugged?"

"I didn't take anything of value. Are you afraid I've somehow manipulated you into my home? Like I planned all of this?"

The confusion on his face morphs into a playful expression, and there's a lightness to his tone that's too handsome to hate.

"Yeah...maybe I am. I mean, it's just weird that a...billionaire would be in some random gas station in the middle of the night that I just happened to be at too. Were you following me?"

When he licks his lips as he smiles, he almost looks sexy, his mischievous expression making me grin in return.

"Now you're concerned about your safety," he says with amusement.

He has a point.

"Listen, Daisy. If you'd like me to leave, I have another place in town I could go to and you'd have the apartment to yourself.

You can also call anyone at Salacious to vouch for me. I have no intention of hurting you or taking advantage of you." Then his expression darkens again as he adds in a fatherly tone, "I'm glad you're interrogating me, though. You should."

I chew on my lower lip as I stare at him, trying to gauge how serious he is. One thing about Ronan Kade is that he seems ridiculously down-to-earth for a man of his wealth and stature. I do believe him, which means he's either sincere or the kind of sociopath who's good enough to make people believe his lies.

After a moment of contemplation, I say, "You don't have to leave. I'm not worried." It's strange how much I don't want him to leave.

"Good. I'll let you get some sleep. I usually rise early, so if I'm not here when you wake up, help yourself to anything in the apartment and Agatha will get you whatever you need."

"Thank you," I mumble.

There's a long pause as he watches me for a moment, the weight of this weird encounter thickening the air with tension. From the doorway, he dons his stern expression again as he furrows his brow at me and says, "Don't ever sleep in the city park again. It's dangerous. Are we clear?"

I stifle a laugh as I link my hands behind my back. "Yes, Dad."

His stiffening expression and momentary pause is proof that I might have just made things even weirder by saying that. I wait one long, torturously awkward second after another before he finally leaves, taking the tension with him.

After he shuts me into my room, I throw my bag on the floor and head into the bathroom. Of course, it's huge, with a sleek, full-size tub, a tiled shower with two showerheads, and a fancy-looking marble counter.

I take all of my showers at the club, but I haven't taken a bubble bath in months, and I'd love to have one now, but I'm so tired, I'm afraid I'd pass out in there and drown. So instead, I kick off my clothes, wash my face, and climb into the giant bed. The mattress is so soft, I almost forget I'm in Ronan Kade's apartment and not sleeping on a cloud.

I'm only alone with my thoughts for a few minutes before I'm swept away into a deep sleep.

I don't move an inch all night. This might be the best I've slept in months. When I do finally peel my eyes open, the bright light of the sun shines through the window and I'm instantly reminded of where I'm sleeping.

No thin foam mattress. No stuffy, poorly ventilated van. No street traffic.

I'm in Ronan Kade's apartment.

What a strange, coincidental twist of fate. It must be a sign, right? I'm here for a reason, and everything I want is within my grasp. All I have to do now is reach out and take it.

I *could* ask him. I probably should ask him. But I've already spent three months working at the club and sort of missed my opportunity to bring up the whole *you knew my mother and left me a million dollars* conversation without now looking like a psycho stalker in this scenario.

But if I could get him to open up about a woman he knew and/or dated briefly in the past, then at least I'd have something. Then I'd be able to move on. I could take the money knowing it was truly what my mother wanted and that I would be taking a piece of her with me too.

I jump out of bed and immediately hear muffled voices down the hall. Gently prying open the door, I listen in on their conversation.

"You're the best, Agatha," Ronan says, his deep voice carrying through the long hallway.

"How long will she be staying?"

"As long as she needs to," he replies warmly. "She won't be sleeping in that van, parked alone in the city."

I roll my eyes at his insinuation that he somehow now controls my life.

"She's as stubborn as she is sweet," he adds, and I laugh silently. He thinks *I'm* stubborn.

"Might be what you need. She'll keep you on your toes," the woman jokes.

"Yes, she would," he replies in a low tone.

As quietly as possible, I close the door and head into the bathroom. My fingers slide easily over the marble counter before I reach into the shower and twist the handle until steaming water sprays from both showerheads. In my head, I hum a tune that's been plaguing me for a few days now, and when I'm standing under the warm spray, I play with different lyrics to assign to the melody.

Showers are always my favorite place to think, and after months of public showers, I'm so relieved to finally have the privacy and time to really brainstorm.

And for the first time in months, the song comes easily. By the time I get out, I feel more refreshed and cleaner than I have in ages. Standing in nothing but my towel, I grab my phone and quickly jot down messy, typo-riddled lyrics in the notes app before my brain forgets them.

After slipping on something comfortable, I run my fingers through my hair while it dries, so it ends up with a wavy, textured look. Admiring my good hair day, I decide to leave it down.

Then I ease out of the bedroom and walk barefoot down the hallway toward the main living area. I'm not sure what's more impressive: the view at night or the bright light that makes this entire apartment feel warm and inviting, as if I'm living on a cloud hovering above the rest of the city.

I'm surprised to find the place empty when I emerge, so I take a few minutes to be snoopy and curious. I mean…who wouldn't?

The intoxicating aroma of coffee pulls me toward the kitchen, but instead of pouring a cup, I continue on through the dining room and into another large living space, this one a little more formal than the other. There aren't any personal photos to inspect. Just some art on the walls, a few pieces of memorabilia that look to be from his travels. There's a bar and a shelf full of old books and—

I gasp, freezing in place as I allow my eyes to drink in the image before me. A black, pristine baby grand piano. Probably the most beautiful piano I've ever seen.

Taking a few steps toward it, I listen for the sound of anyone approaching, but the apartment is silent. I reach out to touch it, and when my fingers brush the cool, clean, black-lacquered wood, I let out a husky breath. This is the kind of piano you only see in movies.

When I was eight, my mom found an old upright piano that someone left in one of the houses she sold. The day she brought it home and shoved it into the tiny, cramped corner of our two-bedroom bungalow was one of the best days of my life. I fiddled with that piano relentlessly, learning notes, scales, and "Chopsticks" on repeat for an entire year.

She gifted me proper lessons the following Christmas with the money she scraped together from her commissions. Every Tuesday after school, I sat with an old woman named Dorothy who taught me the *proper* way to play, but it wasn't long before I went rogue.

When I was truly alone with the piano, I felt connected to it. Like it was an extension of me. To the point where I didn't know if I was the one writing the songs or it was. But together, we pieced together melodies, then bridges, refrains, choruses, and hooks.

The day I sold that piano was the second worst day of my life. But it reminded me too much of my mom.

Just as I let my fingers slide along the ivories, a deep voice echoes from behind me. "Do you play?"

With a yelp, I jump back from the piano, as if I've been caught with my hand in the cookie jar.

"Oh my God, you scared me."

"Sorry," he replies with a laugh. "Didn't mean to."

"It's okay…"

With my hand over my chest, I take in Ronan's casual appearance. No suit or tuxedo, like I'm used to seeing him in. Not even the unkempt, after-work version, where he ditches the jacket and lets the top few buttons loose so he can relax.

Today he's in a tight long-sleeve shirt and jeans over black boots. I feel myself tensing as I quickly assess his appearance. Why am I struggling so much with how good-looking he is? Why can't I just admit that he's gorgeous?

"So, do you?" he asks, his eyes trailing toward the baby grand.

"Um…yes. Actually, I do. Or…I used to." There's something strange about revealing personal details to Ronan, being a *real* person around him, letting my guard down enough to let him see the girl underneath. Maybe it's from always only seeing one another in a work environment.

I see him as nothing more than a rich older man, and he sees me as nothing more than a drink server in a short skirt and heels.

When he pulls back the bench, I tense.

"Well, go ahead then," he says softly.

"Oh no, that's okay. I'm so rusty."

"There's no audience. No one to impress. Just play."

I force a smile and let out a heavy breath, knowing I could argue more, but a part of me doesn't want to. This piano is calling to me.

"Okay…" I mumble, moving toward the seat. When I sit on the bench, he gives me space, leaning against the wall as he watches me with those somber brown eyes.

The keys are smooth against my fingers as I rest them gently in place. It feels as if they're home for the first time in years. After swallowing my nerves, I press down with both hands at once, and the room fills with a rich, intoxicating sound. Instantly, I'm transported. A different time. A different place.

Nowhere specific. The notes take me away as I play a simple

song I wrote years ago, but it's really a feeling I'm whisked off to. The sensation of being free. No worries or fears or stress. The melody drowns all of that out.

My eyes begin to sting with the threat of tears, so I keep my head down.

Even the damper pedal feels like butter under my barefoot as each note melts into the other, and suddenly, I can't seem to stop. I play from memory, deviating from the melody and blending together my own chords and bridges until I find a place to stop. Even after my fingers have risen, I keep my foot pressed, letting the sound coast until I lift it and it's replaced with silence.

And just like that, I'm back. Back in the real world. Sitting in a billionaire's apartment, playing a piano that's not mine.

"That was beautiful," he whispers delicately, almost as if he doesn't want to disturb the tender moment I'm in.

"Thank you," I reply just as softly.

"Did you write it?"

I shrug. "Yes."

"How long have you played?"

When I finally lift my gaze to his face, I find it almost difficult to look him in the eyes. The way he stares at me with interest is intoxicating, and I worry I'm falling into his hypnotic trap.

"I started taking lessons as a kid, but then I just liked to mess around on our piano at home. But I'll be honest…" I say, staring down at the keys, "I think this is the first in-tune piano I've ever played."

When I look up at him, my face pulling into a gentle grin, he smiles back, and for a moment, I swear I forget to breathe.

"You're welcome to play this one anytime you'd like."

I clench my molars together as I swallow down the emotion building in my throat. The opportunity to play again—*really* play—hits me harder than I expected.

"Thank you," I reply, clearing my throat as I look down.

Ronan has this strange way of feeling far more relatable

than he should. Maybe that's his charming trick with women, to deceive them into thinking he actually cares about them or has more in common with them than is reasonable to believe.

The worst part is that I think I'm falling for it.

And I'm sure my mother did too.

Rule #6: Keep your dirty thoughts to yourself.

Ronan

SHE PLAYS FOR ANOTHER HOUR. WHEN I LEAVE THE ROOM, working in my office, she plays even better, as if not having my direct attention gives her the freedom to get even more lost in the music. The sound carries beautifully through my apartment, and for the first time since I moved in, my home feels alive.

I've held parties with musicians, but it was never like this—as if I'm listening to Daisy and feeling her at the same time.

I'm a fool for letting myself get so enamored by it. Or by her. I don't even know the girl.

The entire time she plays, I stare at the computer screen in my office. Emails and reports coming in from my team, but I don't move to respond. The truth is, I don't need to work anymore. There is nothing at my company that requires my attention, expertise, or time, but I do it because I don't know what I'd do without it. That silence is the same demon I fight at night when I try to sleep. Both haunt me with painful memories and I'd rather drown them out with things I can manipulate, like money, work, and sex.

And today, I've discovered that having a twentysomething-year-old playing the piano in my apartment has the same effect. If not more so.

I'm coming to grips with something pathetic, and that's that I don't want her to leave. I haven't even slept with the woman and I'm thinking of ways to get her to stick around longer. Does that make me a creep?

Not that I *wouldn't* sleep with her. Those beautiful long legs of hers wrapped around my waist has riddled my mind nonstop for the last twenty-four hours, but I won't make a move. Not on this one.

I'm a man who takes what he wants. I'm hardly ever told no, and there's nothing out of my reach.

But with Daisy, things feel different. She needs me. Well, she needs *someone*, and I'm in the position to help her. And so what if I like helping her? If we make it physical, then it would only complicate things. Not to mention, I'd lose interest almost immediately.

It's a defense mechanism, really. When there's no real way to tell if someone is interested in *me* or my money, it never ends well. Having my heart broken so many times has formed a callus around it.

I am emotionally bankrupt.

The sudden silence catches my attention, stealing me from my depressing thoughts. The soft pad of her footsteps carry down the hall as she comes to find me. I'm out of my chair and walking toward her faster than I mean to.

She's peering into empty rooms, her tight black leggings catching my eye. I don't think I've ever seen a prettier pair of legs in my life.

When she turns around to find me staring, I watch her expression for a sign. Do I repulse her? Frighten her? I might be dreaming here…but do I interest her?

There's a slight upturn of her lips when our eyes meet, as if she's happy to see me. Then silence stretches out between us for a few moments before she speaks, and I find myself hanging on in anticipation for what she might say.

"I'm sorry. You probably want me out of your house," she mutters quietly. "I didn't realize it's already two in the afternoon."

"Where do you think you're going?" I ask playfully.

"Well, I have to work at eight," she replies with a cheeky grin.

"You're not sleeping in your van again."

I watch her expression harden. "Am I being kidnapped right now?"

"You drove yourself here." I lean my arm against the wall, maintaining my smile.

"I'm serious, Ronan. I can't impose."

"You're not imposing. I have the space, and you need it. Stay warm. Stay safe. End of discussion."

Her eyes take on that sweet, playful look, and I'm fighting the urge to pin her against this wall and kiss that innocence right off her face.

I've been around long enough to know when a woman is playing with me, and I can see it in Daisy's eyes, just how much she likes to pretend to be meek and naive simply to push my buttons.

"Yes, Da—" she starts to say, but I press my hand over her mouth to stop her from finishing that sentence. It might be a joke to her, but it's certainly not one to me. She doesn't want to know just how much that phrase affects me.

When I pull my hand away, her lips fight a smile. "Sorry."

"Are you hungry?" I ask, changing the subject.

"A little," she replies.

With that, I lead her to the kitchen, motioning for her to walk in front of me. Agatha has stepped out to do the shopping, but I can manage lunch. I pull up my sleeves and wash my hands at the sink. Daisy leans against the kitchen counter, eyeing me with interest, as if me washing my hands is the most intriguing thing she's ever watched.

"Are you making me lunch?" she asks with a smile.

"Hey, I'm a good cook."

"Don't you have someone to do your cooking?" she asks.

On my way to the fridge, I shrug. "I don't have time to cook every meal, but I enjoy it when I can. It's calming to me."

"Can I help?" she asks, watching me pull the onions and meat out of the fridge.

"Sure," I reply, gesturing to the cutting board leaning against the backsplash. "Slice these onions."

With a nod, she pulls the large knife from the block and gets to work slicing the onions on the board. I catch her looking back at me while I season and form two hamburger patties on a piece of wax paper. When I notice her quietly giggling, I smile.

"What?"

She shakes her head. "You're nothing like I expected."

"What did you expect?"

"I don't know."

"Tell me," I say, pulling the skillet from the rack over the range and setting it on the burner. As I turn the dial on the stove, it clicks a couple times before the flame gives an audible *whoosh*. I'm standing close to her as I grab a handful of the sliced onions and drop them into the skillet. After a moment, they begin to sizzle as Daisy hides her dimpled cheeks.

"I just find it weird that I'm helping cook burgers in the middle of the day with the richest guy in Briar Point." Then she shifts her hips, turning to face me as she adds, "And you haven't tried to sleep with me once."

Our eyes meet for a moment before I force myself to shift away, looking down at the sautéing onions in the pan. Even while I add salt and a little sherry, I'm letting her words linger, thinking about the right way to respond to them.

Does she want me to try and sleep with her?

"Say something, Ronan. It was just a joke."

I could crack a joke in return. Make light of the conversation. Instead, I shoot for honesty.

"I don't bring women home, Daisy. It's why I have my own room at the club. I didn't bring you home to try and get into your pants. I could have done that at Salacious."

Her smile falters for a moment. When she turns back toward me, her expression is laced with curiosity. "You have a private room at the club?"

"Yes. You didn't know that?"

"No. I've never even been in one of the rooms."

A deep chuckle rumbles through my chest. "You're kidding?"

"Nope. So, wait. You don't bring women home?"

"No."

"Why not?" she asks, sounding genuinely curious. "This place is very impressive."

"Because..." I reply, reaching for the salt, "I don't want to."

After the onions are done, I grill the burgers in the same pan, letting the aroma fill the room. Daisy starts humming after taking a long inhale. "Smells delicious."

When I turn back toward her, I notice she's sitting on the countertop, her legs dangling off the edge, and I have to clench my jaw to keep from thinking very inappropriate things. How I'd love to drape them over my shoulders, feel her soft thighs against my ears, and see just how good she tastes between them.

I wonder if she's a timid lover, moaning sweetly, or if she's wild and bold, unafraid to ask for what she wants. Considering how sweet she is now, I'd like to think she's the opposite in bed. The idea of her digging her fingers in my hair to pull my mouth harder against her has my dick twitching just thinking about it.

Filthy images of her start racing through my mind. The thought of making her come so many times, she's soaked and aching. The sounds she would make while taking my cock down her throat. The way she would look tied to my bed, squirming and begging for relief.

There's something about this girl—she's as sweet as she is

fiery. I could have some fun finding all the ways to make her feel good, and I know I'd love every single second of it.

I'm growing hard behind my zipper, and I feel like shit for it. She has no idea that currently in my head, I'm licking my way into her perfect little cunt.

And it's going to stay that way—in my head.

When the burgers are done, I serve them with leafy lettuce on a grilled bun. With the first bite, she lets out a husky sounding moan, and my dick twitches in my pants again. I guess I just got my answer.

At this moment, I decide that I'm not going to let this woman out of my sight. I may not be trying to fuck her, but I'm too addicted to the sight of her devouring the food I've cooked to let her go.

"You're staying here," I say, not giving a shit that I sound like a fucking caveman.

She's dabbing her mouth with a napkin when her eyes go wide and she stares at me in shock. "You've made that pretty clear."

"No charge. No obligations. You can stay as long as you'd like. But I don't want you sleeping in that van anymore."

Her brows pinch together in worry as she swallows her food and grabs a glass of water to wash it down. For a long time, she stares forward, as if the lunch on her plate holds the answers. "We don't even know each other."

With that, I lean back in my chair and level my gaze on her. "Okay, Daisy. What do you want to know?"

For the next few minutes, we volley innocent questions back and forth. She tells me she's from a small town in Indiana and moved out here in January to start an adventure of her own. She asks about my company, and I explain in far too few words that I own a conglomerate holding company, but that clearly loses her interest quickly, so I shoot back with a trivial question of my own—or at least one that I thought was trivial.

"What's your favorite book?"

The question catches Daisy off guard. Her head turns up and she stares at me with a furrowed brow and a slightly turned-down mouth.

"Just one?"

"Yes."

The expression of contemptuous disapproval doesn't leave her face. "You can't possibly expect me to answer that," she replies with a bite in her tone.

I lean forward, setting my glass down on the table. "Why not?"

"Because it's not a fair question. What's *your* favorite book?"

"*A Moveable Feast* by Ernest Hemingway," I reply without hesitation.

She looks affronted. "Really?"

"Yes…" Now I'm confused.

"No matter what mood you're in?"

"Yes…"

"Out of all the books in the world?" she asks, eyes bulging.

"Well, I haven't read all the books in the world, but out of the ones I have read…yes, that is my favorite." My eyes squint, staring at her with scrutiny.

"Well, I think asking someone to pick just one is a little rude. I could tell you my childhood favorite. Or my comfort book. Or my favorite contemporary or my favorite classic. My favorite poetry book or my favorite fiction."

A smile creeps across my face as she continues, verbally reprimanding me for asking such an unfair question before detailing each of her favorites with delicate precision. *Anne of Green Gables* and *Jane Eyre* and *The Handmaid's Tale* and *The Great Gatsby*.

I can't take my eyes off her. Suddenly, she's melting into the dining room chair, her legs pulled to her chest, as she goes on and on and on.

I soak up every single word.

Rule #7: Don't be afraid of what's behind the curtain.

Daisy

THE CLUB IS QUIET FOR A FRIDAY. WHICH IS IRONIC BECAUSE IT'S spring and I always assumed people were hornier and got it on more in the springtime. Or maybe I'm just remembering that scene in *Bambi*, where all the boy animals got horny for the girl animals in spring.

And...I just compared *Bambi* to a sex club.

That's just how bored I am.

Geo is busy chatting it up with Drake on the other side of the bar, and I'm watching the clientele like a hawk, waiting for someone who looks like they need a fresh drink. But they're all sipping so slow tonight.

Today was surprisingly fun. I was at the piano for most of the day, and when I wasn't playing, I was talking to Ronan. I must be starved for conversation because ours flowed so easily. So now I'm actually hoping he comes in, so I at least have someone to talk to.

Of course, one goes to a sex club for only one reason, so I doubt he'd want to waste his chances of getting laid by chatting with me.

When I spot one of the owners descending the stairs toward the main floor, I force myself to look busy. Grabbing a rag on the other side of the bar, I wipe down the surface and move to an empty table, wiping it down too, although it's perfectly clean. Then I arrange all of the already-straight barstools when I hear someone approach me from behind.

"I've worked in the business long enough to tell when someone is just *trying* to look busy."

When I spin to face Garrett Porter, I force a smile on my face. "It's better than just standing around."

"That's true," he replies. Out of all the owners, Garrett is my favorite. I hardly ever see or talk to Emerson, since he's almost never in here anymore. And Hunter is aloof and not very talkative. Apparently, there was a fourth, but I missed her by almost a year. She left to run the new Phoenix club, but Geo said she was a little strict and always moving, so it doesn't sound like she and I would have become friends anyway.

"I can restock something in the back if I need to," I say, although I know there's not a single box back there to open.

"Nah, you're better on the floor, and I don't want to cut you yet." Suddenly his brows rise as if he has a brilliant idea. "Why don't you go help Marianna upstairs?"

I have to force myself to swallow. *Upstairs.* I've only ventured into Salacious's VIP level once and never behind the curtain, although I know what goes on in there. It's essentially the orgy zone, where everyone is free to do whatever they want, all out in the open like that.

And although the bar and some seating are *outside* the ominous black curtain, the drink servers still have to deliver drinks to the ones inside. Because who doesn't want a gin martini while they're getting publicly railed?

"Um…sure," I answer with fake enthusiasm. I need this job, and although management would never force me to do anything I'm not comfortable with, I'm not openly admitting that I'm uncomfortable with it either. Maybe I'm not. Maybe...I'm a little curious.

"If you're okay with that, of course," he adds to be sure.

"Of course!" With that, I carry my drink tray up the stairs, and I'm only halfway up when I think of Ronan. He mentioned having a private room, but does he ever use the VIP orgy zone? Is that even his style?

Why does the thought of him with someone send a cold chill down my spine? I'm sure Ronan Kade's been with more women than I can count, so why does thinking about it now make me feel sick?

As I reach the top of the stairs, I realize why Garrett sent me up here. It's packed. And maybe that's why it's dead downstairs. The party is on the VIP floor tonight.

"Oh, thank God," Marianna says when she sees me approaching the bar with my tray in hand. "Will you take these to table two?"

"Yep," I reply with a smile. Then I load up the two beers and one cocktail on the tray, carrying them over to the two men and one woman standing close together around the table. They smile at me as I set their drinks down, briefly noticing the way one man has his hand on the woman's bare thigh. I glance up at her face, noticing the lax smile and pink rosiness in her cheeks.

When we were in training for the positions here at the club, they taught us all the telltale signs that someone would give if they were in a situation they didn't want to be in. Avoiding eye contact, nervous twitches, any use of force or being held in place by another person.

None of those signs are here right now, thank God. I haven't had to report anything yet, and I don't want to. From what I've heard, the vetting process at Salacious is strict and the security is top-notch. But snakes are good at squeezing through the cracks.

When I turn back toward the bar, I nearly slam into a man all in black. "Oh, I'm so sorry," I blurt out, just as my eyes trail up to his face. Instantly I recognize him as the man who bid against Ronan in my auction. "Oh, hi…" I stammer awkwardly.

"Well, hello there," he replies with a smile so wide, it creates deep, crevice-like dimples in his cheeks. "Funny running into you here."

I chuckle through my nerves. It was just last night that he was willing to drop thousands of dollars on a date with me.

"I'm Clay," he says, putting out a hand.

I tuck my tray under one arm and shake it. "Daisy."

"Daisy…" He utters my name with a grin, and I get a weird flash of something down my spine.

Clay is very handsome. Big smile and kind eyes. Perfectly coiffed brown hair and expensive-looking clothes. He's not much taller than me. Not as tall as Ronan, although I don't know why I'm suddenly comparing them. I wonder how my night would have gone if Ronan hadn't outbid Clay. I can imagine it would have ended with him and me naked in a room somewhere in the club. That definitely wouldn't have been so bad.

But I can guarantee he would have never asked about my favorite book. Or offered me a place to stay. Or let me play his baby grand piano. Or cooked me lunch the next day.

"Can I buy you a drink when your shift is over?"

Suddenly, I'm hesitating. Why am I hesitating? Clay is gorgeous. Much more suited for me. And probably still rich as hell.

"Umm…I have plans, actually. I'm sorry."

I notice the muscle in his jaw twitch at my response, and I instantly feel bad for turning him down. I bet it's not a common occurrence for him.

Of course, it's a lie. I don't have plans after work. I get off at two in the morning. Unless it's a booty call, who makes plans that late?

"Another time," I say, moving around him toward the bar to do my job. He doesn't follow me, and when I turn back, I notice him already moving on to another woman sitting on the bench along the wall.

"These go to the couple at table twelve in the VIP room. Male and female, round table," Marianna says without looking up at me. On the bar are two glasses of ice water, and I feel my cheeks start to flush with heat as her words settle in. I have to take these drinks to the other side of the curtain, and there's no telling what this couple is doing in there.

I can do this.

She must notice my anxiety because she leans forward and touches my hand. "Don't make eye contact. In fact, don't focus on anything. Just walk in, find the table, set them down, and leave."

With a gulp, I nod.

I've got this.

Feigning confidence and indifference, I load the tray and hoist it up, making my way around the people crowding the bar and walking toward the curtain. One of the bouncers opens it for me and I pass through into the dark space, as if this is just another day and I'm not walking onto the set of a porno.

The sounds come first. Before I see anything, I hear moaning and grunting as well as all the other noises that come with people unabashedly going at it. But I stay focused. I'm looking for the couple on the far left.

Which isn't really enough to go on. The room is comprised of mostly couches, some recessed into the floor to give the room a multidimensional look. Then there are some chairs, a couple tables, but no beds or anything that would allow people to lie on the floor.

After a few steps inside, moving toward the left, my vision adjusts, and I see movement. It's surreal and nothing like I expected. It's not as vulgar or as gross as I figured it would be. Instead, it's almost…beautiful.

Bodies coming together, writhing and moving to find a rhythm, and I find myself wondering how many of these people are strangers and how many are couples out to have a good time.

I'm no prude. I love sex as much as the next person. But I

wouldn't call myself all that adventurous. I've slept with a handful of guys, starting when I was sixteen. My best guy friend and I drank enough of my mom's wine to get up the courage to just take each other's virginity. Since then, the experience has gotten a good deal better but never anything like what goes on at Salacious. And I can't quite tell if I'm not into kink or if I just haven't met the right person.

When I finally spot a couple sitting against the wall, they lock eyes with me, and I know it must be their waters I'm carrying. Judging by the way her hair looks slightly knotted and his jacket is hanging over his arm instead of around his shoulders, I'd guess that these two just finished having a little fun of their own. That explains the ice waters.

"Thank you," the woman mutters as I pass them their drinks.

"Can I get you anything else?" I ask, but they both shake their heads, huddling a little closer to each other.

When I turn around to head back out to the bar, the curtain opens and I watch someone, slightly silhouetted from the light behind him, enter. But I don't need to see his face to know who it is. I've been watching him around this club long enough to know Ronan Kade's gait and posture. Maybe that means I'm more intrigued by him than I'm willing to admit. Or maybe it's just because he comes in here that often, but either way, I know it's him.

And I freeze in my steps as we come face-to-face. At first, a flash of excitement courses through me when our eyes meet. But then that sick feeling returns to my gut when I realize where he's going and what he's about to do.

Rule #8: The VIP room isn't the best place for conversation.

Ronan

"He sent her upstairs?" I snap at Geo, my fist tightening around the glass of whiskey.

"It was dead down here," he replies as he shakes up a martini.

In seconds, I've abandoned my drink and I'm marching upstairs on a mission. I'm aware Daisy works in a sex club. And that she's an adult. And that she's not *actually* mine. What I don't understand is why I suddenly turn into a version of myself I don't recognize where she is concerned. It's only been twenty-four hours since I placed my first bid on a date with her, and already, I'm losing my goddamn mind.

I cannot stand the idea of her in the VIP room. Can't *stand* it.

And it's irrational to be so angry at Garrett for sending her up here. He's just doing his job. If she were uncomfortable with it, he wouldn't have sent her.

Not a single rational thought enters my head as I reach the second floor, weaving through the crowd and searching for her like a crazed maniac. What am I going to do when I find her? Throw her over my shoulder again? She wasn't as big of a fan of that as I was. I'm pretty sure if I do it here, where she's working, I'll really see her furious side.

When I don't see her in the bar area, I know she must be behind the curtain. Without stopping, I pull it back and step inside.

And nearly crash right into her.

First, her expression brightens, as if she's happy to see me.

Then, it hardens.

"Ronan," she mumbles, her eyes glued to my face.

I am rarely at a loss for words or stuck not knowing what to do next, but right now, I'm staring at Daisy, surrounded by sex, and I have no idea what to do.

When I feel someone entering the space behind me, I quickly rest my hand on Daisy's arm and guide her toward a quiet corner on the side of the entrance.

"What are you doing?" she asks.

"I don't want you working in here," I reply.

Her pale blond brows pinch together in that adorable way I've seen them do quite a few times over the past twenty-four hours. "Why not?"

"Because it's just... You're so young."

Her confusion only intensifies. "I'm almost twenty-two, Ronan."

Exactly, I think, although I'm well aware she's using that as her defense.

"Ronan, I *work* here."

"Why *do* you work here, Daisy? I've heard you play. You deserve to be onstage somewhere, not doling out drinks in a sex club."

"You wouldn't understand," she mutters after the initial shock wears off.

Then, someone moans loudly behind me and I press Daisy farther into the corner, as if I can shield her from it. Her eyes widen and I notice a subtle reaction in her face that proves she's a little thrown off by being in this room.

When I lean in, I notice that she doesn't pull away. Instead, she leans a little closer as well, like we're two magnets tempted to collide. "Does this place make you uncomfortable?"

Her eyes snap up to meet my gaze. "Of course not."

A smile pulls at my lips. "Liar."

"I have work to do," she snaps, clearly fighting back a grin of her own.

With that, I let her leave, but just before she disappears through the curtain, she glances back toward me, and I can tell she's wondering if I'm going to follow her or stay in this room of sin.

Letting her wonder a little longer won't hurt her, so I lean against the wall and cross my arms until she's gone.

From across the room, I feel someone watching me, and it's not long before I recognize the person gliding toward me. I smile at Eden when she approaches.

"What was that all about?" she asks.

"I don't know what you're talking about."

"Don't play games with me, Ronan Kade. I know you better than anyone."

At that, I smile. Of course, she's right. I've known Eden since before she was Madame Kink. Hell, I've known her longer than she's been a madame at all. Back when she was just discovering herself, young and ambitious, but just as scared and intimidated by people who liked to take more than they were willing to give.

"All right, fine. I'm trying to help the girl. I think she's fallen on hard times."

"Ah," Eden replies, "that makes sense."

"What's that supposed to mean?"

"You've found a project," she says, and my spine tenses. I hate to hear it put in those terms, no matter how accurate it is. I don't want to see Daisy as a project, but I know myself and I've been doing this long enough to recognize when I've found something to occupy my time and mind.

"I like her," I add, trying not to let it show on my face just how much this young woman has gotten under my skin in the last twenty-four hours.

"I can tell. Just be careful," Eden says, leaning against the wall next to me.

"What's the worst that can happen?" I reply with a tight-lipped expression, and when she touches my hand, I feel the sympathy in the gesture. Eden knows everything, so she knows how much it still hurts.

"Are you sure you don't want to just find someone to play with up here? Might help you take your mind off of it." Eden raises her eyebrows at me, and I smirk with a shake of my head.

"Not tonight," I reply. I don't know many friends who are willing to partake in kinky group sex to cheer me up, but I'm sure thankful for this one.

"Fine. Good luck with your cute little project out there." With a wink, Eden steps away from the wall and presses her lips to my cheek.

Just then, the curtain opens again and Daisy walks in, her eyes finding me right away. I take a good deal of pride in just how jealous she looks as Eden runs her fingers through my hair.

Rule #9: There's no shame in asking for help. Everyone ends up on the bathroom floor from time to time.

Daisy

"You fucked Ronan Kade?"

I nearly drop my tray of drinks and slam into a man passing by when I hear the table of women name-drop the one guy who's happened to infiltrate my entire life in the last twenty-four hours.

First, I walk in on him and Eden St. Claire getting cozy, just moments after I left him in the VIP room, and now this. He followed me out of the room after that, and he's been like a shadow on my tail ever since, never letting me enter the VIP room alone. It's a little over-the-top, if you ask me.

But at the same time…it's almost sweet.

As I'm dropping off the cocktails to a nearby table, I try to listen in on the women nearby, but it's so loud in here and they're just out of earshot.

There are three of them. An older woman wearing a proud expression. A beautiful, young redhead, and a dark-skinned runway model (or so I assume) with a buzzed head and legs for days. I didn't catch which one asked the question, but now I'm practically trying to read lips.

Once my tray is emptied, I make my way closer, pretending to wipe down a nearby table as they carry on their conversation.

"I came so many times I had to beg him to stop," the runway model whispers, and I freeze.

"Older men always know what they're doing," the older woman replies.

"Well, not to mention, he's a pleasure Dom," one of them adds.

A pleasure Dom? What the hell is that?

Thankfully, the redhead is just as clueless. "What does that mean?"

"It means he forces you to enjoy yourself. He gets off on getting you off," the woman replies.

"Sign me up."

The three of them break out in laughter before raising their glasses to drink. I've run out of table to wipe down, but I'm not ready to leave this conversation. It's a major invasion of privacy and probably grounds for firing, to be honest, but I'm too curious to walk away.

None of this is really what I wanted to know about the man, who may have had a romantic relationship with my mother, but I'm not thinking about that anymore. Now I'm just curious…for other reasons.

"Well, he's here tonight. He's right behind you, and he's looking this way," the runway model says with her drink to her lips.

My head practically snaps off my neck when I turn it so fast to find him, and sure enough, he's staring right at me. And since I'm standing just on the other side of the women, it appears like he's looking at them.

Grabbing my tray, I return to the bar, feeling his gaze on my back. I continue my eavesdropping on this table of women, who may or may not try to sleep with Ronan. Not that it's any of my business.

"Should I go talk to him?" the older woman says, and suddenly, I'm detouring, no longer walking to the bar but heading straight toward him. He's sitting alone at a low-set table in one of the blue velvet chairs. His shirt isn't unbuttoned tonight, but he is wearing a blue striped tie and his white shirt fits his arms so snug, it looks like the fabric might rip. How have I never noticed how buff Ronan is?

Thinking about Ronan in that way, considering he possibly dated my mother and I'm here on a mission to get answers, is wrong, but my mind ends up there anyway. Wondering what he looks like under those clothes. Imagining how he makes his submissive come so many times—with his tongue, his fingers, or a toy?

None of these thoughts are appropriate, but I think about them anyway.

I don't even know why I'm walking over here. But as I reach his chair, I stand over him with my tray tucked under my arm.

"Those women at that table are talking about you," I say quietly.

A mischievous smile plays on his lips. "Oh yeah? What did they say?"

"Well, apparently you slept with one of them. And the older one is interested in shooting her shot."

His grin stretches wider, but he doesn't even glance in their direction. His eyes remain on me. "What should I do?" he asks, and it feels like he's teasing me. But why would he? I don't care if he sleeps with any of them, or all of them for that matter. We're just friends.

I force myself to look unaffected. "I don't know. Go talk to them, I guess."

"You could give them a message for me. Or what if I order each of them a drink and have you deliver them for me?"

Okay, he's definitely teasing me. Suddenly, I notice that my neck muscles are painfully tight and I have to force my shoulders to relax from their tense position.

"What would you like to order?" I ask with a cold expression on my face.

He licks his lips, and I feel a flutter low in my belly.

"A whiskey, double, neat," he says, looking up at me.

"I don't think they drink whiskey. One of them is sipping on a spiked seltzer." I can't help but sound judgmental in my response, but Ronan only laughs.

"It's not for them. It's for me," he replies playfully. "And for you, if you'll have a drink with me."

"I'm working."

"So you don't want to make them jealous? I'll let you sit on my lap while you drink it," he replies with a smirk.

I'm struggling to hold my tense expression. Stepping closer to him, I place a hand on each of the arms of his chair, leaning toward him as I whisper, "You're not going to use me to pit women against each other, Mr. Kade."

His knee is between my legs, and with a little nudge, he rubs it against the inside of my thigh, and I let out a little gasp when he does.

"Who says I'm pitting you against them? You'd be surprised what a jealous woman will do to win a man's attention, Daisy." His voice is low with a smoky growl that makes the flutter in my stomach feel more like an assault.

"You're a pig," I reply jokingly, trying to pull away, but as soon as I try, he wraps a hand around the back of my thigh, tugging me closer until my knee lands on the chair between his legs, dangerously close to the spot he definitely doesn't want me landing on.

Suddenly, I'm practically in his lap, straddling one leg, and he's smiling, but instead of that devious grin, it's warm with laughter. "Daisy, relax. I'm joking. But I think I like seeing you so riled up."

"Very funny," I reply, swatting at his chest.

I need to stand up, but it seems to take forever. Forcing myself out of his lap is like jumping into an icy pond. It's far warmer and more comfortable here. The moment I'm standing up, putting space between us, I want to be back in his lap.

His laughter follows me as I walk toward the bar to get his

drink. On my way, I glance at the table of women and find them glaring at me with jealousy-infused hatred, and I know it's awful, but it makes me smile.

At nearly three in the morning, I'm standing under the hot shower in the giant tiled bathroom in Ronan's penthouse.

Not a single song lyric enters my tired brain. It's just a foggy, thoughtless void as I let the hot water warm me to my core. The club was so loud. After hours and hours there, I can still hear the music playing in my head like an echo, when all I really want is silence.

Tonight, there's a new sound infused with the music. The sound of sex, and lots of it.

I can't help but wonder what it might be like in the VIP room, and not as a waitress. But just as myself. I picture myself walking naked across the room. Ronan would never let me do that, of course. He'd find me. He'd shove me against a wall and cover my naked body with his own.

Maybe he'd put me over his knee. Spank me. I can almost feel his harsh palm against my backside.

This is so wrong. I know it, but we all have itches that need to be scratched from time to time. Reaching up to the showerhead, I lift it from the base and turn the intensity higher. Then with my back against the wall, I hold it over the pulsing spot between my thighs that aches after a very long night of being aroused.

It's him invading my every thought.

Ronan lifting my skirt.

Ronan bending me over the sofa.

Ronan fucking me so hard, I scream.

The fantasy is rough and dirty, yet so damn good, I almost don't want it to end.

The steady stream of water pounding against my clit sends me over the edge so fast, I have to bite my lip to hold in my scream. My entire body goes rigid as I come, and I press a hand against the shower wall to keep me upright. The orgasm pulses and pulses and pulses for what feels like forever.

When it finally ends, I lower the showerhead and suck in a lungful of hot, steamy air.

Just as I turn the dial on the shower, a feeling of overwhelming weakness settles in. My arms are like lead as I reach for my towel hanging on the hook. At first, I tell myself it's the steam and the exhaustion making me fatigued, but then the tunnel vision hits like a freight train.

And I know it's not the steam at all.

"Fuck, fuck, fuck," I mutter as every muscle in my body hangs like deadweight, and I pray the episode passes quickly. My forehead starts to sweat, and my hands start to shake. "Not now. Not now," I mutter.

That's when I go down. My ears are ringing with that sort of faint, fuzzy static sound, but when I tumble into the shower door, I know it's loud because it echoes through my ears until everything goes dark.

I'm only out for a moment. Normally when I pass out, it feels like I've been out for hours. But this time, my skin is still warm and wet, so I know it's only been a couple seconds.

And just when I think I'm in the clear, the bathroom door flies open.

"Jesus, Daisy!" Ronan shouts as he rushes over and scoops my frail, naked body off the floor.

"I'm fine!" I shriek, but his hand is on my bare ass, and after the fantasy I just streamed on the dirty movie screen of my mind two minutes ago, it's a little jarring.

"Did you pass out?" he asks, carrying me over to the bathroom counter.

"I'm tired. I just fell!" I sound way too panicked and hysterical. I know that, but I'm deep in the throes of a hypoglycemic episode. My blood sugar is probably critically low, which means my emotions are off the rails.

But he doesn't need to know all of that.

My arms move to cover my breasts as he starts inspecting my head. "I heard that all the way in my room. Are you sure you're okay?"

"I said I'm fine! Will you please get me a towel?" My command is sharp, and it gets his attention. Looking a little stunned, he pulls away, reaches for the towel, and brings it back to cover my body. "Please leave. I'm fine."

His brow furrows as if he's confused, which I'm sure he is. And I can see him hesitating. He doesn't want to leave me, and my guess is, he won't go far. I'm not used to being so…taken care of.

"Okay, I'm going." With his hands up in surrender, he backs up toward the door.

I'm fighting back tears until I hear the click of the door. It takes all the effort I have to stumble toward my bag sitting on the back of the toilet. Once I reach it, I clumsily dig inside for the glucose gummies squished in the bottom alongside the crumbs and receipts. Once I hear the crinkle of the package, I let my back crash to the wall, sliding all the way down as I tear open the plastic, devouring the sugary fruit snacks like an animal.

Then I collapse against the cold tile floor and wait for the sugar to hit my system.

While I'm down here, I think about my mother and how disappointed she would be. I always was bad about eating and watching my blood sugar. And for that reason, I've been blessed with the good fortune of passing out every time it drops. Since I haven't had a bite since the burger Ronan made me, it hit me hard this time.

For no reason whatsoever, I start to cry. Just warm tears sliding down the sides of my face and onto the floor.

That's when it all hits. Grief is a ruthless predator, attacking when I'm at my weakest. Cruel, impossible questions cycle through my mind. Why did my mom have to get cancer? Why did she have to die? Why do I have to be alone?

I don't know how long I lie here and sob, but I slowly feel the energy return to my body as the sugar hits my bloodstream. I rise carefully from the floor and find my pajamas, pulling them on in a drunken haze.

When I open the bedroom door, he's there.

He doesn't say a word, just stands against the wall as if he's waiting for me. It must be obvious just how much I've been crying, and he must be incredibly confused, but it doesn't matter. Because he doesn't say a word, just opens his arms for me, and I step into them like a moth to a flame.

"I'm fine, I promise," I mumble. "It's just...I'm a mess. I don't deserve your help. I got myself into this situation and I don't want to rely on you to get me out. You have no idea how hard it is for me to accept your help, like I'm...useless. A failure." I sob out every word, feeling pathetic, but also safe.

He lets out a heavy sigh, and I'm hanging on every second until he speaks, needing him to say something encouraging. Praying to God he's not about to lecture me or reprimand me or talk down to me like I'm a child.

"You're not a failure, Daisy. Accepting my help doesn't mean you need me to get you out of the situation you're in. It means you've taken care of yourself for so long that you deserve a break. I wouldn't offer to help you if I thought by doing so, I'd make you more dependent on me."

He pauses for a moment before softly adding, "In fact, *I'm* the one who needs out of the situation I'm in. There's no excitement in my life anymore. And hearing you play today...it made me realize how much *I* need *you*."

I let out a shaky breath. Before he can utter another word, I whisper, "Thank you."

Rule #10: Never turn down a free trip to Paris.

Daisy

MY FINGERS GRAZE THE SPINES OF THE BOOKS ON RONAN'S SHELF. He has a floor-to-ceiling bookcase in his formal living room, next to the piano, and I'm browsing the titles while he prepares us both a cup of tea.

Because he knows chamomile helps me sleep.

When I spot *A Moveable Feast*, my fingers freeze, remembering him mention it as his favorite book. With a half smile, I pull it from the shelf. Turning it over, I read the short description on the back. Beneath it is a photo of Hemingway, rugged and brooding, and I smile to myself. Sort of reminds me of someone.

Carrying the book to the front room, I hold it in my lap as I curl up on the oversized sofa, thanking my lucky stars that I'm not suffering through another cold night in the van. There's a clicking sound followed by a delicate *whoosh*, and I glance across the living room as a fire pops up in the sleek white marble fireplace set in the living room wall. I feel the heat right away, but I still tug the blanket off the back of the couch and wrap it around me.

He didn't ask any questions after my fall, and I'm grateful for that. My shame and embarrassment for letting my blood sugar get that low is torture enough. Not to mention, my head is slightly achy too.

Resting it on the side of the sofa, I watch Ronan in the kitchen as he pulls two mugs from the cabinet before turning on the electric kettle. After placing the tea bags in the mugs, he unfastens the buttons on his dress shirt around his wrists and rolls up each sleeve to the elbow.

Why is that so sexy? His thick forearms are on display, and I briefly wonder to myself if this is what seeing cleavage is like to men.

If only Ronan were closer to my age. Would it still feel so strange to be here with him? There are so many barriers between us—age, money, lifestyle. He's a fifty-six-year-old billionaire. I'm a twenty-one-year-old from the Midwest, currently living in her van. My favorite food is Wendy's fries dipped in a Frosty. I bet his favorite food is lobster tails or caviar. The most expensive thing I've ever bought was my van, and I'm willing to bet the couch I'm sitting on cost more.

And, oh yeah, he more than likely dated my mother.

But when he looks at me like he is now, as if he can see right through me, it doesn't feel like those barriers exist.

Even if we did blur the lines and sleep together, it would never be more than a crazy story I tell my friends years from now. *This one time, I had a sugar daddy...*

He sets my cup of tea on the coffee table before taking a seat on the other side of the sofa. We sit in silence for a few moments, and I feel his kind eyes on me. He's not pressuring me or judging me. This sudden feeling of *safety* with him is so strange, especially as it begins to mingle with a subtle sense of attraction. I mean, I masturbated to him an hour ago, so I think it's safe to say that I'm not so opposed to the idea of him anymore.

I still can't quite get a read on what I am to him.

Flipping through the book in my lap, I read a few pages at a time, and it feels as if I'm reading a part of him. It's all short sentences and long words, but I skim through a few paragraphs anyway.

"Do you like it?" he asks in a gentle murmur, and something about those words on his lips sends another flutter to my core, this time lower than before.

I screw up my nose as I turn the page. "You really think this is his best work?"

"I didn't say it was his best. I said it was my favorite," he replies with pride.

"Touché. Have you been to Paris?" I ask, knowing the question is a stupid one. No one would call Hemingway's ode to the City of Lights their favorite without having been there, especially not a man as wealthy as him.

"I have an apartment in the city," he says nonchalantly.

I can't help but roll my eyes as I take a sip of my tea. "Of course you do."

"Was that judgment?" he teases, and I bite back my shame for letting my face express too much.

"No…" I lie. "Call it jealousy."

"So you've never been?"

I scoff. "No. I've never been to Paris."

"You say it like it's so absurd," he replies, one side of his mouth turned up in a gentle smirk.

"For most people, Mr. Kade, it is a bit absurd."

"We should go."

I nearly choke on my tea as he says that, and I let out a chuckle as I set it back on the table. "We should go to Paris?"

"Yeah, why not? You have your passport, don't you?"

I'm gazing at him across the couch, my eyes narrowing as I try to discern if he's being serious or messing with me. It's almost too much to get my hopes up for.

"Yes…" I reply hesitantly. "My mom and I went to Canada when I was sixteen."

"Well, I owe you a date, don't I?"

This time, I laugh in earnest. My high-pitched, squeaky giggle bubbles out of my chest, and I can't seem to stop it. When Ronan doesn't so much as smile in response, I start to get the feeling he's being serious.

"You're kidding, Ronan."

"No, I'm not."

"We can't go to Paris."

"Why not?" He seems so casual about it, as if going to France is as easy as going to the grocery store.

But when I open my mouth to argue and nothing comes out, I realize that I don't have a single good answer for that question. I mean, the most obvious reason *not* to go to Paris has always been a financial issue, but that's not the case here.

But is it wrong of me to take advantage of that? Especially when I'm harboring secrets? And a trust fund I refuse to touch? Probably.

Definitely.

But I'd be stupid to pass up a free trip to Paris, right?

"Umm…okay, I guess," I reply, my face practically beaming as I look back down at the book in my lap. On the cover is a sprawling garden and I couldn't stop smiling if I tried.

When I flip to the back of the book, one of the pages catches on a spot held with a photo instead of a bookmark. I slide the picture out of the book and stare at it. Ronan's cup of tea is halfway to his mouth when he freezes in place.

The photo is older—I can tell by how grainy it is, as if it was developed from film and not taken with a digital camera. It's a picture of a beautiful young woman, holding a little boy on her lap. She looks to be in her early twenties, and if I had to guess, I'd say the boy is about four or five.

"Who's this?" I ask. In my head, I'm being polite and curious. Inquiring about this photo because I want to get to know him better, since I am basically living in his house and all.

But as my eyes rake over the people in the picture and I realize that it was likely hidden for a reason, I'm swallowing dread in my throat like dry cotton.

The silence that follows my question is deafening.

He lets me look at the photo for a moment before gently taking it from my fingers. I glance up at him with regret as I watch him swallow, gazing at the image for only a moment before placing it back in the book.

"That is my wife, Julia, and my son, Miles. They were killed in a car accident twenty-eight years ago."

The floor might as well drop beneath me. My skin is burning with shame and embarrassment as well as crippling sorrow as I stare at him, the threat of tears stinging behind my eyes. I don't even remember bringing my hand to my mouth, but it's there as I softly mumble, "Oh my God, Ronan. I'm so sorry."

When he smiles at me, it's not the full-of-life weightless grin he normally dons. This one is a little sad as if to comfort *me*, which is ridiculous.

"Don't be sorry, Daisy. You didn't know."

As he takes a drink of his tea, I'm still struck almost speechless by this new information. How many people know about this? How on earth does he carry himself so confidently while the rest of us parade around him like fools, not knowing what he's been through, what he's lost?

After finishing his tea, he moves to stand. "It's late. You should get some rest."

"Okay," I mutter quietly.

Then he reaches a hand down and helps me to my feet. Struck by this new information, with only inches between us, I stare into his eyes. Those rich brown eyes are gazing into mine, and suddenly, I feel closer to him than I've felt to anyone in a very long time. Like an entire world exists between us now, and it's only been two days.

I should say something, but I don't even know what to say; I feel so empty without words to express how I'm feeling.

All too soon, he steps away from me, walking to the hallway that leads to the guest room, and I begrudgingly pass by him, walking to the room. Before I shut the door, separating us, I lean my head out and look into his eyes as I say, "Good night, Ronan."

"Good night, Daisy," he replies, and I could be crazy, but I swear he's hesitating too, before he finally turns around and leaves me alone.

Rule #11: If you can't sleep in your bed, try his.

Daisy

THE SUN WILL COME UP ANY MOMENT NOW, BUT SLEEP STILL evades me. No matter how long I lie in this cloud of a bed with my eyes closed, praying that my dreams take me away, I can't seem to fall asleep.

I just keep thinking about that photo. His wife. His *son*. Sadness aches in my chest for him. Right next to shame and regret for opening my big mouth. Why couldn't I just put the photo back and let the moment pass? We were getting along so well and were both so happy with thoughts of Paris in our future.

Then I had to ruin it by bringing up the one thing I'm sure he doesn't ever want to think about.

I shouldn't have gone to bed that quickly. Why didn't I comfort him or say something else, instead of sitting there silent and ignorant?

It's almost five when I finally give up on sleep and climb out of bed. The house is quiet and dark. His office is empty, and I stare at it, considering for a moment that I might find some of my answers in there. But I only get to the doorway before I stop myself.

Why am I doing this? What on earth will I find? Pictures of her? Proof that I might be falling for the same man my mother did nine years ago? Is that what I want? Or do I want a reason to dislike him? Something that makes him anything less than perfect. Maybe he was buying my mother's silence. Maybe he hurt her in some way and offering me a bright future was all she wanted in return for it.

No. Not Ronan. It just doesn't fit.

When I decide that there is nothing in that office that will make me feel better about this, I abandon the idea and turn around. Instead of going back to my room, I continue into the main living area and see a faint light coming from his room.

It would be inappropriate to go in there. Ronan and I are barely even friends. But I admit, we seem to be swimming in unfamiliar water, treading awfully close to something without crossing that line. Why do I suddenly want to?

Curiosity. Loneliness.

Maybe both.

Or perhaps I just want to be someone special to Ronan. Someone he'd find first in a crowded room. And I've never wanted that from any man, but strangely with him, I do.

Without a sound, I follow the dim light across the house and down the short hallway until I'm standing at his slightly open door.

I gently rap my fingers against it, peering farther into the room. "Ronan?"

"Come in, Daisy," he answers in a cool, gravelly tone.

I step in with my arms crossed over my chest as I take in the sight of him, shirtless in his bed, in nothing but a pair of dark gray sweatpants with his laptop resting on his legs. He's wearing glasses, but he slowly takes them off, resting them on the nightstand before closing the computer.

"Are you okay?" he asks, and I'm too busy staring at him. This sudden desire I'm feeling for him is like an intense and all-consuming burn. When did this happen?

"Can't sleep," I reply. The room is silent; the only sound I hear is the thrumming of blood in my ears and the shaky cadence of my breathing.

"Come here." His voice comes out in a cool, low command as he pats the empty spot in his bed.

For a moment, I hesitate. Is this crossing a line? Too intimate? Or is this something two people can do without there being any expectations? After I swallow down my nerves, I cross the room and climb into his warm bed. His familiar scent fills my nose as I rest my head against the pillow next to his.

He moves his laptop to the side table, clicks off the light, and lies down next to me.

"Why are you taking me to Paris?" I ask.

"Because I want to," he replies simply.

"But why me?"

There's a low chuckle coming from his side of the bed as he replies, "Most women don't give me so much grief about it. But then again, most women think they have to sleep with me to get trips to Paris and gifts and jewelry."

"That's not true," I say with a yawn. "Most women *want* to sleep with you."

He laughs again. "Maybe so."

"Those women at the club tonight sure did."

After he lets out a sigh, I roll toward him.

"Can I ask you a personal question?"

He turns my way, his broad arm curling under his pillow, and with the bit of light coming through the window, I can just make out the curve of his bicep. "Of course."

"Are you...a pleasure Dom?" This is what working at a sex club does to you. You no longer shy away from asking blunt, invasive questions, as if it's as casual as *Are you a vegetarian?*

To his credit, he barely reacts. "Yes. Why do you ask?"

"I heard those women say something about it when I was... passing by."

He smirks. "When you were eavesdropping."

"Okay, fine. I was eavesdropping. Don't tell on me." I smile sheepishly.

"I won't."

"So what does that mean?"

He clears his throat, adjusting himself on his pillow. "It means I like to be in control, but I like to bring my partner pleasure. I like being able to control when they come, how they come, and how often they come."

I force my breathing to remain steady as I suck in a lungful of air. Beneath the blankets, my feet rub together—my own little nervous habit because, right now, my kinky mind is going wild.

"The person I'm with has to be submissive, though. It's not like just anyone can fill that role."

"Do you have…a partner? Like someone you do that with all the time?"

"No. Not anymore."

"So you just find random women at the club?" I ask.

"Daisy, I've been around a long time. I've had lots of vanilla sex and I've tried just about every kinky thing a person can try. At the end of the day, I've decided that this is just what I like. I'm not ashamed of it, and I have no problem finding partners."

I lift up on my elbow as my eyes widen and a sense of panic starts to rise up inside me. "I didn't mean to pry. I'm sorry. I'm not judging you, I swear."

With one soft smile, Ronan eases my worries. Then he places a firm hand on my shoulder, letting it cascade down my arm, and I let him ease me back down to the pillow. I know it's meant as nothing more than friendly comfort, but I'm hyperaware of it, noting the way I'm reacting to his touch.

"I know you're not judging me. I'm glad you asked. It's good to be curious."

When he takes his hand away, I immediately feel the absence of his touch. But he quickly distracts me with his next question.

"Have you experimented at all with kink, Daisy?"

"No." The word comes rushing out of my mouth, and he notices my lack of hesitation.

"Why not? Not interested?" He's not pushing or prying, just genuinely curious.

"Um…not uninterested, I guess. Just…"

"Intimidated?"

"Yes."

"I get that. Well, if you ever get interested, Eden is a great person to talk to."

Why on earth was I momentarily hoping he'd offer up himself as a guide? But on the mention of Madame Kink, I remember my next question.

"Do you mind if I ask…?"

"If we've slept together?" he finishes my question, which must mean he gets it a lot.

I nod.

With a little chuckle, he replies, "No, Eden and I are just friends." I breathe a sigh of relief until he adds, "We do play together from time to time."

My feet stop their fidgeting and my eyes are like saucers. "What?"

His laugh is gentle and quiet. "I forget that not everyone is so comfortable with this stuff. It means Eden and I sometimes share a sub or rent a room together."

"Oh, I know what it means," I reply. "I just pictured it playing out in my head and everything."

His laughter grows louder. "Go to sleep, Daisy. I think that's enough talk for tonight."

"Oh, come on…" I reply with a whine. When he reaches out to touch me again, it feels less like comfort and more like connection. His large hand brushes my unruly hair out of my face, then strokes my head for a few minutes, our eyes on each other in charged contact.

"You are so innocent and naive, Daisy. And I think I'd like to keep it that way."

I let those words play over and over in my mind as we both fall off to sleep. I'm not sure if I love the idea of him cherishing me or if I'm terribly disappointed that Ronan Kade has no interest in corrupting me.

Rule #12: Call him Daddy.

Daisy

"Of course it's a private jet," I say with a sarcastic smile.

He grins proudly as we walk across the tarmac, his eyes hidden behind dark aviators.

"Would you rather fly commercial?"

"No, thank you," I reply as we reach the plane. There's a flight attendant standing at the top of the stairs waiting for us, and Ronan gestures for me to go first, while he stops to have a word with the pilot, standing on the ground.

"Welcome." The woman greets me cheerfully.

My lips pull into a tense smile as I step onto the plane. I immediately feel a wave of shame over how stunning this plane is, as if I don't deserve this. I shouldn't be taking a single thing from Ronan, but here he is treating me like a queen.

When we both woke up past noon today, we were tangled in each other's arms, and I could immediately feel how tense Ronan was. I was using his arm as a pillow, my body molded to his, and my butt firmly planted against his groin. My eyes popped open in mortification as I realized our position and quickly climbed out of his bed, hiding my face in embarrassment for the rest of the day.

Getting involved with Ronan really is out of the question. I'm here for answers, not to hook up with the same man my mom might have. He just wants to spoil me a bit, and I'm going to let him. That's it.

The flight attendant takes my bag from my shoulder. "Thank you," I say.

"Please make yourself comfortable and let me know if you need anything."

"Thanks," I repeat. There are two rows of seats and a few in the back that face each other with a small table in between. Just as I sit down in one of the seats, Ronan climbs on board and immediately makes eye contact with me.

"Are you all right?" he asks.

"Of course," I reply with a blushing smile. When he takes the seat across the aisle from me, I feel his gaze on my face and I turn toward the window to hide the urge to grin at him.

Head on straight, Daisy.

When I glance back at him, he's snickering, his legs crossed in front of him.

"What is so funny?"

He leans closer so our heads are nearly touching. "This flight attendant is new. I've never met her before. And she seems to think you're my daughter."

My eyes widen as I lift them to look at his face. "She does?"

"Yeah. She said, 'Let me know if I can get you or your daughter anything during our flight.'"

My cheeks flush. "She was flirting with you!" I whisper.

"No, she wasn't." His brow is furrowed in denial as he looks down at his phone.

"Yes, she was. She was checking to see if you'd correct her, and you didn't."

When he leans away, leaving the aisle clear for the flight

attendant to walk through, I get an overwhelming sense of jealousy creeping through me like fire. When she holds the tray carrying two flutes of champagne, I glance up at her face to find her watching Ronan with interest.

He smiles up at her, and my jaw clenches on reflex.

I reach a hand out and intimately brush it against the sleeve of his shirt for no reason at all. Okay, there is a reason, and it's to assert dominance. I notice the way her eyes track the movement, and it pleases me.

"Will I be making up one full bed or two singles for the flight?" she asks.

"One bed," I bark before Ronan has time to answer.

The woman shoots me a fake smile and I bite back my irritation. I have no claim on Ronan and no reason to stop him from flirting with whoever he wants. But I'll be damned if this woman is going to step in on him while I'm *right here*.

I take my hand away from his arm and take the flute of champagne from the tray.

"We can go straight to the apartment when we arrive so you can freshen up," he says. "And if you're up for it, I think the Louvre in the morning would be perfect." He finally looks up from his phone, and I can't help myself. My next words come flying out of my mouth.

"Whatever you want, Daddy."

The flight attendant's eyes snap toward my face at the same moment Ronan's do, and I'm biting my lip so hard, I'm afraid it will bleed. I'm staring straight ahead as I put the bubbly drink to my lips and take a satisfying sip.

But when I turn my gaze to him, I freeze at the expression on his face. It's serious and nearly in shock. He clears his throat, adjusting himself in his seat as he looks away.

The smile drains from my face. After a tense moment, the flight attendant moves back to the private part of the plane, where she's out of earshot.

"Don't do that again," he mumbles.

My cheeks flood with heat. "What? Why?"

With a stern glance, he replies, "You know why."

It's tense and quiet between us as the plane starts to move down the runway, and I'm so lost in this haze of confusion and strange longing that I don't know which way is up.

Did me calling Ronan *Daddy* really affect him that much?

I can't shake this weird feeling in my belly from being reprimanded by him. Ronan has always been warm and kind to me, but that sudden cold tone of his went straight down my spine like ice water.

The entire time we climb to altitude, I'm stewing in my seat. I don't even know why I'm angry at him or what I want, but I'm fuming. So angry I want to stomp my feet and cause a scene. I want that flight attendant to know that *I* am the one here with him, and I'm not his fucking daughter. I'm the center of his attention. The one he will be focusing on. Even if we're not romantic or sleeping together, right now, he belongs to *me*.

We're cruising at ten thousand feet when I feel Ronan's eyes land on my face, and I know he can tell how upset I am. I hate sitting under his scrutiny, so with a huff, I unclasp my belt and bolt out of my seat.

But I don't get far.

"Where are you going?" he says, extending an arm to stop me.

"To the bathroom," I snap, but he clearly doesn't like that, so he hooks an arm around my hips and yanks me into his lap.

I let out a yelp as I land on his legs, staring down at him with shock.

"What are you—"

His hand grasps the back of my neck and he drags my face so close to his, I expect him to kiss me.

"Stop it," he mutters with his lips near mine.

"Stop what?"

"Stop pouting because I told you not to call me that," he responds.

"What?" I ask, feeling obstinate. "*Daddy*? Why not? Because you like it too much?"

With a strong hand on my hip, he grinds my body against his legs, and when I feel the hard bulge in his pants, I let out a gasp. "Yes, Daisy, I do. I like it far too much."

I'm frozen in shock. I don't know what to say or how to respond. All I know is that my body is on fire with desire and all I want is for him to grind his erection against me again.

And again and again and again.

Judging by the clenching of his molars and the wired look in his eyes, he does too.

So why won't he just do it? What is holding him back? Is this really all about keeping me innocent and naive, like he said this morning? Or is there something else Ronan is afraid of?

With a long exhale, he lets go of my neck and the electricity between us starts to fizzle.

"Daisy, I like the way things are right now. Let's not complicate it. Understand?"

With sex, he means. He thinks that once we start sleeping together, I'll just become another fling.

"No. I don't understand, Ronan," I mumble.

With a huff, I stand, pulling myself out of his grasp. I nearly run into the flight attendant as she appears through the curtain with our dinners on a tray. She stares at me, looking smug, and I grimace in return.

My blood is boiling as I realize that he would rather sleep with her because he has no feelings for her, but he won't sleep with me…because he does.

Rule #13: A good daddy always listens and never laughs.

Ronan

THE FLIGHT ATTENDANT MAKES UP TWO BEDS, PROBABLY noticing the cold shoulder Daisy has been giving me during this entire flight.

After eating our dinners, Daisy comes out of the tiny bathroom in a pair of light blue pajamas, the bottoms so short, I can see the curve of her ass below the hemline. I clench my fists as she walks by.

She's fucking with my head—whether she means to or not.

If she were any other woman, I'd have fucked her a dozen times by now. I'd have put her over my knee for that bratty behavior of hers. If she were someone from the club or a match through the app, I wouldn't be so goddamn conflicted. But she's not just another woman. She's young, naive, and so fucking sweet, it kills me.

And I like her. The more she speaks and the things she says make me like her more, and it's infuriating.

I've been here before. I know this routine. And I don't want to do it again.

I won't survive another heartbreak.

Daisy climbs into her bed without looking at me or even telling me good night. She's still angry that I didn't react the way she wanted to the whole *Daddy* situation. And that she couldn't prove to the flight attendant that I belong to her.

I can't say I blame her. I would have reacted far worse than Daisy if another man was vying for her attention and she shut me down. I'd lose my goddamn mind.

But where Daisy is concerned, I'm always losing my mind.

Daisy has no idea the fantasy she's playing into by calling me that and how much I'm ready to say *Fuck it* and take her right now to show her what it means to me. If I didn't give a shit about what happens to us after this, I would. I'd let her call me whatever the fuck she wants.

It's not like she'd be the first woman to utter that word, but she sure as fuck is the first one to use it in a way that feels so fucking genuine.

Call me a sick fuck, but I want to be her daddy. I'd teach her every fucking thing she wants to know. I'd take care of her and protect her and make her feel so goddamn good.

My cock twitches in my pants, so I jump out of my seat to stop my brain from torturing me like this.

The plane is quiet as I lock myself in the small bathroom. I take a look in the mirror and see a man too old for a girl like her. A man who has lived a long, decent life and would be a greedy asshole to wish for anything more. Daisy deserves better than a quick fuck from a guy like me or, God forbid, getting stuck with me when she has so much life left to live.

I've spent so much of my last few years in that damn sex club that it has my brain all kinds of fucked up—I don't need to screw every person I get close to.

When I come out of the bathroom in my blue satin pajamas, the lights are out and Daisy is facing the wall. But when I reach the two separate beds, one on each side of the aisle, I can't bring myself to climb into mine alone.

So against my better judgment, I climb into hers. She stiffens as I drape my body behind hers, pulling her tight to my body.

"What are you doing?" she mutters.

"I sleep better with you near me."

"Last night was the first night we slept next to each other," she argues.

"I know, and I slept great," I reply coolly.

"Fine," she replies with a yawn, and I can't help but smile.

After pulling the blanket up around us both, I tug her closer, so she's resting against my body, the same way she was when I woke up today.

I'm playing with fire here. For a man afraid of growing attached and getting his heart broken, I'm certainly not acting like it. Somewhere in my mind, I think that I can keep Daisy just like this—whatever *this* is.

"Go to sleep, and we'll wake up in Paris," I whisper.

Under the blankets, I feel the gentle rubbing of her feet, the same thing she did last night, and I find myself smirking, my face practically buried in the mess of blond waves on my pillow.

"Night, Ronan," she replies.

"Night, Daisy."

Daisy and I are strolling through the Luxembourg Gardens, my favorite spot in Paris and the first place I brought her when we woke up in the city this morning. After a quick stop at the apartment, of course.

I love the look of awe and excitement on her face. I think I even caught a few tears in her eyes as the car drove us through the city. The pleasure it brings me to see her so happy makes me want to do it forever.

"So what on earth made you move into your van?" I ask as we walk.

She's biting into the croissant in her hand as she contemplates her answer. "You're going to think it's stupid," she replies, taking a sip of her coffee.

"No, I'm not."

"Promise not to laugh at me?"

"I would never laugh at you," I reply with a furrow of my brow.

After a long, heavy sigh, she crumples the paper her croissant was wrapped in and wipes the crumbs off her face with the back of her hand. Then she pauses near a large fountain before speaking. "Three years ago, my mom passed away. She had breast cancer."

"I'm so sorry, Daisy," I say, interrupting her as she plasters a fake smile on her face, something I've noticed she does a lot. Forcing herself to appear brave and unaffected.

"Thank you." She looks down at her hands as she continues. "I was supposed to go to college. The plan was music school, but she passed just after I graduated high school. It was all too much at once. Then, I just got stuck for a while. And I thought the only way to get myself unstuck would be to just run away. My life was so dreary, and I just wanted it to be…poetic."

I find myself leaning closer until I'm standing almost pressed against her, her hip against mine and her hair near my nose again, so I can inhale her delicate scent. "Poetic?"

When her eyes lift, her gaze finding mine, I feel something shift. "You know…something adventurous, with art and music and poetry. I had these big dreams about driving around the country in my van and collecting these rich experiences. Going to museums and hearing musicians play, and then I could just write my music, journal my experiences, and be truly free, without any idea where it would lead to next."

"I think that sounds beautiful," I mutter, my eyes not leaving her face for a moment. Then I touch her little button nose. "You are a dreamer, Daisy."

Then her expression falls. "Yeah, well, dreams are just dreams, and life is not poetic at all. I ended up serving martinis in a sex club, so…"

She steps back, and I hate the listless expression on her face.

"Life can be very poetic, Daisy. But that doesn't mean it will always be pretty."

With a shrug, she shoots me a small smile. "I guess."

"Give it a chance. It just might surprise you." My hand is itching to reach for hers. It would be inappropriate to hold her hand, but I'm struggling to get through an hour without touching her. She crawled into my bed that night, and it was all over for me. Waking up with her in my arms was the nail in my coffin.

We act like friends, but friends don't feel the overwhelming urge to protect the other, not like this. I want to take care of her. I want her to be mine in a way I haven't felt in a very long time.

I want to own Daisy. I bet she would submit beautifully.

But if I fuck her the way I desperately want to, can I promise myself I won't push her away after?

Can I promise my stupid broken heart that it won't get hurt again?

No.

My fists clench subtly as we continue our walk. I let her lead the way, wishing for an opportunity to touch her again.

"Did you grow up in Briar Point?" she asks, making small talk as we stroll through the park. The sound of children playing nearby grows louder as we reach the larger fountain, little remote-controlled boats streaming across the water.

"Yes, I did," I reply. "Not far from the club, actually."

"Really?" she asks, stepping closer, so our arms graze each other's.

"It was just my mother and me. She had to work two jobs to make ends meet. I wanted to give back to her when I grew up, but instead of going to college, I met Julia, and we got married very young. A couple years later, Miles came along. I was just getting started in business and doing pretty well. Well enough to support them."

I pause, taking a deep breath before continuing on. It's not hard to talk about them anymore, but it does cost me a bit of my peace. When I feel ready, I go on.

"Then one morning, she was taking him to the store and they were hit by a driver speeding the wrong way in their lane. Just like that, they were gone."

"Ronan…" she mumbles, as if to tell me I don't have to talk about it.

I don't know why I feel the need to tell her this part. I guess I've never felt so comfortable with other women before. But it's so easy with Daisy.

"It's all right. I can talk about them."

With a small smile, she loops her arm through mine, and I fight back the grin that aches to come out. The tension slides off my shoulders like melting wax.

"Keep going," she whispers.

Slowly we meander our way toward the busy city street.

"After my wife and son died, I buried myself in my work. It allowed me to hide from the pain and loneliness, so that my life became nothing more than business, money, and success."

She squeezes my arm. "Did you ever marry again?"

"A few years later. Her name was Lydia. It was a mistake and was over in three months."

"Did you have any more children?"

I swallow. "No."

"You don't want any more?" she asks with gentle curiosity, as if asking that would be offensive to me, which it's not. Her sweet boldness is refreshing.

Turning toward her, I gaze into those big, blue, innocent eyes. "I wish I had. I'm afraid it's a little late for me now. But I always think about that, who will inherit everything when I'm gone."

She doesn't say anything, her mouth set in a thin line. I place my hand on her arm, realizing we've put ourselves in another bout of awkward silence.

"Did you ever fall in love again?" she asks quietly, barely loud enough for me to hear.

"Yes," I reply without hesitation, thinking immediately about that summer with Shannon.

"What happened?" she asks with softness in her eyes.

"Right person, wrong time."

Her arms squeeze around mine again. After a few minutes, she randomly changes the subject.

"How do you say *I'm hungry* in French?"

"*J'ai faim*," I reply in my clunky French.

She lets out an adorable gasp. "Oh my God. Do you speak French?"

I laugh. "A little."

"You must spend a lot of time here," she replies as we make our way up to the tourist-heavy street lined with restaurants. I keep her close, my eyes shifting back and forth to watch for anyone suspicious.

"I used to spend a lot more. It's been a while."

"Where is your favorite place to go?"

I chuckle, squeezing her closer. "You really want to know?"

"Yes, of course."

"Well, what if I told you there's a club like Salacious here in Paris?"

She gasps again. When she stops and stares up at me with her wide, sky-colored eyes and her mouth hanging open, I already know what's going to come out of her mouth. "I want to go!"

"No," I reply without hesitation. I don't know why I even brought it up.

"Oh, come on. Ronan, I *work* at a sex club. I think I can handle going to one."

"This one is a little different than Salacious."

"How so?" she asks. We cross the street as I take her hand in mine, leading her to a restaurant on the other side.

"Never mind. I don't want to talk about it anymore." My tone is clipped and impatient, realizing that I just opened myself up to this. I genuinely did not think Daisy would be interested in a sex club.

"Well, you have to take me," she argues obstinately. "I want to see it. And I have to brag to everyone back home that I went to a Parisian sex club."

I grumble to myself while she's beaming next to me. Why the fuck would I tell her about that club? I'm sure as fuck not taking her. Because, deep down, I know if I do, it'll have me breaking all my rules.

Rule #14: Play with fire and you'll get burned.

Daisy

OH, HE'S TAKING ME TO THAT CLUB. WHETHER HE LIKES IT OR not. He can't possibly keep treating me like some naive little girl. It's not like we'll be the ones having sex, but I still want to see it. I mean, who wouldn't?

After we eat at this adorable café on the street with little brown wicker chairs under the canopy, he has the driver come pick us up to take us back to his apartment.

It's even more beautiful than his apartment back home, with its tall ceilings and intricate white crown molding. I poke around the apartment, looking at old artwork and trying to figure out how the hell I wound up in Paris with Ronan Kade. This feels like a dream. All day I tried to memorize every little detail. Every moment felt like a line in a song. The warm flaky croissant. The sound of children playing in the park. The way his strong arm felt with mine wrapped around it. The comfort of his protective touch on my back.

Ronan's bedroom door is open, so I wander my way in and find him opening the door of his room that leads to a wrought-iron balcony with a near-perfect view of the Eiffel Tower. Two steps into the room, I gasp.

"It was supposed to be a surprise," he mutters when he sees me. "This room has the best view."

My mouth is hanging open as I approach him. "It's breathtaking."

Pointing to the two chairs and small table, he adds, "You can have your coffee here. It would be a great place to journal or write your songs."

I bite my bottom lip as I let my fingers dance over the iron railing. "That sounds perfect. Will you take me to the tower tonight? To see it sparkle?" I ask as I feel him step closer. I've noticed the way he eats up the space between us lately, and I love it. It's like his will to stay away from me is wearing thin. It's the little things that tell me this. Tiny touches and lingering glances.

Like the way he is right now, stepping up behind me until he's so close, I could lean on him. But he doesn't give in. It's like this is all he wants—nearness, contact, connection.

"Of course," he replies as I feel his fingers gently stroking the strands of my hair.

Suddenly, his phone rings, shattering this tender moment. He reaches into his pocket and glances down at the screen for a moment before turning away from me and hitting the answer button.

"Hello," he says in a curt greeting. I hear a man's voice on the other end of the call, and I crawl onto the bed, although it's clearly Ronan's, watching him with a weird sense of anxiety in my belly. It's ridiculous for me to be jealous of whoever is on the other end of that call or to be concerned that they will take Ronan's attention away from me, but I can't help it.

What if the man on the line wants to meet with him? What if he leaves me? What if he goes to that club and finds a woman who knows how to be his sub? What if he gets tired of me?

Have I become so dependent already? This is ridiculous.

Still, I wait in discomfort while they talk business, and when he says, "Tonight?" I stop breathing.

He glances back at me for a moment, and I hope my face conveys just how pathetic I feel.

"Yes, we can meet tonight. Eleven works."

"But you said—"

He clenches his jaw and furrows his brow as he stares at me with pity. "See you then. Bye."

"Who was that?" I ask, as if I have any right to know.

"It was an old friend and business partner," he says gently, as if he's afraid of disappointing me. Too late.

"You're meeting him tonight, aren't you?"

"Yes."

"Where at?" I reply, afraid of the answer.

"A club." The word sounds heavy as it escapes his lips. He might as well have slapped me with it.

"A sex club?" I reply, my voice sounding weak.

"Yes."

The blood drains from my face as I swallow down my rage. I'm such an idiot. My fears were valid. He doesn't care about me. He wants to find a better woman. What on earth am I even doing here?

I climb off the bed in a fury. "It's fine. I'll go see the tower by myself."

When I try to storm out of the room, he snatches me by the wrist and yanks me back, and I want to hit him. I'm so angry at him, and for what? For not giving me the attention I want? For not wanting me? This has all gone too far. The sooner I'm out of here, the better.

"No, you won't," he bites back.

"You can't tell me what to do, Ronan. I'm an adult. You're not really my daddy."

A high-pitched yelp flies out of my mouth as I'm suddenly thrown onto the bed, landing with a bounce before he's on top of me. The weight of his body is a welcome sensation, but in this moment, I'm too worked up and angry to enjoy it.

My wrists are pressed against the mattress by his hands as he hovers above me. "I told you not to call me that. Didn't I?" he grits out before clenching his teeth.

This power I have over him is intoxicating. And I realize at this moment just how much control I have. I can have his attention and his time, even if I have to push his buttons to get it.

With a devious grin, I reply, "Or what? What are you going to do, Ronan?"

He leans closer until his mouth is just an inch from mine. "I'm going to put you over my knee and spank your ass until you learn."

A wicked laugh bursts out of me as I smile up at him. "Sounds like something a daddy would do," I tease in return.

With a tight expression, he lets out a growl, grinding himself against me. My body lights up with desire, my legs falling open as I welcome him between them, so close I know he can't back out now.

I let out a whimper, tilting my hips to feel the rock-hard proof of his arousal against my core.

"What are you doing to me, Daisy?" he whispers as he lowers himself over me, his mouth going to my neck, instead of my lips, where I truly want it. When I feel his warm breath hovering over my skin, I'm afraid I might go crazy with need. He keeps my wrists in his hands, pressed into the mattress above my head. I'm squirming wildly beneath him, and still, his lips won't make contact with my skin.

"Please…Daddy," I cry out in a high-pitched plea. I know it's a form of manipulation, to use the one thing he can't resist against him, but I'm growing desperate.

And it works. That's what does him in. His eyes find mine, and they are wild and hungry, rich brown irises gazing down at me, and I realize I've never wanted someone so much in my entire life.

His mouth crashes against mine like thunder. He tastes like bourbon and *him*, warm and heady. I'm devouring his kiss like I need it to survive. Hips grinding, fingers grabbing, teeth biting—we are a mess of desire and lust.

I'm practically dying of pleasure already, just from the pure satisfaction of his touch and how *good* it feels to experience him finally letting go. This is happening, and I'm not going to let him stop.

But just as I reach for his belt, he rips his body out of my grasp. It's like being doused in ice-cold water.

"Fuck, Daisy," he barks, standing away from the bed and glaring at me with anger.

"Ronan, don't stop," I beg as I sit up and reach for him.

"I told you not to call me that. Why won't you just listen to me?"

He's pacing the room, looking frustrated and disoriented, not at all like the confident, levelheaded Dom he usually is.

Suddenly, I'm flooded with guilt. Ronan looks as if he's mentally punishing himself for every move with me, and it's my fault for preying on his weakness. Maybe he really does want to protect my innocence. Or maybe he's really been hurt so many times, he'd rather have sex without emotions.

Either way, it kills me to see him hurting—knowing I'm the cause.

I quickly climb from the bed and close the distance between us.

Pressing myself against him, I rest my hands on his chest and gaze up at him with my eyes soft and pleading. "Okay, okay. I'm sorry," I whisper. I'm not making a move to kiss him or touch him like we just were.

With a big exhale, he relaxes. I keep my hands there on his chest as I draw myself closer, resting my cheek where I can feel the erratic pounding of his heart.

His arms draw around me and he squeezes me tightly. And just like that, we feel like friends again. Or whatever we are—not quite friends but not quite lovers either. After a few moments, he speaks.

"It's not that I don't want you, Daisy. You have to understand *just how much* I want you."

Placing his fingers under my chin, he lifts my face until I'm staring up at him. His next words turn me from solid flesh and bones to a melted puddle of nothingness on the floor.

"But the things I want to do to you, baby girl, are dirty, filthy things. And you're too fucking sweet for me."

I move my lips to argue, but not a single word comes out. Because it doesn't matter what those filthy, dirty things are or how much I want him to do them to me.

All that matters is that he knows what's best for him—and I trust him. It's strange that it happened in just a few days, but I do trust him. I trust him to take care of me. To protect me.

Even if that means from him.

Rule #15: Follow the rules.

Daisy

"You have maids in Paris too?" I ask as I wake up from my nap to find a woman cooking in Ronan's kitchen. He's drinking a glass of what I assume is bourbon as he sits in the oversized leather chair in the living room.

"They're called employees, not maids. And no. She works for a friend. I'm paying her well and feeding you at the same time." He looks up from the book in his hand. I'm pleased to find a touch of warmth in his expression, which means he's not still mad at me. "Any more questions?" he asks with a smirk.

I bite my bottom lip. "Can I go to the club with you?"

He lets out a groan and his smirk disappears as his eyes trail back down to the book. "No."

Dammit. Crossing the room with a frown, I lean against the arm of his chair. He sets the book down and I watch his eyes graze the bare skin of my thighs and scan their way up to my face. Then he pats his leg like an invitation, and I find myself climbing into his lap.

Nothing like the plane incident, where he was shoving his

erection into my hip to prove a point. This is far more innocent. I'm done trying to manipulate him and force his hand. Besides, I like this. Being able to nuzzle into his chest, my face close to his neck, so I can breathe in his cologne, his broad arms around me, holding me close.

"I'll be good," I reply quietly. "I'll stay by you the whole time. I won't talk to anyone. I just want to see it and I don't want to be here alone."

His head rests against mine as he strokes my arm, but he doesn't answer. And it guts to me to have to ask this because I'm terrified of the answer.

"Is it because you want to be with…someone else there?"

He pulls his head back and looks down at me. "Absolutely not."

"So take me with you."

We sit in silence for a while as he contemplates before finally replying with a groan. "Fine, but there are going to be rules, Daisy. I know you work in a sex club, but this isn't Salacious. And you won't be there as a drink server; you'll be there as a patron."

Inside, I'm practically screaming. A shudder of excitement is growing deep in my bones. Just the thought of being on his arm all night and seeing God knows what, I almost can't believe it.

"Are you happy now?" he asks as he picks his book back up.

"Yes, Ronan. Thank you," I reply with a smile.

"You're welcome, Daisy."

I rest my head back on his chest. "Will you read to me while we wait for dinner?"

His hand strokes my back gently as he reads. It's something about the history of France during the war. I'm not paying much attention to the words but letting the deep timbre of his voice soothe me as I daydream about all of the possibilities that tonight could bring.

––––––––

The driver stops in front of an old building in a somewhat touristy part of town. When we get out, my long dress nearly touches the cobblestones, and Ronan is there in a heartbeat, putting his hand on the small of my back like he always does.

"It's here?" I ask, looking around at the people passing by. There are restaurants and nightclubs lining the street, but nothing that looks like a sex club.

"This way," he replies, guiding me down a narrow side street. When we reach an old bar that looks more like a speakeasy-type of jazz bar than a sex club, I stare at him in confusion. Without answering my questioning gaze, he just presses me into the club and guides me around the crowd until we reach the back, where an elevator waits for us. There's a man guarding the elevator, and Ronan simply says, "I'm meeting Matis."

The man in the suit nods before pressing a button, and the elevator opens. Ronan ushers me inside and keeps me close to him as the doors close.

"Who's Matis?" I ask.

"The owner," he replies without inflection.

"How do you know him?"

He glances toward me, a quirk in his brow. "Business."

Now it's my turn to look confused. "What kind of business do you have with a sex club owner? Don't you work with like mega-billion-dollar corporations or something?"

He chuckles to himself. "I own a portion of this club, Daisy. Is that what you wanted to hear?"

My lips part as I stare at him in shock. Of course he owns *part of* a sex club. He probably has his money in everything. Is there anything he doesn't own?

Without warning, he turns me toward him, lifting my chin again. "You will stay next to me the entire time, understand?"

I bite my lip to keep from smiling as I nod. "Yes, sir."

His nostrils flare as he lets out a low noise that sounds like a growl.

"I can't even say *sir*?" I ask.

Ignoring my question, he continues. "There aren't as many boundaries here like you're used to at Salacious."

"What does that mean?"

His grip on my back tightens and he pulls me closer. "It means that just because you're seen with me, it doesn't mean people won't try to proposition you."

A playful smirk pulls at the corner of my lips. "And what should I say if they do?"

A sour, dark sort of expression transforms his features as he lets go of my back and moves a hand to my face, cupping my jaw. My head tilts back more as I stare up into his eyes. "You tell them your *daddy* said no."

"Oh, so you can call yourself my daddy, but I can't say it?" I ask in a teasing tone.

As the elevator chimes and the doors open, he turns away from me and adjusts the sleeve of his suit. "Yes, Daisy."

I'm still smiling as he leads the way out of the elevator and onto the club floor. Nothing like the loud but chill aesthetic upstairs, this club is energetic and alive with music and dancing.

The partitioned dance floor is dark and crowded, bodies gyrating and groping one another to the rhythm of the music. Everything about this club has an old art deco sort of vibe, and it reminds me of something out of *The Great Gatsby* or *Moulin Rouge*.

On the wall, in a large neon cursive sign, is the word *L'Amour*, which I assume is the name of the club. While I'm busy staring at the sign, I nearly miss the shadows and silhouettes of the people moving on the dance floor, who are definitely getting it on, VIP style.

My cheeks heat with a blush as I look back at Ronan, who's watching me with a mischievous smirk.

"Okay, so it's not *that* different than Salacious," he says in a low, ominous mutter.

I follow him around the large room until we reach some round tables along the back wall of the club. These are clearly meant for important clientele and owners. It's when we reach the second table that a man takes one look at Ronan and lights up with excitement.

"Monsieur Kade!" he shouts with a thick French accent.

Ronan smiles at the man, who is so completely surrounded by women that he can't even stand from the booth he's in. Instead, Ronan reaches out a hand and the man shakes it emphatically.

"Matis, good to see you again," he replies before turning toward me. "This is my friend, Daisy," he adds, and I'm so caught up on the word *friend* that I'm staring at Ronan too long before reaching out a hand toward Matis.

"Lovely to meet you, Daisy," the man says, holding my gaze as he presses his lips to my knuckles.

He's very handsome and surprisingly a lot younger than Ronan—maybe in his thirties. He has shoulder-length black hair that is slicked back and curled behind his ears, a chiseled jawline, and sharp cheekbones.

When he doesn't let go of my hand, I feel Ronan's touch on my hip, pulling me back toward him, and I remember what he said about people in this club neglecting relationship boundaries.

Why does that idea suddenly excite me?

"Champagne!" Matis yells as one of the servers passes by his table. She nods her head at him before scurrying off toward the bar.

It takes some shuffling of seats, but soon, Ronan and I are sitting in the round booth with Matis and a few of his friends. Except, as we were arranging ourselves in the seats, somehow, I ended up next to Matis with two people between me and Ronan, who is currently flanked by two stunning women.

And just like that, I'm the one feeling territorial.

Matis puts his arm around me. "Is this your first time in a sex club, little flower?"

My lips tighten in a tense smile. "I work in a sex club," I reply, turning toward him. His eyes widen as he glances back at Ronan.

"Are you a performer?" he asks, and I break out in a laugh.

"I'm a server."

He reaches out a hand and strokes my hair out of my face, looking into my eyes as he murmurs, "You could be a performer. Such a sweet little flower."

I'm practically in a trance, staring at him as he caresses my hair. There are conversations happening around us, but for just a moment, it feels like it's only the two of us. Then I sense a pair of serious brown eyes laser focused on our every move.

When I glance toward Ronan, I have to admire how collected he appears to be. Reclining in the seat, one arm resting on the back of it and one leg folded over the other. His body language says *unbothered*, but I know his face well enough by now to know that if Ronan is *not* smiling, then he's angry.

Well, actually, I don't know if *angry* is the right word to describe it. It's more like he's…unsettled. Wired. On edge. If he didn't want Matis touching me or talking to me, he'd be hauling me out of here over his shoulder. I've learned that much about him.

But he's not yanking me out of my seat, and his friend hasn't taken his hands off of me since I sat down. So either Ronan really doesn't want to upset his business partner, or he's *okay* with me being fondled by a stranger—a stranger to me, at least.

"So, what do you think of Paris so far, little flower?" Matis asks.

I turn toward him, biting my bottom lip and tasting the shimmery pink lip gloss. "I love it."

"Has he taken you to the Eiffel Tower yet?"

"Not yet," I reply, glancing toward Ronan with a playful glare. "But he promised to."

"Make him," Matis says with sincerity. "It's the most romantic city in the world. A perfect place to fall in love."

My breath catches in my chest as I stare at Matis, those words feeling heavy and frightening.

When he says it like that, it sounds both exhilarating and terrifying. Life-changing and traumatic.

Perhaps because I know I'd fall first. Maybe I already am.

Which is insane, when I remember how far apart we are in age. I'd be far more excited about falling for him if I wasn't harboring a secret about Ronan that will shatter it all.

I'm building a house of cards around my heart, and *when* he learns the truth, it will all fall apart.

"Don't look so frightened," Matis whispers, leaning in closer. "You've never been in love before, have you?"

I shake my head, gazing up into his eyes.

"I've known Mr. Kade for many years, and I can tell you I've seen plenty of women fall in love with him. He makes it very easy."

If that was supposed to make me feel better, it doesn't. I'm willing to bet every single one of those women, probably even my own mother, wanted to feel special to Ronan. As if they were different. As if they deserved all of his time and attention. But where are they now?

I don't want to fall in love with him if that's what will happen to me. I'll be replaced by the next starry-eyed girl to come along.

"Although I'll admit," Matis adds, "I've never seen him look at any of the other women like he's looking at you right now."

I glance over at Ronan and see him leaning forward now, his eyes focused on my face, his mouth set in a straight line.

When I feel Matis's fingers drift over my bare shoulder, a shiver runs through me.

"You are so exquisite, little flower."

I'm staring at Ronan as Matis's lips graze my earlobe. And I'm just waiting. Why won't he put a stop to this? Why won't he snap?

Not that I *want* Matis to stop. He's gorgeous, and I'm definitely attracted to him. And he clearly likes me. So why would I stop him?

Is that what Ronan is waiting for? For me to put an end to this first? Like some sort of game of jealousy chicken? If so...I'll gladly win.

I turn my head slowly toward Matis, putting our lips so close to each other's, I can feel his champagne-scented breath on my face.

"Let me make love to you, Daisy," he whispers casually.

Oh my God. My eyes nearly bug out as his words spin around in my head. I've never been spoken to so forwardly in my life, and it's incredibly jarring. I literally just sat down. I've only been speaking to Matis for five minutes. And he asked to sleep with me like he was asking to buy me dinner. At least do that part *first.*

"That's enough," a dark, familiar voice bellows, and I pull away from Matis to see Ronan standing up with his jaw clenched and his hands balled into angry fists at his sides.

"Oh, Ronan. You used to be so good at sharing," Matis adds with a laugh as he sits back in the booth and takes a sip of his drink with a smug smile.

"Not with this one," he replies, and I have to remind myself to breathe. "Let's go, Daisy."

He holds out a hand for me, but I hesitate. "But we just got here."

His eyes darken. "Now, Daisy," he barks, and I quietly stand, squeezing my way out of the tight booth and moving toward the man currently glaring at me more like a disgruntled parent and less like a loving friend.

"Au revoir," Matis murmurs in a singsong tone before scooting himself closer to one of the other girls at the table.

"Until next time," Ronan replies casually, nodding to each person around the table.

Then he practically drags me away, and my heart sinks at the prospect that we're leaving so soon. We just got here. I haven't seen a thing.

"Oh, Daisy," he mumbles with more softness than he was showing at the table.

"What? I didn't do anything. It was your friend laying all the moves on *me.*" I'm dragging my feet as he pulls me toward the front of the club. Watching the crowd of *dancers* on the floor, I can't help wishing I could be among them.

Ronan and I reach a crowded area around the bar, and he tugs me toward an empty corner. "You are a brat, Daisy."

My head snaps backward as my wide eyes bore into him. Did he really just call me that? "Excuse me?" I retort in a defensive shriek.

He chuckles in return. "It means a submissive who acts out for attention. You never listen to me."

"It works, doesn't it?" I reply with a half smile, and he laughs to himself as he shakes his head and looks away.

"You have a lot to learn, baby girl."

"So teach me," I reply.

"That would be a dangerous decision, Daisy."

It feels like another step backward, but I don't push it. Not after today.

But that pit of disappointment in my gut is still there. "I don't want to leave yet, Ronan," I say in a plea.

A large hand touches the small of my back, and the rebellious feeling starts to fade. "We're not leaving. I just had to get you away from that smooth talker, Matis. He'd have you on that table, devouring you like a meal in minutes, if I hadn't stepped in."

My brow furrows in confusion as he pulls me farther into the club. "Wow," I reply sarcastically, "thanks for saving me from that."

Rule #16: Help her when you can.

Ronan

"Where are we going?" she asks as we reach the back of the club. There are some things I'd like her to see. Things that are more than just explicit displays of carnal debauchery.

L'Amour is deep and intricate, like a maze. Unlike Salacious, which was obviously well planned to be a sex club, this establishment feels a bit more like a converted nightclub that they made up as they went along. The entire floor is dark and cavernous with dim glowing lights around the perimeter. It operates much like Salacious's VIP room but less discreetly and on a much larger scale.

That is not where I'm taking Daisy. She wouldn't last a minute in there. I'd have to hide her in my coat to keep their dirty hands off of her, and I don't have the patience for that tonight.

Instead, I want Daisy to appreciate the other side of kink.

This part was *my* addition. It's a smaller section of the club and much like the voyeur hallway of Salacious, but instead of a hallway, it's a grand room with large partitioned stalls inside. Each one is open, not even a plexiglass window between the partaker and the audience. Although it's not about voyeurism and exhibitionism here. It's about something deeper and more meaningful. Almost like artists in a museum—Daisy did say she wanted more art in her life.

As we enter the BDSM level of the room, I watch her eyes grow rounder as she takes in the sights. She hugs herself closer to me as we walk, and I'm forced to remember that I've been desensitized—Daisy hasn't, and it's a bit much to take in at first.

So we take it slow. Starting a good distance away, I let her curiosity lead us. There's a bondage performance that catches her attention for a moment before she wanders toward an intense impact-play scene, which surprisingly piques her interest.

She watches with rapt attention as the man strapped to the St. Andrew's cross is taking a lashing with the bullwhip. His Dom is attentive and slow with the swings, checking in on his sub after every few hits.

"He likes that?" she whispers to me as we walk slowly across the room, away from the two men who seem to be coming to the end of their scene.

I'm not so sure how to answer that question. "In short, yes. But...sometimes it's not always about what they *like*. It helps them to understand themselves better...or to heal from trauma, to build their confidence, to strengthen the communication with their partner. There are a lot of very positive reasons why people *like* it."

"Did being a Dom help you?" she asks, gazing up at me with that sorrowful expression. And I know what she's referring to. Did it help me to heal from the trauma of losing my family?

How on earth do I explain to her that it didn't just help me heal? It saved me.

"Yes, it did. What started as just sex quickly became something far more powerful. Even I doubted it in the beginning. I thought being a Dom was all about feeling powerful and superior, but domination is really about control. And it allowed me to control the things I could and accept the things I couldn't."

Her gentle blue eyes are focused on my face as she nods with understanding. As we reach a dark wall on the side of the room, she slowly presses her back against it, her blond brows drawn together in contemplation, and I'm dying to know what is going on in that adorable head of hers.

"Even the pleasure parts?" she asks, and the corner of my mouth twitches upward at the innocence of her question.

Putting my arm against the wall over her head, I press myself closer. "Yes, even those parts. After I lost my family, I lost my purpose. Finding this lifestyle and becoming a Dom gave me back my purpose. As strange as that sounds."

"It doesn't sound strange," she replies, leaning in. "You're…a giver." There's a playful smirk on her face that's far too tempting. So I avert my gaze, focusing on the wisp of hair in her face as I continue.

"Most Doms take their own pleasure from their subs, and that's fine. Their subs enjoy it. That's what their subs need. But the control and power I feel when I can make a person come, not just once but over and over and over, until it's like I control their body more than they do…is *intoxicating*."

Her bottom lip is pinched between her teeth in that way she so often does, but her eyes are glued to mine, a hint of the red light overhead glinting in the blue irises of her eyes.

"I think that's healing for me," I continue. "To take care of someone. To make them feel good. To provide what they need. And to give me a purpose I've lost along the way."

Her throat moves as she swallows and softly nods. "That makes sense."

Our eyes are locked for a few moments, and I wish I could keep her here forever. In Paris. In this club. Mine.

But that's impossible, so I'll savor every sweet moment I do have.

Sliding my hand down her back, I whisper against her ear, "That's enough for tonight. Let's go home."

———

Daisy is restless during the entire car ride back to the apartment and not in a worried, anxious way. She keeps readjusting herself in her seat, her fingers rubbing at the locket around her neck. I have half a mind to ask if she needs to use the restroom, but I refrain. When she hums a tune and mumbles a little song to herself, I turn her way. "What was that?"

"Nothing," she replies, looking out the window.

"Were you just writing a song in your head?" I ask, a smile tugging shamelessly on my lips.

With a slightly embarrassed blush in her cheeks, she replies, "Yes."

"About me?"

She snickers. "About Paris."

"Let me hear it," I reply, nudging her arm.

"No way! It's just…thoughts and ideas. It's not even good yet."

"How long does it take you to write a song?" I ask.

She shrugs, twisting her pretty pink lips in a little knot. "A few days, maybe. Sometimes less."

"Why don't you ever record them? Or perform something?"

"It's just a silly little hobby," she argues.

"No, it's not," I snap in return. "It's a talent not many have. You shouldn't waste something like that."

"I'm not wasting it if *I'm* enjoying it," she replies smugly.

"Well, other people could enjoy it too is all I'm saying. I certainly would."

Her head shifts in my direction. "You want to hear my songs?"

"Very much," I say as the car pulls up to the apartment building and the driver gets out to open my door. Just like last time, Daisy opens her own door, facing the street no less, before I can rush over to open it for her.

"Will you stop doing that?" I mutter sternly at her.

"I'm capable of opening my own door, Ronan." Her tone is sweet but obstinate.

"I know you are," I reply with a sigh as I lead her to the door. I'd still like to open it for her. I want to say that, and maybe I should. But Daisy doesn't need to know all the things I'd like to do for her—literally everything if I could.

When we reach the apartment, I notice her yawning on her way inside, and I'm surprised to see her walking toward the guest room. We might be keeping it strictly in the friend zone for now, but we've shared a bed nearly three times now, if you include the plane ride and the four-hour jet-lagged nap earlier today.

"Where are you going?" I ask, hoping I don't sound too desperate. I was looking forward to having her next to me tonight.

She starts to shuffle toward the bedroom when I notice something strangely erratic about her behavior. As if she's worriedly weighing the option of what bed to sleep in, like it's a matter of life and death.

"I...uh, think I should sleep in the guest room tonight," she stammers.

"Okay," I reply, loosening my tie. "That's fine. Is everything okay?"

Heaving a sigh, she looks at me in disbelief. "Don't you need to...be alone?" she asks awkwardly.

"Be alone?" I'm confused.

She seems exasperated with me by the time she finally comes out with it. "We were just in a sex club, Ronan. I don't know about you, but I'm in a severe state of arousal, and I am dying for relief!"

I'm not often struck speechless, but she's done it. I don't know what's more stunning—her basically admitting that she has plans to masturbate or the realization that she's excessively aroused.

"Okay," I reply dumbly before she scurries off to the guest room, probably mortified at what she just declared she's about to do. In a state of shock and confusion, I shuffle into the master bedroom and begin undressing.

The entire time I'm getting myself ready for bed, I have these questions roaming around in my head. Is she doing it right now? Is Daisy somewhere in my apartment touching herself under her covers? How does she do it? Does she roughly finger herself, curling them to find her G-spot? Or does she circle her clit with her thighs pressed together? Does she have a toy in there? Is she watching porn?

I'm going mad. Absolutely fucking crazy.

My body feels strung tightly, wired and anxious, ready to tear down the doors of this apartment to see what she's doing. It's obvious to me now that the more I deny myself what I want with Daisy, the more intense it's going to get. Before long, she will have me literally insane with need for her.

I try to crawl under the sheets of my bed and go to sleep alone, ignoring what I know she's doing a couple doors down the hall. I try, but I fail miserably.

Why did she have to tell me that?

In a fury, I throw off the blankets and storm across the room. There's not a rational thought in my mind to justify what I'm about to do. I have absolutely no right in the world, but I don't care.

I don't know what I'm about to find as I march to her room like a savage. I'm fully aware of how rude and brutish it is for me to barge in the way I am, but she has me wild beyond decorum. As I throw open the door to the guest room, I'm shocked to find her lying silent and still under the covers, on her side.

She gasps as I enter the room, jumping up to stare at me in shock. "What are you doing?"

"What are *you* doing?" I reply with accusation.

She responds with a roll of her eyes, dropping back down to her pillow. "Relax. I'm not doing anything. I was too humiliated for even saying that. Sort of killed the mood." Then, her brows furrow as she glares at me from her bed, her eyes raking over my half-naked appearance. I'm standing in her room in nothing but a tight pair of gray boxer briefs with my rock-hard cock pointing upward. It's obvious that I've been thinking about her masturbating for the last five minutes—which is exactly what I was doing.

"Why are you here? Am I not allowed to have privacy?" she complains.

I don't answer her. There simply isn't a response for that question, not one that makes sense at least.

So I walk silently around the bed and climb in behind her, sliding under the sheets until my body is nearly touching hers.

"Let *me*," I say in a bold request.

She stares at me over her shoulder, a rightfully perplexed expression on her face. "Let you what?"

I nuzzle closer. "Let me relieve your ache, Daisy."

Her breath hitches, just as her eyes meet mine, hope and anticipation coloring her features. As her lips part, I know she's itching to say something, but she stops herself. Instead, her head tilts into a slow nod.

"I need to hear you say it, baby," I say, using a soft, authoritative tone.

Her eyes are moist and her pupils dilated as she licks her lips and softly mumbles, "I want you to touch me, Ronan. I want you to make me come."

My cock twitches in my boxer briefs and all of the reasons in my head that have been telling me to keep my distance seem trivial and useless now. Self-preservation and defense mechanisms have nothing on those beautifully wanton words leaving her precious lips.

"Lie back, Daisy."

I can't believe this is about to happen, even as I pull her back so close to my body, we're practically fused together. Then, I ease my right hand under the covers and over her soft hip. She's in nothing but a small T-shirt and a lace thong. As my fingers skate over her belly and down to the warmth between her legs, she lets out a strangled gasp.

"I'll stop if you want me to," I whisper.

Her hand covers mine as she shoves my fingers over the moist center of her panties and says, "Don't you dare stop."

My jaw is tight as I ease the fabric aside and run my finger through the delicate lips of her precious cunt. She's already soaked, pools of arousal at the entrance, her clit so swollen and sensitive to the touch that she flinches and gasps every time I graze it.

"Oh, Daisy." I growl. "You're suffering, baby girl. Do you want Daddy to make you feel better?"

What the fuck am I doing? I'm throwing caution to the wind. I'm sailing headfirst into a storm, and I don't know if I'll make it out alive. But those words just slip through my lips so effortlessly, like I was made to utter them to her. And it's not wrong, perverted, or sick—it just feels right.

Judging by the way she groans and shoves her backside against my aching cock, she doesn't think it's so wrong either.

"Yes, Daddy," she cries with a needy hum. "Please help me."

My middle finger plunges deep inside her, just as her hand grasps at my forearm, her nails digging into my skin as I pump it slowly to find the rhythm she craves.

"Like that, baby?" My voice is strained. I'm struggling to maintain my composure. She feels so good in my hand—soaked and trembling. Fuck, I've been craving this longer than I should. But this isn't about me and what I want. No matter how much I love it.

"Yes," she gasps, practically riding my hand. Determined, I add a second digit, thrusting and curling until she's moaning loudly.

My self-control starts to slip as my lips find her neck, trailing hungry kisses across her jaw and cheek, then up to her ear. She's writhing against me, and I can tell by the way she jerks my hand tighter against her skin that it's the clit stimulation she wants.

So I pull my soaked fingers from her depths and drag them to her swollen clit, rubbing fast and hard circles that have her practically gasping and shaking.

She's breathtaking like this. So vulnerable and real. Blond waves cascade over her pillow as her pink cheeks dimple from squeezing her eyes closed. Her legs are fidgeting under the blanket, squirming and writhing in desperation.

A desperate-sounding yelp escapes her lips right when I know she's there. "That's my girl," I murmur against her ear. "Come on Daddy's hand."

The cries of pleasure get louder as her thighs seize around my hand, her body contorted in pleasure. Her cunt pulses against my fingers as she comes, her fingers still gripping my arm so tight, I can feel the marks of her nails already.

I'll gladly wear those scars with pride.

We lay like that for a while as I kiss her neck again, listening only to the sound of her rapid breathing. The shape of her body is curved against mine so perfectly I don't want to move.

I wait for her to come down fully from the orgasm before reluctantly slipping my hand from between her legs and sliding her panties back in place. I mistake her for being asleep when she whispers, "What about you?"

Her hand slides across my hip as if she's reaching for my cock, but I grab her wrist to stop her. Placing it back at her chest, I hug her close.

"Don't worry about me, baby girl," I reply comfortingly.

Not another word is spoken before I hear her breathing change, and I know she's asleep. I lie awake for a while, reliving the entire thing, hearing the word *Daddy* on her lips over and over until it lulls me to sleep.

Rule #17: If your sugar daddy wants to spoil you, let him.

Daisy

THIS MUST BE A DREAM. OR HEAVEN. OR SOME STRANGE TWIST OF fate because it's the second day I'm spending in Paris with Ronan Kade, and I still can't believe this is happening.

Hell, I can't believe last night happened—his hand between my legs. Those expert fingers that knew all the right things to do. Coming faster and harder than I ever have in my entire life.

Of course, I was practically edged all day long, with the plane ride, and the moment on his bed, and then the sex club. The need was so painful. I hate the analogy, but I quite literally felt like a cat in heat.

And his hand alone did the trick.

Well…as much as it could, I guess. It didn't stop my ache for *him* completely.

But I'm not pushing it.

After we woke up today, my body still cradled against his, we didn't talk about it. We just continued on the way we were before.

He promised me food, which is what brought us to a cute little café about a block from his apartment. It must be good because it's filled to the brim with customers, and the waitresses are running around like mad.

"Ronan!" one of them yells from behind the bar when she spots us.

"Bonjour, Ilsa," he replies with a wave and a smile.

"It has been so long," she says in perfect English, and I feel Ronan's hand at the small of my back, leading me toward a table by the window. I smile at the waitress watching us, and it feels as if I'm walking around with a celebrity.

When we sit down, I stare at him with scrutiny. "Why does it feel like everywhere we go, everyone knows you?"

He picks up his phone to read a message and answers without looking at me. "I don't know what you're talking about."

"That night at the gas station, you were talking to the owner like you knew her name."

"Her name is Sherie."

"See. How do you know that?"

He sets his phone down and looks at me with a smirk. "Because I take the time to get to know people. Why is that strange to you?"

I open my mouth to reply, but nothing comes out. A moment later, the waitress, Ilsa, brings us menus, but Ronan waves them away. "No need, Ilsa. You know what I like."

"A raclette, two plates?" she asks with a smile.

"Yes, please." He shoots her a dashing smile, and I bite my lip, staring at him across the table. "Champagne as well."

"Oui, monsieur."

After she leaves, he glances toward me, his arms folded on the table.

"What did you just order?" I ask curiously.

"You'll see."

About fifteen minutes later, Ilsa brings an entire contraption to our table, and I almost can't believe my eyes. It's half a wheel of cheese tilted over an open flame, so it melts slowly over an assortment of cooked potatoes, bread, and sliced sausage.

"Oh, I definitely died and this is heaven," I say as soon as the first bite of warm, gooey cheese hits my tongue. Ronan watches with a pleased expression as I savor each delectable bite.

"You like it?" he asks after a sip of champagne.

My mouth is full as I hold back a giggle, covering my face with a napkin. "I'm so happy right now," I reply, and when he grins back at me, it becomes even more true.

It's not about the luxury or the age difference or anything other than how incredibly good I feel around him. Someone else's happiness has never mattered so much to me in my entire life.

And it's very clear by the lavish meals and what happened last night that Ronan really does find pleasure in spoiling me. Just the way he's contentedly watching me proves that.

But I can't help but wonder—who spoils him?

"I'm going to write a song about this cheese," I say with a mouthful, and he laughs.

"I'm glad you like it, and I look forward to hearing that song."

As he refills my champagne, he shoots me a wink before handing it to me.

"Eat up, baby girl," he murmurs.

"Yes, Daddy," I reply sarcastically.

I'm still feeling a little tipsy from the bubbly we had with lunch as we take another walk around the city. Ronan's apartment is near the same part of town as an old bookstore that we spend over an hour in. It's like a dream, stacks of dusty old paperbacks in every little nook and cranny. I pick up a French songbook as a souvenir, and he finds an old edition of Emily Dickinson poetry. When he tries to pay, I nearly tackle him away from the register. It's not much, just a couple books, but it means something that I can at least get him this.

When we're done at the bookstore, we continue our stroll. My fingers itch to touch him, so when our hands brush, I take the opportunity to link them together, which he doesn't seem to mind. His large hand is soft, and I nearly melt when his thumb strokes the back of my hand.

From time to time, the people passing us stare for a moment too long, but I actually sort of love it. I'm sure they're thinking that I'm much too young for him, but I don't care. I feel like his, and I want them all to know it.

As we reach a promenade near the Louvre, I hear a piano playing in the distance, and I don't even realize I'm walking toward it until we're watching a young man play a purple upright piano covered in graffiti. A small crowd is gathered around him as he does his best to get through a simple classical piece.

I can't help the smile that pulls at my lips as I watch. His fingers stumble on certain chords and transitions, but it's clear he was classically trained.

When the song ends, the crowd cheers, and he stands from the bench and walks away with a small group that I assume is his family.

The piano sits on the cobblestones in silence as the mass of spectators disperse.

"Go ahead," Ronan says with a nudge.

"No," I object, shaking my head and staring at him in shock.

"It's for everyone to play, so play it."

"I don't…like to perform for others," I say, pushing back against him.

"Then, perform for me."

I lift my eyes to his face and we share an intimate look. Then, he curls a strand of hair behind my ear. "Go, Daisy."

And I can't *not* listen to him. While everyone on the street passes by without a second look, I ease my way up to the lonely piano and have a seat on the bench. It's covered in dents and scratches, but as I set my fingers on the keys, the sound is surprisingly beautiful.

Even with all that it's been through on the streets of Paris, this instrument makes a perfect sound. So with my eyes on Ronan, standing just on the other side of the promenade, I play a song. This one is upbeat, fast and melodic, and without thinking about the people passing by or anyone hearing the little notes I mess up, I keep my focus on him. Even when I look down at the keys, I imagine that he's the only one listening.

But before long, he's not the only one. In my periphery, I see the crowd starting to collect in a circle around me, but I keep my cool. Just like in his apartment, I let the music take me somewhere else.

And I can't stop. I feel like an old version of myself, and I'm practically weightless as the song continues. When I glance up and see someone drop a bill on the top of the piano, my eyes widen. I glance at Ronan, who's beaming with pride.

As the song ends, everyone standing around me erupts in cheers and applause. I'm swimming in the celebration as I rise from the seat and take the coins and bills dropped on the top of the piano and rush into Ronan's arms.

"That was amazing," he says, squeezing me tight.

"Thank you," I whisper into his neck. When I pull away, I gaze into his eyes. "For everything."

Rule #18: Paris is the city of lights (and orgasms).

Daisy

"IT'S NOT SPARKLING," I SAY AS RONAN LAYS THE LARGE PLAID blanket on the grass.

"As soon as it gets dark, it will." The sun has set over the city, but its light still warms the sky, and I'm getting anxious to see the infamous twinkle of the tower. Even though we could see it from the apartment, he still insisted that we enjoy it from here.

"Oh," I reply, taking a seat next to him, trying to maneuver my legs to the side in this knee-length dress, so I don't flash the other people sitting around us. It's not too crowded, but there are a lot of people here with the same idea as us. As he uncorks the bottle of wine he brought, I pull the extra blanket over my legs. Then he reclines one arm behind my back, so we're nestled close to each other.

After he passes me a glass of chilled white wine, we tap our glasses together in a silent toast, then fall into a delicate silence, the sound of people chattering around us like soothing white noise. The tower looms in the darkening sky, and I suddenly feel a wave of unexpected emotion rolling over me.

My mother would have loved this.

The thought hits me like an assault, mostly because it comes with a sense of grief that I'd rather not be feeling in this otherwise romantic moment. Emotion gathers heavily in my throat, and my eyes start to sting with tears.

Not now, I internally beg myself.

Turning my face away from Ronan, I quickly try to blink the tears away. I'm in Paris for goodness' sake. I should be elated, but I can't seem to understand why all the happy things that happen to me suddenly feel like sad ones.

Ronan's hands lightly slide up my arms. I expect him to ask if I'm okay or hassle me into telling him what's wrong with me. Instead, he pulls my face toward him.

"You're thinking about your mother, aren't you?" he asks, and I feel momentarily gutted by the mention of her. How he just knew the thoughts in my head without even trying.

I nod my head.

His mouth tenses, those full lips of his pressing into a straight line, as if he suddenly understands. "Traveling really brings out the grief. It's normal. It took me three years to take a trip after my family died. For so long, the guilt I felt for being happy kept me from ever being truly happy. But you don't need to feel guilty, Daisy. You're allowed to be happy."

"I know," I whisper, another wave of tears trailing down my face. He pulls me between his open legs, so I'm using his body as my own personal blanket, and he squeezes his arms around me.

"But being sad is okay too, baby girl."

I draw in a lungful of air, and it feels like the first deep breath I've taken in a very long time. With my back against his chest, I stare up at the tower and try to be in the moment. With him, like this, I feel safe—physically and emotionally.

How long can this last, though? Is it stupid of me to wish for something longer? We haven't even defined what we are, but I know it's something. To me, it feels like everything.

But what am I to him? A fleeting moment? A momentary companion? A weeklong fling?

It feels like more. It has to be more.

Suddenly, I notice a woman staring at us from her own blanket about ten feet away. Her eyes dance back and forth from Ronan's face to mine, and seeing as how she's closer in age to me than him, I'm guessing the harsh expression on her pretty face is judgment.

But she can judge me all she wants. I've stopped seeing his age. I don't see his years, his wrinkles, his gray hair, none of it. I just see him. The number of years a person has lived seems like such a trivial detail when you find someone who lights a spark in your soul and makes life worth living again.

He has one arm slung over the top of the blanket I'm holding up to my chest, but I casually shift my arm, putting his under the blanket and snugly holding it against my stomach. Instead of pulling it out, he squeezes me tighter.

When I move my head just slightly to the side, I feel his breath against my cheek. We are teetering on the edge of something big. As much as I hate to push him, I think we're both ready to take the leap.

"Ronan," I whisper.

"Yes, Daisy," he replies, his mouth against my ear.

"I'm not sad. Not anymore. Not like this." My fingers rest over his until our hands are clasped, and I wonder if he can feel how badly I want him, how much I'm aching for his touch.

"Neither am I." He kisses the side of my head.

I can practically feel his heart beating and the slow but heavy cadence of our matching breaths as I lean into him. I squeeze his hand in mine before ever so slightly nudging his hand downward.

His body shudders against me as he lets out a husky exhale. "Baby girl, you make me crazy."

"Why are you fighting it so much?" I reply in a whisper.

"I don't know anymore. You make me forget."

"Then, touch me. Touch me like I know you want to."

"Fuck," he mutters darkly against my ear in a tone so low, I know only I can hear it.

His hand trails down from my belly, and I release my hold as he reaches the hem of my dress, dragging it upward until I'm exposed. Thankfully, the blanket lying over our bodies has his movement hidden from view.

As dusk starts to turn into darkness around us, his soft touch eases closer. When his fingers brush the soft fabric of my panties, he murmurs in my ear, "Take them off."

"Out here?" I whisper, looking around.

"Now, Daisy. Take them off."

I swallow, easing my arms under the blanket, and as gracefully as possible, I shimmy my panties down my legs, quickly snatching them up in my hands once they're past my bare feet. I hold them in my fist before he takes them from me, pressing them to his nose with his ravenous eyes on me before shoving them into his pocket. Then he eases me back against his chest.

"Spread your legs for me, baby girl."

I let out a quiet whimper as I lean against him, his fingers going straight to the aching core between my legs. His touch feels like heaven, soft and gentle, teasing me to the point where I start to writhe.

"Be still, Daisy. We don't want anyone to know what I'm doing to you under this blanket."

I have to bite my lip to keep from moaning as his fingers circle my clit for a moment before leisurely sliding inside me. Ever so slowly, he plays with me, his touch unhurriedly exploring me. My eyes close, savoring the delicate intimacy between us. We might be in public, surrounded by people at one of the most famous attractions in the world, but right now, it's just me and Ronan.

I nearly yelp as his thrusts grow more powerful, my body buzzing with need. He's playing me like an instrument, and his fingers know all the right notes.

"I miss your moans," he whispers in my ear. "Tell me how that feels."

"It feels…so good," I reply breathlessly between gasps for air.

"I love the way you soak my hand, Daisy. You're so wet for me."

I bite back a whimper.

When he adds a second and then a third finger, I feel so full and stretched around him. He picks up speed, keeping his motions small but intense, so it's not overly obvious. But soon, I'm strung tight. The inability to move or squirm or cry out is making it ten times hotter, and I'm about to explode.

When my eyes fall closed with my face pressed against his neck, he nudges me to open them.

"Watch the tower, Daisy."

"I can't," I whisper. "I'm gonna…"

Just then, the Eiffel Tower illuminates in glowing white light, sparkling in the dark night sky. At that very moment, Ronan moves his fingers to my clit, circling hard and fast, forcing me to come so violently, I let out a muffled scream. Thankfully, the crowd cheers for the lights, drowning out my cries.

I squeeze my eyes closed, leaning hard against his chest as pleasure floods every inch of my body. Wave after wave, I ride out the orgasm until I'm fully spent and trying to catch my breath. The tower sparkles for a few more minutes, and before it stops, I feel Ronan's hand, still wet with my arousal, as it slides around my throat.

He pulls me backward, turning my face as he kisses me hard. I'm drunk on his touch when he finally pulls away. His lips are still touching mine as he mumbles, "We need to go back to the apartment. Now."

Rule #19: Rules were made to be broken.

Ronan

I'M PRACTICALLY DRAGGING HER OUT OF THE PARK. I MAY HAVE A great view of the tower from the apartment, but we still have to get there by car. The driver is waiting for us as Daisy and I climb in, in a rush.

Thank fuck the partition is already up because the moment my ass hits the seat, she's on my lap, her legs straddling my hips as I pull her lips to mine, ravenous for her mouth. She tastes delicious and so sweet as our tongues tangle, and I'm eating up every little moan and yelp she emits.

Fuck the rules. Fuck trying to protect myself from heartache. Fuck the past, and fuck the future.

Right now, it's just about her and me, and this boiling hot passion that neither of us can seem to ignore any longer.

I need Daisy. I feel as if I might die without her touch because life certainly isn't worth living without it. She's come by my hand two nights in a row now, and I don't think I can wait another second before I have her coming on my cock.

She's writhing against me now, grinding her hungry little

pussy against the hard length in my pants, and it's both the cutest and the hottest fucking thing I've seen in my life.

"You're making a mess on my pants, baby girl," I say with a laugh between kisses.

"I don't care," she replies, barely breaking the contact between her lips and mine. "I need you, Ronan."

"Ronan?" I ask, kissing my way down to her neck, licking up the salty-sweet taste of her skin.

Letting out a sexy laugh, she digs her fingers in my hair. "I need you, Daddy."

"God, I love it when you call me that." I grunt against her throat.

"I thought you hated it," she replies, pulling back and stilling the motion of her hips.

I grab on to her waist, grinding her down on me. "No, baby. The problem is that I like it too much."

The car pulls up to the apartment, and she climbs eagerly off my lap as the driver opens the door for her. I'm right behind her, and we're rushing into the building together, her hand in mine as we reach the elevator. The moment it closes, her back is against the mirrored walls, and I'm devouring those perfect lips again.

Just knowing there is nothing under her dress, no barrier between me and her perfect cunt, makes me crazy. Everything about Daisy drives me crazy. Her sweet and her stubborn sides. The way it sounds when she calls me her daddy. Those little humming sounds she makes as I kiss her.

It makes me want to get more than a hum.

My body takes over, and the next thing I know, I'm on my knees in front of her. I don't care that we're in an elevator that could stop for anyone. I need her taste on my tongue. I drag up the hem of her dress while I lift her left leg, and suddenly, I'm unhinged.

I lunge for her, dragging my tongue through her perfect pink folds. Like a wild animal with his first taste of a woman, I don't lick her sweet cunt for her pleasure—like I normally would. I do it because I'm desperate for a taste. I warned her about this. That the things I wanted to do to her were filthy, and this is nothing compared to what I really have in mind.

"Ronan!" she shrieks, her trembling fingers clutching my hair at the scalp.

But I don't stop. My tongue laps at her core like a starved man, and when I close my lips around her pussy, plunging my tongue inside her, she lets out a husky groan that sets my body on fire.

God, I need more. I need it all.

All too soon, I hear the bell of the elevator chime at our floor. After jumping to my feet, I toss her over my shoulder, carrying her into the apartment with her bare ass on display. I take her straight to the bedroom, tossing her onto the mattress and grabbing her legs to yank her to the edge.

Her cheeks are flushed and she's wearing a lust-filled expression as she stares up at me. Everything about her is perfect.

She keeps her eyes on my face as I pull her upright, dragging her dress over her head. Then I find the clasp of her bra, quickly unhooking it so that it falls away and I have a full view of her.

"My perfect girl," I say adoringly, letting my eyes rake over her entire body. Then, I trace my fingers over her pert breasts and down her soft stomach. She shivers in the wake of my touch, biting down on her bottom lip.

I make quick work of my clothes, too goddamn eager to feel the bare skin of her body against mine. My cock aches behind the zipper of my pants, and I pull them down in a rush, noticing the way her eyes trail downward as it bounces free from my boxer briefs.

"On your hands and knees, Daisy," I say in quiet command. Her eyes light up in anticipation as she shifts to kneeling and hovers near the edge of the bed for me.

Leaning down, I kiss her sweet lips. Then I stand upright and gently guide her mouth to my cock.

She moves her lips hungrily toward me, but I hold her back by her chin. "Easy, baby," I grunt in a warning. With her mouth hanging open and her tongue out, I ease my cock toward her, watching her eyes darken with lust as I slide easily into her mouth.

The suction of her lips around my shaft, pulling toward the head, draws a low growl of pleasure from my body. When she adds a sweet hum, I nearly lose it.

"Oh fuck," I mutter in a low, husky moan. "Your mouth is like heaven, baby."

She drags her lips up and down my hard length like slow, warm ecstasy. I wish I could stay like this forever, but after she swirls her tongue around the tight head of my dick, my control snaps.

Yanking her mouth away, I hold her by the chin. "Turn around for Daddy," I say in a controlled command. As she quickly turns on all fours, I climb onto the bed behind her.

Once I have her beautiful pink pussy in my sights, my cock leaking with anticipation, I pause.

"Daisy..."

"Yes?" she replies sweetly.

"I have condoms in my side table drawer."

She hesitates for a moment. "I...I don't want to," she says, and my brow furrows with concern.

"What do you mean you don't want to?"

"You've been tested, right? So have I. I'm on birth control."

My hands are on her sexy round hips as I stare down at her. I shouldn't. But where this girl is concerned, I can't think straight. And just as I open my mouth to argue, she utters the words that ultimately do me in.

"I don't want there to be anything between us. I want you to come...inside me."

Fuck. How does she do this? How, with just a few words, does she completely dismantle my resolve and turn me into a desperate, dirty man?

"Oh, baby girl. Daddy wants that too." My voice is so strained, my tone is like gravel. I'm at the end of my fuse, ready to explode.

Yanking her back toward me, I line up my cock and notice the way she starts to squirm and writhe. Easing my hand down her spine, I hold her still as I slide my way in, savoring the sight of her body taking every inch of my cock.

She lets out a cry of pleasure once I'm seated as far as I can go, shoving her hips back against me.

"You take me so well, Daisy." I groan. As I pull out and thrust back in, this time with a little more force, she lets out a husky, wanton yelp.

"That's it, baby. Let me hear you." With a firm grasp on her hips, I do it again, and she lets me know just how much she loves it. Her sounds are filthy and beautiful, her fingers gripping the sheets tight as I fuck her.

I keep my movements slow but forceful, and when I stop moving altogether, she slams her hips back against me. "Goddamn. My girl is so eager. Do it again."

She keeps it up, fucking herself with my cock, her moans and cries getting louder. It's fucking amazing, but I know what my girl really needs.

Without warning, I pull out of her, and she lets out a desperate gasp. Quickly, I flip her on her back, shoving a pillow under her ass before I plunge back inside.

Then, I press my thumb to her clit, rubbing hard circles as I pick up my movement again. I watch with delight as her face morphs into divine pleasure.

"Come on Daddy's cock, Daisy," I mutter breathlessly. "Let me see it."

And just like that, the orgasm takes her like an assault. Her legs start to stiffen, her spine curling, and I watch her body climax for the second time today.

At that very moment, I realize something. I could never come again for the rest of my life but spend every single day making her do that, and I'd die a very happy man. I *love* the way she comes. Everything from the way she squeezes her eyes shut to the way she curls her toes. I love it all.

Her pussy pulses around my cock, sending me over the edge. A carnal moan escapes my lips as I spill every single drop inside her, the intensity of it shaking me down to my core.

We are breathless and exhausted as I slowly lower myself over her, resting my head against her chest, just to hear the lively beating of her heart.

Happiness like this doesn't last for long—I know that much. But I'm going to do everything I can to savor every second of it.

It's going to hurt like hell when she breaks my heart, but fuck…she's worth it.

Rule #20: Enjoy the view.

Daisy

WHEN I PEEL MY EYES OPEN THE NEXT MORNING, EVERYTHING feels different. I'm curled up under the covers in Ronan's bed. But when I roll over to lay my hands on him, I find his side cold and empty.

Normally, I'd feel panicked or paranoid, but I don't with him.

Instead, I sit up and look around the room. The windows are open, bathing the room in warm light, and when I grab my phone off the nightstand, I read the time. Only nine in the morning. Which is impressive, considering we stayed up half the night trading orgasms, wrapped up in each other's bodies until the exhaustion hit.

My sleep cycle is definitely a mess, but who cares? I had the most amazing night and the most amazing sex of my life, and it feels as if I've only scratched the surface of what we could be.

For the first time in months, I feel alive.

After jumping out of bed and cleaning up in the bathroom, I toss on one of my spring dresses I packed and do some poking around the apartment. There's a desk in the bedroom by the french doors that lead to the balcony.

The thing that catches my eye on the desk is my open lyric journal. There's a pencil lying in the center to keep it open and I come closer to find someone else's handwriting scrawled across the page.

> You want your life to be poetic, so here you go.
> I'm not a poet but I've been dying to tell you this.
> Your eyes are not as blue as the sky.
> The sky is as blue as your eyes.
> You write the rest.

A smile stretches across my face as my fingers trace the thin gray lines on the page, rereading them over and over and over. Ronan wrote this.

I can't stop smiling as I pick up the journal and stare at the blank lines under his note. Grabbing the pencil, I carry the journal out to the balcony, curling up in the wicker chair and placing my feet against the wrought-iron railing. In the distance, I keep the tower in view as I let words spill out of me like water, soaking the pages.

I can't remember the last time I felt so in tune with my pencil and the lyrics I'm scribbling. It feels like someone else is writing this song. Like I'm possessed.

I write about dusty bookstores and the Eiffel Tower at night. I even write a line about melted cheese over potatoes.

It's all so fluid and effortless. And nowhere in my mind is there space for grief or pain. I'm not even thinking about the *big secret* anymore. Night will come eventually, but for now, I want to bask in the sun.

I barely even notice when the front door slams. I'm finishing a stanza, when I feel him standing over me.

"It worked," he whispers, and I finally look up to smile at him.

"What worked?" I ask. It's then that I notice he's in a pair of jogging shorts and a tight, sweaty T-shirt. Did he really go for a jog after the sex marathon we pulled last night? What is this man made of?

"My little note. I told you...I'm not a poet."

I'm gazing up at him with the morning sun beaming over the city, and for the hundredth time since I met Ronan, I admire just how dashingly handsome he is. Streaks of black in his mostly gray hair, a crisp jawline, strong cheekbones, and eyes so gold they radiate warmth.

"I love it," I reply, just as he leans down to press his lips to mine.

"Good."

He walks away, lifting his shirt from the back and pulling it over his head before tossing it into the hamper by the closet. I'm staring at his defined back muscles, replaying the events of the last few days.

Should I be ashamed of this whole...*Daddy* thing? What started as a joke became something that not only has us both very aroused but also has given me a sense of security and comfort that I haven't felt in a very long time, if ever.

Is that worse? That I call Ronan *Daddy* because he literally watches over me and treats me like his little girl?

Even if it is, who cares?

Clearly, he and I share a kink for it, and we both enjoy it, so why should I feel weird about calling him that? It has nothing to do with Ronan being my actual father and every-thing to do with us giving each other something we're clearly both craving. He feels best when he's needed, and I feel safest when he's there to protect me. If people think that's weird, then fuck them.

When I hear the shower come on in the bathroom, I abandon my journal and pencil on the patio table and follow the sound.

I turn the corner into the bathroom with its glass shower walls currently steaming up from the hot water. Without a word, I peel off my dress and pull open the shower door. He's watching me with his back to the tile wall as if he was waiting for me.

I freeze, gazing at his face with the water running in rivulets from his thick gray hairline down to his coarse beard. Then, with my bottom lip pinched between my teeth, I let my gaze stray over his tan, muscular chest coated with a thin layer of hair and across his soft abs, all the way down to his hardening cock. I notice the way his chest hair darkens from white to black as it trails downward.

I've never found an older man so attractive in my entire life, but Ronan Kade has somehow rewired my brain.

"Enjoying the view?" he asks in a teasing tone.

"Yes," I reply with a smile. "Do you sleep with a lot of women my age?" The question pops into my head and I don't even fully understand why.

His brows pinch inward. "Not a lot. I'm not *only* interested in twenty-one-year-olds, if that's what you're wondering. Do you only date men my age?"

I chuckle. "The oldest man I'd slept with before yesterday was twenty-five."

He scoffs. Then, he reaches for me, scooping me up by the waist and dragging my body against his. "Well, that is unfortunate, but your standards are much higher now," he replies, and I giggle again.

Ronan cuts off my laugh with a kiss. I hum against his lips, loving the way his trimmed beard scratches my nose and chin. His body is both hard and soft, with toned muscles that he clearly works hard to maintain, but also a thick layer that proves he indulges in life at the same time. I think I prefer the soft parts anyway, especially as he circles his arms around me and holds me tight.

When he turns us around, so my back is against the tile wall, I open for him. He hooks an arm under the leg I have raised, then with our eyes on each other, he slides in, eliciting a long, breathy moan from my body. At this angle, with the pressure against my clit, I can feel my body warming with pleasure.

"You feel so good, Daisy. Like you were made for me."

I run my fingers through his wet hair as he moves slowly inside me. I love the idea of him savoring me, deriving pleasure from my body. It's a slow build toward something explosive. For a long time, I just ride this slow, gentle wave along with him.

"Harder." My voice is nothing but air and moans, but when Ronan pounds into me, knocking my backside into the wall, I lose the ability to speak altogether.

"Like that, baby girl?" he says with a groan. "I want you to tell me exactly how you want it."

"Yes." I force out a sound, resembling an answer, as my body tightens like a spring ready to explode.

"Yes, what?" he replies, and I'm too busy holding my breath against his relentless pounding, waiting for the climax to knock me down, that I miss his response. "Yes, what, Daisy?" His voice is loud and deep, harsh with his own exertion and desire.

When the words finally do find their way to the surface, I'm practically screaming. "Yes, Daddy."

Fireworks detonate behind my closed lids as I ride out my orgasm, wishing it could last forever. But all too soon, it's over, and he's groaning loudly into the crook of my neck, shuddering against me. We're both breathing raggedly when he finally pulls out of me, his warm cum leaking down my legs.

His fingers find the mess along my inner thighs, sliding it upward, like he's trying to put it back in. "Seeing my cum leak out of you makes me want to fuck you again, baby girl."

I gaze up at him, speechless, consumed by the inferno burning inside me from that statement alone. Then, he lifts his cum-coated fingers and trails them across my bottom lip. I quickly swipe my tongue across my lip, tasting him. Leaning in, he kisses me, his own cum mingled between our lips.

It's so erotic and sexy and makes me want him all over again.

"Do you think I'm depraved, Daisy? For wanting to fill you up every moment I can?"

Wistfully, I shake my head. *I want that too.*

"If you're depraved, then I'm depraved," I reply.

With a smile, he kisses me again, this time deeper, with a hint of desperation. When we finally do pull away, there's something in his expression that worries me. Something that makes me feel as if he's not as enthusiastic about this as I am.

"Everything okay?" I ask, as if he'd tell me.

He hesitates.

But a moment later, he just nods and presses his lips to my forehead. "More than okay, Daisy. Much more than okay."

And with that, I smile and try to force my worries away.

Rule #21: Don't be afraid of hope.

Daisy

"WHAT ARE YOU READING?" I ASK. WE'RE ON A BENCH IN THE middle of the same park we visited on our first day—his favorite park. It's our last day in Paris before we go home tomorrow, and I'm not ready to leave. I feel weightless here. Like I've finally found the freedom I was longing for after my mother died. It's the city and it's him. I'm living in a snapshot of the life I've always wanted to live, and tomorrow, I'll have to wake up from this dream.

My feet are in his lap as I rest my head against the side of the bench, watching the people passing by. He turns the old book in his hand to show me the cover. It's the collected works of Emily Dickinson that I bought for him yesterday, and I feel a blush warm my cheeks.

"Are you brushing up on your poetry?" I ask.

"Might as well."

"Will you read me something?"

"Of course," he says before flipping through a few pages. When he lands on one he likes, he clears his throat and reads it out loud in a gentle tone.

On the first line, my throat tightens and my eyes sting.

"'Hope' is the thing with feathers that perches in the soul and sings the tune without the words, and never stops—at all... '"

It was my mother's favorite. Hearing it in his voice is like an invasion. Two worlds colliding.

While he speaks, the thumb of his free hand runs along the top of my foot to my ankle then back up, and I stare at him as if my heart is being slowly pulled out of my chest.

Even without confirmation, I've accepted the possibility that my mother loved Ronan. And I hate the reminder because it means I have no right to love him the same way. He's not mine. How much would it hurt her to know that he and I are together? To know what we've done? If she were alive, would she be angry with me? Jealous, even?

His voice offers warmth and comfort as he reads, and I try to find something new in the poem that I never found before. But hope feels like a trigger. I wasted hope on my dying mother, so it feels foolish to hope for anything now.

To wish for happiness like this to last more than one week in Paris. Is it too soon to hope for more? Is it foolish to hope for forgiveness when I decide to come clean?

When I turn my head toward Ronan, he finishes the poem and looks at me. "What do you think?"

"That was beautiful," I reply, shoving down the rising despair inside me.

"Yeah," he agrees. "I like that one."

"Can I ask you a personal question?"

He tilts his head, resting the book on his lap before linking his fingers with mine. "Of course."

"Do you still feel the pain? From losing your family."

His fingers squeeze mine as his eyes narrow. "Yes. It never goes away. There are moments when I feel like they were just here. Like they should still be here."

I force myself to swallow, watching the way his face changes when he brings up his grief, how his features grow heavier and more weary.

"But over the years, those moments don't come as often. And everything in between is fine."

"Just fine?" I ask, resting my head against the back of the bench.

"Sometimes better than fine," he replies with a soft smile. When he brings my knuckles to his lips, I feel that tug on my heart again. "I'll be honest, Daisy. I used to think I could replace them. That if I got married again and had other kids, it would eclipse the pain I felt. But I did fall in love, many times, and I did get married again, but nothing ever dissolved the grief completely. So I stopped trying."

"Stopped trying to find love?"

A smile pulls at his lips. "You don't want to hear about the women I've loved, Daisy. I know you don't."

I sit up a little. "Yes, I do. I know you had a life before me."

"Really?" His face twists in confusion as he stares at me from across the bench, and I realize that he has no idea my motives are twofold. On one hand, I want to know everything about Ronan Kade that I can possibly know for my own lovestruck curiosity.

But also, because I know somewhere in those stories is a memory of my mother that I have never seen, and Ronan is a vault I'm dying to open.

"Yes, really," I reply with confidence.

"To be honest, Daisy," he says carefully. His hand reaches up to tug softly on one of my unruly blond waves that's fallen out of the clip holding it all back. "Nearly a decade ago, I stopped trying to find love to replace what I had lost, and that's exactly when I did find it. But it didn't work out anyway, so then I really gave up."

"What happened?" I reply eagerly, hoping it's my mother he's talking about.

"She already had a life that didn't include me. And as much as I wanted her, I had to accept that ruining what she had was no way to love her."

"Was she married?"

"No, she had a daughter."

I have to hold in the gasp that wants to escape. I suspected this. I knew it was possible, but to hear him talk about her, knowing how much he loved her…it stings.

"It's all right. That ship has sailed, and I've made peace with it. Can you imagine me now, though? If we had gotten married, raised a child, you probably wouldn't have seen me at Salacious."

It's taking everything in me to keep still, without crying as he talks, even while I know that the child he's referring to is mostly likely me.

"Do you regret it?" I ask, my voice not more than a whisper.

"No," he replies without hesitation. Then he leans forward and brushes his thumb across my cheek. "Just because I wanted her, doesn't mean I deserved her. And it doesn't mean we were meant to be. I loved her…a lot. But I refuse to live in the past. I'm here now, and this is exactly where I want to be."

There is no holding back the tears that fill my eyes now. When he notices them, he pulls me closer until I'm sitting in his lap. Then he kisses my cheeks, one at a time, before kissing my lips. Without pushing or prying, he just holds me and strokes my hair as I cry.

In moments like these, my mother's death still feels like an open wound. An open wound I'm trying to hide.

"Don't be sad, baby girl. Not for me."

"I'm not," I reply. "I just…don't want to go home tomorrow. I want to stay like this forever."

"Me too, Daisy."

"What's going to happen to us back home?" My voice sounds weak and hesitant.

"Whatever you want to happen," he replies.

I drag a breath into my lungs as I feel the relief of that response. Turning my head, I find his eyes with my own. "I want this. Us. Like this."

His eyes shine with satisfaction as he brushes a wisp of hair off my forehead. "Me too."

"What are you thinking about?" I ask, and the corner of his mouth tics upward.

Letting out a soft laugh, he kisses the side of my head and whispers, "Just all the rooms I want to take you in at Salacious when we get home."

The blood in my veins grows hot with the thought.

After a few moments, we get up from the bench and walk hand in hand through the park, on our way back to the apartment. If people are staring, I'm not paying them any mind. All I'm thinking about is how good it feels to be his.

I don't know when it started, but I feel like we're about to embark on something that is guaranteed to be amazing. As long as it doesn't all fall apart first.

Rule #22: Listen to what she wants.

Ronan

"I don't want to go home." She whines from the seat next to me as our plane flies over the Atlantic.

"I'll bring you back," I whisper, kissing the side of her head. Her hair smells so good, like lavender and mint. It's a scent I've come to love in just under a week. Everything about her is familiar to me now, like she's imprinted herself on my skin, already a staple in my everyday life.

Something is off with Daisy today, though. I noticed it yesterday, and I'm afraid that when she says she doesn't want to go back home, what she really means is that she doesn't want to return to reality.

For me, I'm nervous that this dream ends in Paris, and the moment we return to our regular lives, she'll lose interest. The novelty of a much older man will wear off and the electric connection we share will fizzle.

It's hard to trust your emotions when luxury is involved. Is she truly that interested in me? If I couldn't fly her in private jets or put her up in a penthouse suite, would she still feel a spark between us?

On top of all of that, I'm afraid that Daisy is still dealing with so much residual trauma from losing her mother, and if that's the case, she's probably so desperate for an escape, she'll do anything to get it.

Either way, I'm nervous. This week has been like a fantasy, but there's a hard road ahead for both of us if we're going to turn this dream into a reality.

When the flight attendant comes by with our drinks, Daisy perks up, affectionately clutching my arm. She clearly loves the idea of making this woman jealous, and I'm not going to stop her.

"Did you have a nice stay in Paris, Mr. Kade?" the woman asks.

"Yes, we did. Thank you."

"Just make up *one* bed please," Daisy interjects.

The attendant forces a smile as she nods. "Yes, ma'am."

Then Daisy links her fingers with mine and grins sweetly in return. A moment later, the woman is gone, and I'm laughing to myself. It's cute that she's so possessive. Is she going to be like this back home? If I go into Salacious, will she still cling to my arm, or will she be embarrassed to be seen with me? Being around strangers is one thing, but showing her interest in a much older man around people she knows is a different story.

"Is that how you're going to be at Salacious?" I ask, my brow furrowed, and my voice laced with a hint of humor.

She takes a sip of her champagne and before setting it down, she scrunches up her face in contemplation. "I guess the real question is why you're coming to the club in the first place."

"Well, sometimes I go because I like being there. I don't always go for the sex."

Her brows are arched expectantly, as if she's waiting for me to continue, so I do—because I know what it is she's really asking. "The only person I'll be sleeping with at the club is you, baby girl."

Her lips tighten in a pleased smile.

"Are you okay with everyone knowing that we're together?"
I ask.

"Of course," she replies on an exhale. "Are you?"

"Fuck yes." Leaning forward, I pull her face to mine for a kiss.
There's a heaviness to her expression now, as if it's suddenly sinking
in that she's entering into an actual relationship with a man in his
fifties. I just hope it's excitement I'm seeing and not regret.

"So," she whispers, "what exactly do you have in mind at
Salacious?"

Oh, so we're having this conversation now?

My cock twitches in my pants from the thought alone, so I
take a long drink before replying.

With my hand on her knee, I give it a gentle squeeze. "If we
start talking about this, I won't be able to keep my hands off of
you."

"Who said I wanted you to?" she says with a wicked grin.
We're sitting next to each other at the dining table, her hand on
mine as her legs start to part ever so slightly.

"The flight attendant could walk in at any moment, baby girl.
You've got a little exhibitionist in you, don't you?" I reply, letting
my hand skate up her thigh.

"Well, you did make me come in front of half of Paris the
other night, so I'd say that's a yes." She lets out a little gasp as my
fingers graze the fabric of her panties.

"Does that mean you'd let me take you in the VIP room?"

"Maybe…" She hums.

"Or the voyeur hall?" I add, rubbing her with a little more
pressure.

"Yes." She's struggling to keep her composure now as I tease
her, stroking her over her panties for a while, before slipping
them to the side to feel how wet she is. "What about…?" A tiny
mewling sound escapes her lips as I slide my finger in an inch,
just enough to drive her wild. It takes her a moment to regain her
composure. "What about the punishment rooms?"

I pause, gazing at her in surprise. "Would you like that, Daisy?" Biting her lip, she nods. "I mean...I'd like to try it."

My cock throbs in my pants at the mere thought of it. Punishment isn't my style. It's not usually what I like...but if it's what she wants, I'll do anything for her.

With her featherlight touch hovering over the top of my hand, she writhes in her seat, and I see the way she's fighting between asking me another question and urging me on.

"What is it, baby? What else do you want?" I ask, picking up my slow movements again.

With a hooded, lust-filled gaze, she says, "Everything. I want you to teach me everything."

I have to force myself to swallow. Pulling my hand from the warmth of her pussy, I lift Daisy from her seat and set her on the table in front of me, her legs hanging on either side of mine. She's staring down at me with a wrinkle between her brows.

"Daisy, I'll teach you anything you want to learn. You know you can trust me, right?"

With warmth in her eyes and those wild blond waves hanging around her face, she nods. "I want to learn about everything you do. I want to be what you need."

"Baby," I reply, keeping my tone soft, "you *are* everything I need."

Her shoulders sag. "Ronan, you know what I mean."

"I know what you mean," I reply, running my hands up her thighs. "And like I said, I'll teach you everything you want to know. Whatever you want to try, I'll do."

"You're a...Dom, right? So make me your sub."

"Is that what you want?" I ask with intrigue.

"Do you think I'm submissive enough?" she replies with a shrug.

Leaning forward, I pull her face to mine. "Being submissive is not a personality type, Daisy. It's a role, and one you have to *want* to fulfill. It's not something I need, if that's what you're afraid of. What I like, baby girl, is making you feel good. Giving you as much pleasure as I can."

I squeeze her thighs with my fingers, tugging her closer to me on the table. There's a hitch in her breath as I do.

"Nothing turns me on more than the thought of having complete control over your body—to play with, to test, to... fuck." I add that last part in a low mutter, watching her reaction.

She lets out a little moan, her round eyes hooded with desire.

"With some boundaries, safe words, and clear communication, I think we can do that. Does that sort of submission turn you on, baby girl?"

"Yes, Daddy," she replies in a whisper, and I start to lose my cool. I watch her throat move as she swallows, letting out a delicate breath with her eyes on me.

"Good." Then I pull her face toward mine and kiss her so hard, she turns to melting wax right here on the table. As I pull away, I whisper against her lips, "Now be quiet so no one hears you."

Then, I drape her legs over my shoulders and drag her to the edge of the table, pulling her panties aside and taking a long, slow lick of my favorite pussy.

As she bites back her moans, I find a rhythm, thinking about how beautiful she's going to look strapped to my bed, completely at my mercy. Even the overwhelming trust she puts in me turns me on. For a moment, the fear of what lies ahead is gone. It's just us, my face in her lap and her muffled cries.

When it's like this, I let myself believe that Daisy and I could be more than a fling. Maybe this one doesn't have to end in pain and regret. The pure, honest soul of hers that longs for poetry, freedom, and color in her life matches mine enough to mean she cares more about me than the money or the pleasure.

What we have could be so much more.

I'm a fool to hope.

But I've been a fool before. And I'd be even more of a fool to pass up the opportunity to not play the hand I have in hopes of winning the whole pot. I'd risk it all for her.

Her legs tremble around my head, her breathing growing

labored and desperate, and I know that when she lets out a squealing, "Yes, Daddy," it's not an accident. It's her way of claiming me. Marking what's hers. Making it clearly known who I belong to, a message to the single person within earshot. And although it's a little excessive, it makes me pretty fucking proud. I would have done nothing less for her.

And that gives me more hope than anything else.

Rule #23: All dreams come to an end—some more abruptly than others.

Daisy

Stepping foot back in Ronan's apartment feels like coming home from one vacation and immediately starting another. Somewhere in the parking garage below the building is a white van in desperate need of a cleaning, packed to the brim with belongings I don't ever want to see again. Everything I need is in this raggedy old backpack.

I'm staring out the large window, overlooking the city, when I feel a pair of arms wrap around me from behind.

"Are you okay?" he whispers in my ear.

I nod. I'm better than okay, really. I'm in this luxurious apartment with a man who is crazy about me and a journal full of songs I've written. Life is good.

So why do I feel unsettled? As if my feet have touched down but I haven't fully landed.

"I'm fine," I reply, wincing as I flex my neck from side to side. "Just a little tired." I slept plenty on the plane, but I can't shake this *run-down* feeling that's starting to creep up on me.

"Why don't you go lie down for a little while?" he suggests.

"We're going to the club tonight, right?" I reply eagerly.

"No. We're taking the night off, Daisy. Now, go rest."

"What if I don't want to?" I say with a coy smile.

"Then I'll put you over my knee." He growls in my ear.

"Promises, promises."

"Go, baby," he says, this time with a tone of sincerity.

"Okay, okay, I'm going." Reluctantly, I pull myself away from his warm embrace and walk toward the bedroom—*his* bedroom.

I feel pathetic for not having a room of my own. Or a *home* of my own. Does he think I'm pathetic? If he's not sick of having to take care of me now, when will he be?

Trying to shove the thoughts away, I shut the door behind me as I stumble toward his bed. Sitting on the edge, I realize a moment too late that my sudden onslaught of weakness and overall raggedness is due to the fact that while I slept on the plane—and enjoyed two orgasms—I didn't eat anything except for a buttery chocolate croissant before we took off. I was so caught up with the conversation we were having and his expert fingers, I didn't even think about it.

To be honest, I'm actually a little relieved. I'd rather it be my cursed low blood sugar than something more serious. So, instead of lying down, I stand from the bed and start toward the door.

"Ronan," I call, ready to explain—and that's when it hits me.

I stood up too fast. Ears ringing, vision tunneling, head spinning, I go down fast.

Trying my best to break my fall, I reach for the dresser but only manage to knock nearly everything on it down to the floor in a deafening shatter. It all feels so far away to me as the room diminishes to a tiny circle, until I'm completely swallowed in darkness.

When I peel my eyes open again, there are voices around me. I'm still on the floor of Ronan's bedroom, my head burning from where

I must have landed against the rug. My vision is blurry, as if my eyes are filled with water. But I can hear a familiar, frantic voice.

"I don't know. I just found her on the floor. She passed out."

Ronan. God, he sounds terrified.

"Is she all right?"

"Ma'am, can you hear me?" There's a light being shined in my eyes, and I squint against it, murmuring to the person standing above me.

"I'm fine."

"Do you remember what happened?" he asks. "Ma'am, did you take anything?"

Take anything? Who is this? It feels like I've been out for hours. My head is throbbing so badly that I can hear it hammering in my ears.

"Blood sugar," I mumble, but my words are slurred, and moving my lips feels impossible.

"Blood sugar?" the man asks. "Are you diabetic?"

I shake my head, which makes it pound more. This is the worst I've ever felt after one of my fainting episodes. I must have hit my head pretty hard.

"I have...low...blood sugar," I stammer. I'm so weak I can barely finish a sentence. My voice feels heavy. *Everything* feels heavy.

My eyes find Ronan standing behind the man in blue. *I'm sorry*, I try to say with just the expression on my face, but the way his jaw clenches and his eyes narrow, I can tell he's mad.

I must have really scared him. Just thinking about him finding me like this makes my throat sting and my eyes water.

The paramedic rattles off some more questions while I lie there and hate myself. That pathetic feeling from earlier only intensifies, adding both shame and embarrassment to it. I'm so bad at taking care of myself; I can barely keep myself alive. Eating is the most basic of human needs, and I can't even handle that.

"She needs to go to the hospital," Ronan says angrily.

"No," I force out from the floor. "I'm fine."

"You're not fine, Daisy."

"I just need to..."

"Daisy." His voice is stern, and he speaks my name with a bite to it. When I look up at him, I feel the tears brimming, and with one blink, they slide down the sides of my face and onto the floor. Feeling defeated, I just nod.

A moment later, my limp body is being hoisted onto a stretcher, and I have to drape my arm over my eyes to hide the fact that I can't keep the tears in anymore.

I knew the dream ended in Paris. I just didn't realize it would end this abruptly.

There are no billionaire connections or VIP treatment at the hospital. I'm wheeled into the overcrowded ER, shoved into a tiny curtained area, and situated with an IV that must be pumping glucose into my veins because, within minutes, I'm feeling human again.

The entire time, Ronan hovers, but he won't speak to me.

I want to send him home, but part of me is terrified that if I let him out of my sight, then I'll be living in my van again. No more weekends in Paris. No more poetry. No more *him*.

I'm too young. Too irresponsible. Too sick and sad and broken for a man like him.

"Daisy," he whispers, when he notices me silently crying on the hospital bed.

"I'm sorry," I reply without letting him finish.

"Do you have any idea how fucking scared I was? I found you on the floor. You looked—" His words stop as he turns away, and all I can see is the click of his jaw as he clenches his molars.

"I said I was sorry," I reply with a quiver in my voice.

He lets out a heavy sigh. "I want to take care of you, Daisy. But I need you to take care of yourself too. I need to know you can."

"I'm not a child, Ronan," I reply with force. "It was a mistake. It happens all the time."

I've never seen him look so angry, and for a moment, I think it's over. He's realizing at this very moment that he's too old to be taking care of an irresponsible woman who can't even remember to eat.

So when he rushes toward me, I'm taken by surprise. His strong hands grip my face as he forces me to look at him.

"You're not going to let that happen again, you understand me? You're going to eat better. Three square meals a day. Are we clear?"

"I will. I promise," I choke out.

"I can't…" Whatever he was about to say is lost, his words trailing off as he presses his lips together. After he looks away for a moment, like he's composing himself, he turns back toward me with a stern expression on his face. It looks as if he's about to say something, but just then, the curtain opens and the doctor walks in.

She talks fast and goes over my test results in a rush. She talks more to Ronan than me, and I get a little irritated. I don't know if she thinks he's my dad or if she's checking him out—not that I would blame her. Even in these hospital lights, he looks gorgeous. But I want to yell at her that it's *my* health. My fault. My issue to fix.

I don't, of course.

Basically, she says I'm fine. No sign of diabetes or a concussion. I just had a major blood sugar crash, and I need to learn to eat better. Stress and travel can throw off my system—it's all the same things I've heard many times before.

It's another hour before we're finally going through the discharge process and climbing into Ronan's car to go home. I can't tell if he's still mad at me, but when he pulls me into his arms in the back seat, I take it as a good sign. But there are still traces of anger there—I can tell.

There has to be some way for me to make it up to him. He can't stay mad at me forever.

Rule #24: Teach her a lesson.

Ronan

I SQUEEZE MY FISTS FOR THE TENTH TIME SINCE LEAVING THE hospital. My palm is itching. And not because I'd like to take my anger out on Daisy or hurt her in any way. I'm not a fucking monster.

While we were in the hospital, I saw the sad, regretful look on her face, and I could see just how bad she felt for letting me find her like that and for scaring the ever-loving shit out of me.

I have plans for her when we get home. Mostly I'd like to just hold her. Kiss her. Feel her heartbeat and her breath and soak in just how alive and healthy she is, but I can't. Not yet.

Daisy wants to know what it's like to be mine, and I intend to show her.

But before I do that, I have to take care of her first.

"You need to eat," I say in a cool command when we get into the apartment. She's standing by the door, looking defeated. Her long blond hair is pulled into a messy bun on the top of her head.

"Okay," she replies compliantly before disappearing into the bathroom to wash up.

While I pull out the meals Agatha prepared for us, putting them in the microwave per her instructions, I think about how much things have changed with Daisy in such a short period of time.

In just a week, she's become so much more to me than a mysterious girl that fascinated me. She's quickly risen to a place in my life that scares me. More than Julia. More than Shannon. More than my ex-wife and more than any other woman in between. I wish I could understand why.

Aside from the fact that Daisy is beautiful, smart, and funny. This is about more than her good qualities. It's about the way she makes me feel when we're together. The way she makes me feel about my own life.

"Hope" is the thing with feathers that perches in the soul and sings the tune without the words, and never stops—at all...

That's how Daisy makes me feel. Like I have more life left to live than I let myself think. Like I might have more love left to give.

The microwave beeps and I pull out the plate, setting it on the table for Daisy, with silverware and a glass of water. After she comes out of the bathroom, I point to her plate and say in a cold, emotionless command, "Eat."

She swallows, moving toward the table without arguing.

I might be overstepping, but Daisy told me she wanted me to be her Dom. Fuck, she calls me *Daddy* like she's been dying to do it since the moment we met. Well, if she wants me to treat her like she belongs to me, then this is what she gets.

And she hasn't seen anything yet.

Wait until I get her to the bedroom.

I'm letting my anger force my decisions, and I shouldn't. I need to calm down. Think clearly.

But then I keep seeing her on the floor of the bedroom, fearing the worst. She doesn't take care of herself. She treats herself like she's expendable, and it grates on my nerves more than I expected it to.

After today, the whole thing will be forgotten and we'll go back to the way things were. But for now, she owes me.

When she's done eating, I take her plate and kiss the top of her head.

"Are you still mad at me?" she asks, and it nearly breaks my heart. She must feel awful because this is not the same girl who fought me off when I tried to carry her home with me after finding her sleeping in her van. The remorse on her face is real.

"No, Daisy. I'm not mad at you."

"Yes, you are," she argues weakly.

"No," I bark. "I'm not." But I can see why she thinks I'm angry with her. I *sound* angry.

Her innocent, round eyes gaze at me as if she's waiting for more. "But..." she whispers.

"But I still want to punish you."

Her soft white-blond eyebrows pinch together as she whispers, "Punish me?"

My cock twitches in my pants. "What did I tell you I was going to do if you were bad, Daisy?"

She swallows, her lips parting as she leans in ever so slightly. "Put me over your knee."

"I think you deserve that. What do you think?"

"Yes," she replies without hesitation.

She looks petrified, her eyes wide and her breathing shallow.

"Yes, Daddy," she adds in a small voice, and at that, my cock practically jumps.

"Good girl, Daisy." I kiss her forehead. "Now go take your clothes off and wait for me on my bed."

She nods, forcing in a deep breath as she walks away.

After she's disappeared into the room, I take my time cleaning up the plates from dinner. I want her to wait. I want to take my time with her, and if I rush in there too eager, she's going to see me crack. And I can't have that.

So when I'm ready, I unbutton the sleeves of my shirt and walk into the bedroom. She's sitting on the edge of the bed, staring down at the floor while she waits. At the sound of my footsteps, her head snaps up to stare at me with anticipation.

I stop in the doorway. We're doing this a little backward, but everything with Daisy has been unconventional, so I'm not really surprised. Even still, I need to make sure I don't *really* hurt her.

"I need to know you consent to this, Daisy."

"I do," she replies quickly. Her voice is a sweet wisp of warm air. It almost makes this both harder for me and more appealing. I know behind that innocent face and pretty voice is a girl who is tough as nails. She's been through hell. She's survived on her own. She doesn't need me, but I know she wants to pretend she does.

And more importantly, I know that she wants *this*.

The punishment, the penance, and the forgiveness.

"If it becomes too much for you, just say *red*, and I'll stop. Understand?"

She nods, those big blue eyes gazing up at me wantonly.

"You have to say *red*, Daisy. If you tell me to stop or that it hurts, I won't stop. Is that clear?"

I watch her chest rise and fall with each breath. Her knuckles turn white as she squeezes the down comforter in her fists. I can see her trembling from here.

"Yes. I understand."

As I walk toward her, her breathing picks up, but her eyes don't leave my face. She's gazing at me as if she's searching for something. When I sit down on the bed next to her, I don't say a word. I just pat my lap and stare at her expectantly.

Without a word, she lays herself over my legs, baring her naked ass to me. My mouth practically waters at the sight.

Everything about this feels different. We're not at the club. This isn't a woman experienced in being a sub or being punished. This is someone I have intense emotional feelings for. In some way, I feel as wholly unprepared for this as she is. But I still want it.

Probably ten times as much as normal.

My hand rubs large circles over each cheek of her ass, loving the way she squirms and trembles with my touch.

"We're doing twenty, and you will count each one. Is that clear?"

"Yes, Daddy," she murmurs.

"Nice and loud," I say just before raising my right hand and letting it land with a smack against her ass. She lets out a squeak, but mostly bites back any other response.

"One," she announces.

Without giving her a break, I do it again. And again. And again. Each time hearing her count through gritted teeth and a low whine.

She starts to writhe, letting out a yelp each time. Her ass is a solid red now, and I take a break to rub the raw flesh, watching the way the color changes to white with my touch.

My cock is so hard, it's aching beneath her, and every time she shifts it feels like heaven and hell combined.

"You know why I'm doing this, don't you, Daisy?"

"Because I didn't eat today," she says in a high-pitched whine.

"Because you scared me, baby. You scared the fuck out of me. Now I want to hear you scream and cry and thrash, because at least then, I'll know you're alive and well. Scream for me, Daisy."

She shivers under my hands before whispering, "Yes, Daddy."

With that, I lift my hand and spank her right on her raw, red flesh. It's easily the hardest smack, even making my hand sting, but she does as I said. She lets out a pained scream, kicking her feet on the bed so that I have to hold her tighter against me with my free hand.

"That's my girl," I reply, before spanking her again.

"It hurts!" she cries against the mattress.

"Count, Daisy. Or I'll have to start over."

"Sixteen," she sobs.

The last four smacks hurt me as much as they hurt her. I know she wants it to be over. I know she hates it, but I can tell by

the way the sweat beads on her back and how even when she begs
me to stop, she knows I won't, that Daisy likes the punishment.

It may not be in my nature to want to bring her pain, but
seeing her take it so well has an arousing effect on me.

She's thrashing against me, screaming into the bedding as I
rub her tender ass. When I slip my fingers between her legs, I feel
the pool of arousal there, and I let out a growl. At my touch, her
screams turn feral, low and needy. I drag my hand back up to her
ass, and her hips move in search of my touch.

"Tell me what you want, baby girl," I say, squeezing her ass
in my hands.

"Touch me," she cries out.

"Did you learn your lesson?"

"Yes, Daddy," she whines. "Just please, touch me."

"My girl is so needy," I mutter, sliding my fingers back to her
aching core. I spread the moisture of her cunt through her folds,
opening her up and teasing her with my touch. She's squirming
and moaning, her breaths coming out as pants and gasps. I'm
being gentle when I know she wants it rough.

As I plunge one finger inside her, she lets out a husky groan,
stretching the sound with the movement of my hand fucking her
slowly. When she gasps, I know I've found the spot, and I add a
digit, thrusting in a rhythm that renders her speechless.

"Is that the spot? Right there? Tell me, Daisy."

"Yes," she replies breathlessly. "Right there. Don't stop."

Her legs are spread open, and her weight on my cock is exquisite as I watch her unfold on my lap. The muscles in her legs tense
and her toes curl, right as I feel her body tighten with her cunt
pulsing in my hand.

"Yes, baby. Come for Daddy."

She lets out a gasp for air, just as her body begins to soften,
letting her breathe.

I can't hold back another moment. Shifting her body
facedown on the bed, I stand up and quickly unbutton my pants,

unleashing my aching cock. She lets out a yelp as I yank her ass to the edge, her toes barely touching the floor as I center myself on her wet core and force my way in.

The feel of her body swallowing my cock is breathtaking. Her cries and yelps as I fuck her, thrusting in hard, mixed with the sound of my body slapping against hers, is the most beautiful sound I've ever heard.

"Look what you do to me, Daisy. You make me fucking crazy." My words come out in clipped grunts with each thrust. I'm going to lose it if I don't slow down. So I pull out, leaving just the tip at her entrance, and freeze there for a moment.

She moans and writhes, pushing back to impale herself on my cock, and a groan crawls up from my chest at the sight.

"Jesus Christ, baby girl."

I pull out again, and she thrusts back hard, her needy pussy chasing my cock.

"Fuck," I groan. "Tell me you want it, baby."

"I want it, Daddy," she cries. The bedding is a mess now, her fingers clenched tightly around it as she uses the bed as leverage to fuck herself with my dick.

My balls begin to tighten, and my cock threatens to blow, so I grab tightly onto her hips and pound into her hard. Slamming her body against the mattress, I shout, unloading inside her.

When I'm finally fully spent, I lay my body against hers. She can probably feel my heart beating against her back. Feeling my breath against her ear, she turns her head and finds my mouth, kissing me softly with her perfect lips.

That was the hottest thing I've ever done, and I've done a lot of shit. Daisy has me rethinking everything I thought I knew about myself. And while I don't ever look forward to hurting her like that again, I have to admit that seeing her grow with that pain and struggle changed me. And here I thought I was too old to learn something new.

Rule #25: Age really is just a number.

Daisy

"It's not too hot, is it?" Ronan is holding my hand as I sink my toes into the water, my whole leg being swallowed up by lavender-scented bubbles.

"It's perfect," I reply. Just hot enough to feel the sting but not too hot to hurt.

Of course when my ass hits the water, I'm singing a different tune. I let out a squeal as the hot water stings my tender backside, and I notice Ronan's evil grin when I do.

"I'll rub something on it after your bath that should help, but I can't promise it won't bruise."

"I sort of hope it does," I reply, resting my chin against the side of the tub.

"Why? You want a bruised-up ass?" He smiles, while grabbing a white fluffy towel from the cabinet.

"Sort of. Like a trophy."

He freezes for a moment and closes his eyes before reopening them and taking a deep breath, which makes me laugh. I do like the idea of him leaving marks on my body, and I'm not entirely sure if that's a good thing or not. That was my first time being properly spanked as an adult, and while I was a little terrified, it wasn't because of the pain. I was more afraid of what it would do to our relationship. Would him punishing me make me resentful of him? Would it make him angrier, since he doesn't like doling out punishment?

Clearly, neither of those things happened. While he had me pinned to the bed, his hand landing hard against my ass, I loved the thought of him making me pay for what I had done more than I ought to. Not all of our issues can be resolved with a spanking, but the fire that burned in that moment was like an inferno, and I don't think I've ever been so aroused in my life—albeit a filthy, degrading sort of arousal.

It's not something I want to feel all the time, and now I really need him to pamper me a little to make up for it, but the guilt and embarrassment of what happened earlier today is gone.

Hence the bubble bath and the doting behavior. Things between us went back to normal. For which I'm very grateful. I hated him being so upset with me.

I've never been in a relationship like this, one that feels so comfortable. Yes, Ronan acts like my *daddy* from time to time, but for all of the moments when he doesn't, he treats me as his equal. He doesn't laugh at me or talk down to me or treat me like I can't do things. Our connection is refreshingly balanced.

And as much as I worried about it before, I know Ronan doesn't think I'm too young or too irresponsible for him. All the fears I've had about him, he's proven unfounded.

Realizing that only reminds me I'm falling deeper and deeper into a relationship that is doomed to fail when he learns the truth.

The harsh reality is that I'm faced with two options now.

One, come clean about my mother. Eventually, it's going to come out. If we truly stay together long enough, he'll find out who my mother is, so I can't hide it forever.

Two, I lie and pretend I know nothing. But that option makes me sick to even think about it. I hate lying. And just the idea of outright lying to *him* is unthinkable.

So I have to be honest...eventually. And there's a good chance that when I am, everything between us will change and he won't want me anymore. I need to be ready for that, but I don't know if I can truly prepare myself for that outcome.

I'm not just falling for Ronan Kade. I'm *addicted* to him. I crave him in a way I don't fully understand. He doesn't make the pain of my grief go away, but he does make me forget about it for a while. And when I'm with him, I'm not wading in the water alone. He's right there next to me.

"Will you get in with me?" I ask, reaching a bubbly hand toward him. "This tub is more than big enough for both of us."

He's leaning against the bathroom counter, his arms folded in front of his chest as he stares down at me with a quizzical notch in his brow. He's thinking about it.

Then, one by one, he unbuttons his shirt before sliding it off and starting on his pants.

When he's naked, he slides into the hot water behind me, pulling my back against his chest, and I relax in his arms. We're silent for a moment, the hot water calming us both.

"That wasn't too much for you, was it?" he asks, referring to the spanking.

I shake my head. "Not at all."

"How are you feeling now?"

Taking a long breath and a moment to think, only one word comes to mind. "Content."

"Good," he replies. "Is there anything else you'd like to try? Maybe something at the club that piques your interest?"

With my head resting against his chest, I give it some thought. Before Ronan, everything at the club sounded impersonal and intimidating. Now the idea of being in there with him changes everything. I adore the prospect of exploring all the possibilities, knowing that he will keep me safe and make me feel good.

"What do you like?" I ask, turning my head toward him.

"It's not about what I like. I'm asking you."

My face stretches into a smile. "Well, you have to have some tastes of your own."

"My taste is watching the person I'm with get off, Daisy. If you get off with whips and paddles, I want to do that. If you get off when people are watching you, then I want that too."

When I let out a small laugh, he turns my chin to face him. "What was that for?"

"Nothing," I reply. "I just…don't think you'd really paddle me. At least, I don't think you'd like it."

"You're right. I wouldn't." He's very blunt and matter-of-fact with his response.

"But you'd still do it?"

His features twist in thought before he licks his lips and gives me a pointed stare. "Would you ever let someone else join us? Someone who *would* like to do that?"

My jaw nearly drops to the floor. "Like a threesome?"

He pauses, his brows pinched inward. "Not necessarily. More like a scene. I think I'd love to watch, but I don't know if I could be the one to do it."

Goose bumps erupt along the flesh of my arms at the idea, and I try to control my excitement as I eagerly reply, "Yeah, I think I might like that. As long as it's someone you trust. And they go easy on me."

"Always at your pace, baby girl. I'd never let anyone hurt you."

He presses my sweat-soaked hair back from my forehead, and I can't help but ask, "That wouldn't bother you? To see me with someone else?"

"Again," he replies, "it's not sex. But yes, the thought of you wanting to be with someone else does bother me."

He dribbles water down my arm, watching the rivulets slide off my skin and into the soapy water, and I let his words replay in my mind. That was incredibly vulnerable of him, and as much as I loved hearing it, it drove this knife of guilt in a little further. As much as he portrays confidence and control, there's a part of Ronan that feels insecure, which guts me to think about.

I reach for his fingers, squeezing them tightly in mine. "That would bother me too. But," I say, kissing the back of his hand, "I don't want anyone else."

"No?" he asks so nonchalantly. "Not someone younger?"

My chest aches at that question. "No. Do you want someone older?"

He presses his lips against the side of my head. "No."

Then I lean back against him, feeling his hard body wrapped around mine. "Close your eyes, Ronan."

His head rests next to mine, his breath on my cheek. "Okay, they're closed," he says with a chuckle, clearly humoring me.

"Mine are too," I whisper. Our fingers are mingled, rubbing and touching each other. Our legs are pressed together, and I can feel his heartbeat through my back, so we're practically fused.

"Right here, in this moment, do you feel any different than me? Just because you're older?"

"No," he whispers in my ear.

Then he wraps our clasped arms around my body, squeezing me tight.

"It's just years," I say. "Who cares about the difference when it feels like this?"

"That's right, baby girl." His voice is soothing in my ear as he holds me.

We sit together in silence until the water cools, not saying another word and not touching each other more than this. I've never enjoyed silence with someone so much in my life.

Eventually, he gets out, drying himself before wrapping me up in a towel, our warm bodies pressed together. Then he lifts me like a child in his arms and carries me to the bed.

As we crawl under the covers together, I write another song in my head as I drift off to sleep. This one is about a man who looks good in hospital lighting and the weight of secrets so heavy, they nearly drown me in the bubble bath.

Rule #26: Best friends know everything.

Daisy

"Paris?" Geo asks, his eyes wide and his jaw hanging open. "As in Paris, France?"

"Oui," I reply with a smile. My elbows are resting on the bar, and I can barely stand still. I can't remember the last time I've felt so happy.

"Most girls get an hour upstairs in the VIP room," he replies.

My grin grows wider, so much that my cheeks are starting to burn.

"Look at you," he says, setting down the bottle in his hand and shooting me a soft expression. "You're in love."

I can feel the blush rising as I bite my lip and try to hide my silly, lovestruck face. Which only makes Geo double down.

"Holy shit. You are *really* in love."

"Oh stop," I reply, glancing around me to make sure no one overheard that. "I'm not *really* in love."

He laughs as he picks up the bottle and gets back to work making the drink. "Yes, you are."

I shrug with a smile. "Okay, maybe a little."

"Take these to table two and then you can tell me all about it," Geo says, sending me on my way with a tray full of drinks. I'm practically bouncing with the six champagne flutes balanced on the tray, and the entire time I'm walking, I'm thinking about what details I'm going to share with my friend and which ones are too personal.

Should I tell him about L'Amour? Or getting fingered in front of the Eiffel Tower? Should I tell him that I was spanked like a bad, little girl and *liked* it? A lot.

Okay, maybe I'll just gloss over these topics, skipping the details.

After dropping off the drinks at table two, I turn around to see Ronan walking through the heavy black curtain at the front of the club. Immediately, my heart skips at the sight of him. Never mind the fact that I've been with him for a week straight. I've been at work for an hour and I'm already missing him.

Tugging my bottom lip between my teeth, I fight back the ear-to-ear grin that threatens to stretch across my face. Suddenly remembering what we did last night before the bath, and then after the bath, and this morning…and just before I left for my shift at the club.

Seeing Ronan from across the room in that fitted suit, I freeze in my spot, admiring him. His right hand is in his pocket and his left is skating over his beard as he stops and scans the room. He never does that. So I freeze, waiting for his eyes to find me, and after a moment, our gazes meet.

As he slowly walks toward me, I glance sideways at Geo, who is grinning and shaking his head. Ronan and I agreed that we wouldn't hide our relationship, but we weren't eager to flaunt it either. Secrets are more fun anyway—well, these kinds at least. I told him I would have to tell Geo, but other than that, we're not going to make it public yet.

I'm ready to break that promise right now, though. I don't know if I'll be able to keep my hands off of him. He looks so good in that suit.

"The apartment was so quiet and boring," he says quietly as we meet in the middle of the floor.

"I've only been gone an hour," I reply, grinning like a fool.

"It was a long hour."

"So…what are you going to do?" I ask. I know he's not here to partake in any activities with anyone, but I can't help but ask.

"Have a drink. Watch you. Admire how cute your ass looks in that skirt." He leans in a little closer. "Then…when your shift is done, I'll take you upstairs and tie you to my bed."

My cheeks burn with his words and the image he's promising.

"Then I hope it's a very slow night."

"I'll pay Emerson to close the club right now," he replies with a smile, and I laugh.

"You can wait, Mr. Kade. I still have a job to do."

"Fine," he mutters before passing by me to take a seat at his regular table near the back. The same table he sat at the night he won a date with me.

I feel his burning gaze on my ass as I walk to the bar, and Geo is there, laughing to himself when I approach to get the bourbon neat he has ready for Ronan.

"What's so funny?" I ask.

"I love the sight of you eating your words."

"What are you talking about?"

"Only a week ago you said you *weren't into older guys*," he teases me.

"I found one who changed my mind." Even I can hear the dreamy pitch in my voice.

"Obviously."

"Ronan made a compelling argument," I reply with a smile.

"Yeah, with his dick."

My jaw drops. "Geo!" I squeal before glancing back at Ronan to make sure he didn't hear that. Although I guess if he did, he wouldn't be too offended. Geo's right, although it wasn't really the sex that changed my mind, was it? It was changed before then.

The night he tried to carry me over his shoulder to his apartment.

The day he wrote a line of poetry in my journal.

The way I felt in his arms last night in the tub, when we both held each other with our eyes closed.

All very compelling arguments for why I no longer care about Ronan Kade's age.

Setting his bourbon on my tray, I carry it over to his table. I love the way he's watching me as I walk. Like I'm the only person in the room. Like he literally came to a sex club just to watch me serve drinks all night.

I pass the drink to him with a wicked smirk.

"What's that look for?" he asks.

"Nothing," I tease, thinking about Geo's remark about his dick.

"How are you feeling? Did you get enough to eat before your shift?"

This is how he's going to be now, isn't it? Always checking that I've eaten enough and not skipping meals anymore.

I lean over him, my hands on either side of his chair as I hold my lips near his ear and whisper, "Yes, Daddy."

He responds with a groan.

Before I can back away, he hooks a hand around my leg and tugs me closer, putting me between his knees, bringing our faces just inches apart. So much for being discreet.

"I don't have to wait until the end of your shift," he says in a cool, sexy warning.

"I would lose my job."

"Think I care? You keep calling me that and I'll fuck you right here."

I smile at him before dropping a couple inches and pressing my lips to his for a quick kiss.

"You can wait, Mr. Kade. Drink your bourbon and behave."

His jaw clenches as his fingers trail up and down the back of my leg. I hate to walk away now. I'm too addicted to his touch. But I have to. The floor is getting busy with thirsty patrons.

But as I stand up and turn away from Ronan, I catch the eye of someone across the room. Clay, the man who *tried* to win a date with me, is standing alone near a high-top table, staring at me with curiosity in his gaze. His eyes track downward toward Ronan, then back up to me.

I suddenly feel exposed and uncomfortable as I force myself to look away and head back to the bar. While I serve drinks and take orders, I feel them both watching me, but I try to focus solely on Ronan. Every few minutes, I sneak a glance and a smile in his direction, and for the most part, I don't think he notices Clay's pointed attention on me.

I can't avoid him forever, so after serving the table next to his, I stop at Clay's.

"Hey there," I say with my customer-service voice and smile. "Can I get you something to drink?"

He doesn't answer right away. Instead, he narrows his eyes and bites his bottom lip. "Hey, Daisy. Haven't seen you around in a few days," he says, stepping closer to me.

"I was out of town," I reply cheerfully.

"Oh nice. Where'd you go?" My smile starts to fade. He must notice because he lets out an anxious laugh. "I'm sorry. That was inappropriate to ask. Don't answer that."

I laugh in response, trying to keep it as casual as possible. "It's okay. I, uh…went to Paris, actually."

His eyes widen. "Oh, wow. Paris? That sounds amazing. Good for you."

"Thanks," I reply with a tight-lipped smile. "Can I get you a drink?"

"Sure…" he says, and I sense by the way he's hesitating and chewing on his lip that he's working up the nerve to ask me something. "Maybe you'll have a chance tonight to have one with me?"

When I spot the anxious hope in his eyes, a feeling of sympathy washes over me. I take a moment to appreciate Clay's sweet nature and handsome face.

Is this the type of man people think I should be with? If I were dating a man like Clay, there would be no anxiety. No fear of judgment. I wouldn't hesitate to take him home to my dad and no one would question if I was with him for the *right* reasons.

But nothing about him sets my soul on fire. He's handsome, objectively sweet, and he's in a sex club, so I'm willing to bet he has a kinky side.

"That's really sweet," I reply, glancing down at my feet before scanning my eyes upward. "But I can't."

After a moment, he nods knowingly. "It's that rich guy, isn't it?"

"Yes," I say under my breath.

As his eyes glide slowly from Ronan to me, I can only imagine what he's thinking. That it's unfair for the "rich" guys to get the girls or that I'm only with him for his money.

"Be honest," he says, resting his elbow on the table. "If I had won that night..." Before finishing the sentence, he clenches his teeth. "You know what, never mind. I don't want to know."

I remember the day after the auction when I saw Clay and considered how my night might have ended differently if he had won. It makes me sad to even think about it. To have missed out on the greatest, most romantic week of my life. That auction changed my life forever. I can feel it.

"I'm sorry," I whisper, but I'm not sure why.

When he leans in as if to say something intimate, my skin grows hot, and I start to panic. All I can think is that Ronan is watching, and I don't want him getting jealous or angry, seeing someone talk to me for so long.

Abruptly, there's a hand against Clay's chest and someone pressing themselves between us. I half expect it to be Ronan, but then my eyes focus on the long black nails and delicate fingers of the woman touching Clay's chest.

"Down, boy," she says in a soft, sexy command.

I turn my head and gaze into the eyes of Eden St. Claire as she levels her dominant expression on Clay, who's currently surrendering with his hands up and a smirk on his face.

"Yes, Madame."

My face gets ridiculously hot as I stare at them both. *What on earth is going on here?*

"Give Daisy your drink order and let her get back to work."

When Clay's eyes slowly cast upward to my face, he looks apologetic and much smaller than he did a moment ago. "Gin and tonic, please."

I nod before glancing toward Eden. "Nothing for me. Thank you, Daisy."

My mouth opens but nothing comes out. Instead, I scurry wordlessly toward the bar to get his drink. To be honest, Madame Kink intimidates me. That much confidence and prowess scares me because I can't help but feel that's how much confidence I'm supposed to have, but I don't.

She's an icon at Salacious—beautiful, kind, dominant, sexy, fearless. She's everything I wish I were.

On my way to the bar, I catch Ronan's eye and he gives me a questioning expression with a wrinkle in his brow. My response is nothing but a shrug and a smile.

When I return to the table where Clay and Eden are still talking, I deliver his drink, and she quickly catches me by the arm before I leave. We walk together for a few steps until we're out of earshot of Clay.

"Come to room nineteen when you get off."

My eyes are as wide as saucers and my heart feels as if it's now pumping ice instead of blood. Suddenly, Eden lets out a laugh.

"Oh my God, your face," she howls. "You look terrified. I just meant to hang out with me. Have a glass of wine with me. I want to talk to you."

"You do?" I reply, still in a daze of confusion.

"Well, you are dating my best friend. I just thought we could get to know each other."

"Oh…"

Is this real life?

With her hand on my arm, she leans in toward my ear and whispers, "You might tell Geo everything. Well, Ronan tells me everything."

With that, she just walks away. And I glance toward Ronan, still wide-eyed and in shock, to see him smirking shamelessly in his chair.

Rule #27: If you want a man's heart, you have to win over his best friend first.

Daisy

It's past two when I'm cut from the floor, and I nervously ascend the stairs toward room nineteen. "She has a private room like you?" I ask Ronan. His hand is delicately resting on the small of my back as we go.

"Yes," he replies.

"You're not mad she's stealing me away?" I say, when we reach the hallway in between rooms nineteen and twenty-one. He pulls me in for a kiss.

"I did have plans for you, but they can wait."

Just then the door opens, and Eden is standing there, staring at us with a lopsided smile. "Oh, what plans? Can I join?"

"Maybe next time," he replies with a wink.

"You can stick around, you know," she tells him.

He shakes his head, looking at me. "Nah. You probably want to talk about me anyway."

"We do," she says with a wicked smirk.

"Where will you be?" I ask.

"Just next door." Then he fishes into his back pocket and pulls out a matte black card. "Come in when you're done. No rush. Have fun." Then he presses his lips to my cheek as if he's dropping me off for a playdate.

As I'm shut in with Eden, I try to relax as much as possible. When I heard she had a private room, I was sort of expecting a literal sex dungeon, but this is cozy and feminine. The bed is a rich blue and gold piled with pillows and on the right side is a soft-looking sofa and a large lounge chair with a fuzzy white rug in front of it.

"This is not what I expected," I mumble as I walk slowly into the room, looking around. She's at the wet bar on the opposite side, uncorking a bottle of wine.

"Well, don't poke around too much," she replies with a laugh. "It's just well disguised."

I chuckle to myself as I step closer to the bed, noticing the metal rings bolted to the headboard.

"Have a seat," she says sweetly as she carries two glasses of wine to the couch. I can't stop looking around, wondering what she must do in here. I've heard enough stories about Madame Kink to know it must be very...well, kinky.

"I hope you don't mind me stealing you from Ronan tonight. I was just excited to get to know you, now that you're dating."

Something about that word *dating* makes my blood run cold. Not that I don't want to be dating Ronan. Hell, at this point, he has my heart. There is no fear of commitment in this case. But that secret I'm harboring from him feels louder and more ominous every time I think about how good things are going with him. My happiness is salt in the wound.

"I don't know if I'd really call it dating," I say awkwardly, as I climb up onto the sofa and take the glass of wine she's poured for me.

"Well, aside from the fact that you're living with him and he just took you to Paris." She laughs as she takes a sip and watches me over the rim of the glass.

"Okay, you've got a point," I reply.

"He seems really happy, and he obviously cares about you a lot." That statement feels like a punch to the gut. I swallow, my heart pounding in my chest.

"And you want to make sure I'm not just leading him on for his money?" I reply as a question.

"Bingo," she replies before taking another sip.

"I'm not," I say, trying to sound convincing, which isn't hard because it's the truth. I'm not using Ronan for his money. I don't even want it. I mean, if she knew the truth, she'd know that I already have more than a little bit in my name. But that's not really something I want anyone to know at this point. "It was never about the money."

She tilts her head to the side. "It's hard to take a personal jet to Paris and claim the money doesn't make a difference."

When I start to defend myself, she holds up a hand. "Listen, this isn't about you, I promise. I'm sure you really do care about him, but I've been friends with Ronan for seven years. He pulled me out of a really bad place and gave me a chance to start over, and it meant more than you could ever know. He never asked for a thing in return because everything he does is selfless. And for that reason, he's had his heart broken again and again. He acts tough, but he's—"

"I know," I snap, interrupting her. Suddenly, I feel territorial, hearing her talk about him as if I have no idea who Ronan is or what he's like.

She looks affronted for a moment, her eyes widening, but then she relaxes her expression and gives me a nod. So I continue.

"I know how selfless he is. I know what he's capable of. We both tried to stay away from each other, and I really don't give a shit about his money. Yes, we enjoy it because we can, but if Ronan woke up without a dime to his name tomorrow, I'd still love him."

My eyes widen, and I stare at her with shock at the words that just came out of *my* mouth.

She's wearing a shocked expression as well. "Does he know how you feel?"

I grab the glass of wine from the table and nearly gulp it down.

"No," I say after the glass is empty.

I should be happy or excited about this revelation. I do love him, and it's not really all that surprising. Ronan didn't just capture my heart; he ruthlessly stole it right out of my chest. He didn't even have to try. He did it by being genuine. By just being him.

He might be the best person I've ever met in my life.

No, he is. He definitely is.

So why am I filled with dread and anxiety?

Because I'm lying to him. Every single day I'm lying by omission because of this secret that I've held on to since the moment I started working at Salacious. It was fine then because there was no reason for me to come forward, but now…

Now I love him. And I'm going to lose him.

"Are you worried about what people will think? He's a lot older than you," Eden says, her scrutinizing gaze on my face.

"A little," I reply, which is the truth. Ronan is older than my dad, a detail I'm sure my dad won't love whenever I do introduce the two. But my mind won't even let me get that far because Ronan will never meet my dad. The minute Ronan finds out about my mom and the fact that I know they were together and have known this entire time, he'll be done with me.

Just thinking about that makes it hard to breathe.

"Are you okay?" Eden asks, her eyes narrowing on my face.

I force myself to nod, shoving away the dark thoughts and pasting a fake smile on my face. "Yeah. I'm fine."

"So…" she says, refilling my glass. "You love him, huh?"

My fake smile slowly morphs into a real one. "Don't tell him I said that," I reply, chewing on my bottom lip.

"You got it."

For a moment, we sit in comfortable silence, and I let my gaze scan the room, then her. Eden is not like anyone I've ever met, but in some strange way...she reminds me of my mother. My mom was headstrong like Eden, unafraid to take what she wanted and say what was on her mind. It makes me miss her—a lot.

So for a moment, I imagine it's my mom sitting across the couch, sharing a glass of wine with me, talking casually about the man I'm dating and seriously falling for. It feels so natural, putting her in this scenario.

"Have you ever been in love before?" I ask, making conversation.

Eden's face takes on a surprised expression. "Yikes, no."

A laugh bubbles out of me. "No? Never?"

"Never. Love is a trap—no offense—and not one I ever plan to be caught in."

My body sinks into the couch as I laugh again. Maybe it's the wine or maybe it's the ease of the conversation, but I'm suddenly seeing Madame Kink as Eden, just a woman who faces the same fears and insecurities as the rest of us.

"You love Ronan, don't you?" I ask.

She takes a sip and nods her head. "Yes, but that's different. He's my friend. It's easy to love him."

"It's really no different. Loving a friend and being in love," I reply. "Just add sex."

This time, she laughs. "See, when I add sex, love is the last thing on my mind."

I pull my legs under me and perch myself up higher. "Speaking of..." I say, feeling bold from the wine. "What on earth was that with Clay downstairs? Did you two...?"

She waves a hand at me. "Oh, him? We shared a room a couple days ago."

Then she gives a little shrug, and I know I probably won't get any more information out of her than that. I doubt Madame Kink kisses and tells. But hearing him say *yes, Madame* downstairs was confirmation enough.

If that's what he likes, he and I would have never worked out.

When I look down, I notice my wineglass is empty. So I set it on the table and give her a smile.

"Thanks for the wine…and the conversation."

"Thanks for joining me," she replies. "I don't get a lot of female friends around here anymore. So I hope we can do it again."

"I'd love that."

As I stand up, ready to turn toward the door, I'm surprised to find Eden pulling me in for a hug. It's sweet at first, but as she pulls away, her green eyes find mine. "Please don't hurt my friend."

Her tone is solemn and serious, and my heart plummets to the floor. I don't want to hurt him. I hate the very thought of it. But I'm cruising down a hill without brakes, and I know there's a crash waiting for us at the bottom.

"I won't," I mutter, and I hope she can sense just how desperately certain I am.

I'd rather die than hurt Ronan, but at this point, I don't know if I can help it.

Rule #28: Return the favor when you can.

Daisy

I'M STANDING OUTSIDE RONAN'S ROOM, THE BLACK CARD IN MY hand. All I can think about is how deep I'm falling, knowing the further I go, the more it's going to hurt. My throat is tight, aching with the pain of unshed tears. If this is what love feels like, I hate it.

I love him. Sitting in Eden's room was the first time I voiced it but not the first time I realized it. This is not a crush or an infatuation or an addiction. I care about this man more than I care about anyone else.

And I think he feels the same. When he walks into a crowded room, he looks for me. I am special to him. That's all I ever wanted.

Ronan leads with his heart. So I know this is not a fling or merely a hookup to him.

Surely, we can work this out. We'll get through it. He might be angry about the secret I'm keeping, and it might take him time to get over it, but I have faith that we will overcome this.

We have to.

I press the black card against the panel on the door, and it beeps before I hear the lock click. When I step into the room, I see him sitting across the room in a large chair, staring down at his phone. As he spots me, he moves to get up, but I hold up a hand.

"Don't," I say in a soft command. "Just stay there."

His head tilts in confusion, but he doesn't move.

I could tell him everything right now…or I could savor this moment, indulging in what I have in my grasp right now. It's not a hard choice to make.

"Just let me look at you," I say in a slow, sultry tone.

His expression melts into a soft half smile as he leans back in his chair, staring across the room at me with a hooded gaze. He's so perfect, I want to worship him. I want to fall into his arms, give myself to him, make his pleasure my only purpose on earth. If only for tonight.

Slowly, I drop to my knees near the door, and his eyes darken at the sight. As I start crawling toward him without a word, his tongue peeks out to wet his lips before he tugs the bottom one between his teeth, biting down hard as he watches me move toward him on all fours.

When I reach him, I rest my cheek against his thigh, gazing up at him with adoration.

"My beautiful girl," he whispers, brushing his fingers through my hair. I could stay like this forever, but I'm desperate for his pleasure. I *need* to make Ronan feel good.

Sliding my hands up his legs, I reach for his zipper. He catches my hand and holds them in place.

"What are you doing, Daisy?"

"Let me, Ronan," I plead softly.

"You don't need to do this." There is no inflection in his voice, so I know he's serious. It's clear he's not used to letting other people spoil him. Ronan is so used to taking care of others that he's uncomfortable letting others take care of him. It makes me want to do it that much more.

"I know," I reply. "I want to. Let me make you feel good, Daddy."

There's something intoxicating about using that term in a way that's not playful or for the sake of being sexy. When it comes out of my mouth, it's genuine, and judging by the sincerity in his eyes, he feels that too.

After a moment of hesitation, he loosens his grip on my hand, still touching me as I slowly peel open his pants. His cock is already hard behind his boxer briefs. Dragging down the elastic, I find his solid length and gently ease it out until I'm holding him in my hand.

His breathing grows shallow and labored as I stroke him slowly. I love watching the effect this has on him—grunting, squeezing, trembling. I'm desperate for more. Leaning forward, I run my tongue along his shaft, and immediately, he hisses, sucking in air between his teeth. So I do it again, teasing him and noticing the way he's holding himself back. I'm drunk on his reactions.

Then, I take his swollen head between my lips, and he loses an ounce of control, digging his fingers in my hair and darkly muttering, "Fuck, baby girl."

He keeps up his hissing and groaning as I suck, bobbing my head up and down on him. I think about everything through his perspective. How he gets off on my pleasure. Playing with my body to make me come. Finding my climaxes like little hidden pieces of gold.

With that, I suck harder on the head of his cock, watching his reaction as I do. He lets out a long, loud groan, his head hanging back, so I do it again and again. My thighs grow slick with arousal at the sight of him slowly coming undone.

After picking his head back up, he watches me as I suck and lick and play with his cock, enjoying his reactions to every little thing I do.

"Jesus, baby. Look at you," he murmurs. "You're my filthy little girl, aren't you?"

With a sweet hum around his cock, I gaze up at him as I nod.

He's losing control, like my very own sexy Jekyll and Hyde, letting out his vulgar side when he's usually so sweet and kind.

"You love Daddy's cock, don't you?" he grits out.

Arousal tickles its way down my spine, spurred on by his dirty words, and I pick up my speed, humming my response. Clearly, I love Daddy's cock.

His shaft is slick with saliva now as I wrap my hand tightly around him, stroking eagerly as I suck on the head. One of his hands grips tightly to the arm of his chair while the other holds gently to the back of my head.

I wish he'd push me down. I want him to choke me on his cock.

But he doesn't. So I take him so far into the back of my throat that I gag, coughing as I come up, and he grunts in response. Then I touch the hand holding my head and show him how I want him to push me down.

"You want me to fuck your throat, baby girl?"

Gasping, I pull my mouth off of him. "Yes, Daddy."

"I don't want to hurt you," he mutters through clenched teeth.

"I trust you," I reply, affectionately rubbing my hand up his leg. I watch the muscles in his jaw twitch as he grinds his molars. Then his hand guides my mouth to his cock again, and I relax my throat as he shoves my head down. I gag again, saliva coating his cock, and I feel his head swell against my tongue.

His raspy groans and grunts fill the room as he holds my head in place, fucking my throat. My core pulses with need. I wish I understood why I love letting him use me like this. Maybe it's a form of penance for my guilt. Or maybe it's because Ronan is wholly perfect, and I love feeling him use my body for his own pleasure.

But I know what it costs him to let go like this. How much he's going to pamper me later to make up for it, more for himself than for me.

More than anything, I want Ronan to know that I crave this

as much as my own pleasure. I want it all—the good, the bad, everything.

Suddenly, he moans loudly before trying to pull me off.

I swat his hand away from my head and I grip his cock in my hand, stroking him until I feel his body stiffen.

"Daisy, I'm going to fucking come."

I moan louder, my lips vibrating around him. My stroking picks up speed, and when I feel the head tighten even more, I know he's there.

With my mouth open and my tongue out, I let him unload all over me. Salty jets of his cum land against the surface of my tongue and face.

"Oh fuck," he mutters as he shivers out the rest of his orgasm.

He tears off his tie and uses it to clean the mess off my face, caressing my cheeks and chin as I close my mouth and swallow what landed on my tongue. His gaze darkens as I do.

"You really are Daddy's girl, aren't you, Daisy?"

I respond with a smile as he drags me up onto his lap, so I'm straddling him. Then he kisses a pattern around my neck and chest and up to my mouth. It's not heated, it's not leading anywhere. He's literally kissing me to worship me.

Making him feel good quiets the shame and guilt, but only temporarily. Because feeling his love for me has it rising to the surface again.

Rule #29: You should always trust your partner—and your gut.

Ronan

I HOLD HER IN MY LAP THE ENTIRE WAY HOME. CARESSING HER soft hair as she leans against my chest, I shove down the feeling of regret for using Daisy so vilely. I'm not corrupting her, I know that, but I can't help but fear that her reasons for wanting me to use her like that aren't entirely kink related.

Daisy is hiding something.

When we were in Paris, things seemed great. She was happy, bubbly even. But it seemed the closer we became to each other, the more she tried to distance herself. I can see hints of anxiety and fear in her eyes.

I'm not pushing her for answers, mostly because I hope I'm wrong. I hope there's nothing threatening to drive us apart.

There's that foolish hope again.

Once we get back to the apartment, Daisy is asleep in my arms. She's clearly still working through some jet lag, so I carry her inside. She stirs awake but only cozies herself farther into my arms.

Reaching the bedroom, I set her on the bed.

"Stay with me," she murmurs, and I try to resist, but I can't bring myself to pull away. Shedding my clothes down to my boxer briefs, I climb under the covers with her, letting her sleep against my chest.

But I don't drift off. Sleep evades me as I lie awake with her in my arms, thinking about all the things that could go wrong. Projecting every scenario until I feel hopelessly certain that I will lose her. All based on suspicion and instinct.

I can't helplessly lie here. Before the sun rises, I climb out of bed and go to my office.

The first thing I do is search Daisy's social media accounts, but she keeps them all private. And since I don't have any active accounts of my own, I haven't requested access to them.

As I craft an email to an old friend, who occasionally does investigative work for me on the side, I swallow down this crippling guilt. It's the money that's done this to me. The money and the heartbreak, never knowing if a person's interest is genuine. Never knowing what they see when they look at me. That gnawing fear that I'll never be anything more than a bankroll to anyone ever again is always living in the back of my mind.

So I quickly ask a favor—for him to look into Daisy, giving him all the information I have.

My stomach turns as I type. This feels like a betrayal.

And when my mouse hovers over the Send button, I remember lying with her in the bathtub, eyes closed, feeling more connected to her than I've felt to anyone in my life.

Fuck, what am I doing?

Before I can hit Send, I close out my email and shut off my computer.

What did I think he would find? A criminal background she's hiding from me? Some secret family or life I don't know about? No. Not Daisy.

With that, I head out of my office and walk back to the bedroom. She's still sleeping peacefully in my bed, so I crawl back under the covers with her, absorbing her warmth as I kiss her head.

She stirs, clutching tightly to my body. Daisy trusts me. She needs me. Not only to take care of her, but also to give her a safe space to explore this new part of herself and her desires, without having to worry about someone taking advantage of her.

This pain and degradation she craves could be part of her healing process. I want to give her everything she needs, but I don't know if I have it in me. It's just not my style.

Perhaps if I do this, if I scratch this itch for Daisy, my doubts and fears will be silenced. I know exactly who I can ask for help, but I don't know if that's something Daisy will be open to.

"What's wrong?" she whispers, gently peeling her eyes open and gazing up at me.

"Nothing, baby girl," I reply in a whisper.

"You're restless."

"I'm just thinking. Go back to sleep."

"Thinking about what?" she murmurs, ignoring my command.

I decide to forgo discretion and answer her questions. "About who I trust with you."

Her eyes pop open as she lifts herself onto her elbow to stare at me. "You mean Eden, don't you?"

My expression grows solemn as I nod. "Daisy, can you tell me why you like the idea of pain? Is it curiosity or something else?"

Her brow furrows. "Should I not—"

"No, baby girl. Never mind. You shouldn't feel bad for what you want to try. I'm sorry for asking that."

Her features relax as she rests her head against my chest. "I trust you, Ronan. And as long as you're there to protect me, I'll trust anyone else you want to join us."

"I'll always protect you, Daisy." With that, I kiss her forehead and squeeze her body closer.

It only takes a few minutes before I hear her breathing slow to a sleeping cadence. She really does trust me. So why can't I trust her? What is wrong with me?

I'm letting my jaded heart ruin something perfect. So I shove the worries away and close my eyes. This time, my fear and anxiety are gone, so within minutes, I drift off to sleep.

Rule #30: Give her orgasms at work. If she gets fired, it'll be worth it.

Ronan

SWIRLING THE BOURBON IN MY GLASS, I WATCH THE VOYEUR HALL with a keen eye. I need to speak to Eden, but she's a little tied up in room five at the moment. So I bide my time, having a drink at the bar, keeping up casual conversation with Geo and Emerson while I wait.

When I hear Daisy's name, my interest piques and I lift my eyes to where Geo is smiling while drying a glass with a bar towel.

"Oh really?" Emerson asks with curious interest. I wasn't paying attention, so I have no clue what they said, but I'm willing to bet Geo is telling the club owner everything about me and Daisy.

"I guess Garrett didn't tell you Ronan took our drink server to Paris for a week," Geo says.

Emerson grins wickedly as he takes a sip of his drink. I send Geo a scowl. "You're the only one spreading gossip," I mutter.

"It's hardly a secret," Geo replies. "You've both been wearing heart eyes since you got back."

I can't exactly argue with that. Instead, I shrug and toss back the rest of my drink. Emerson claps a hand on my back with a laugh. He looks pleased with himself, as if he's somehow responsible for this.

"I'm happy for you," he says astutely, and I nod in return.

"Thanks."

It's easy for him to seem so casual about it. He's happily married and settled down. Every ounce of my happiness still feels so fragile, as if it could all dissolve into nothing at the drop of a hat.

Out of the corner of my eye, I see Eden emerge from the voyeur hallway, looking a little more worn-out and red-faced than she normally does, so I seize my opportunity.

I say good night to Emerson and Geo, slapping a bill on the bar, before hopping up from the barstool and meeting my friend halfway across the room.

"Uh-oh," she says when she sees me coming. "What's that face for?"

I smile. "Got a minute? I want to talk to you."

"Sure. Let's go to my room so I can relax."

We walk together up the stairs, and I catch sight of Daisy delivering a tray of drinks on the second floor. I shoot her a wink and she blushes in return, just before I disappear down the hallway.

As soon as we're shut in Eden's room, I remove my coat and walk directly to the bar, where I know she keeps her good wine, uncorking a bottle she must have already opened.

"Let me guess," she says from behind me. "You're curious what Daisy and I talked about yesterday."

"That's one thing."

"Oh. There's something else?"

I take a deep breath. Why am I nervous about this? Eden and I have done this dozens of times. It's nothing out of the ordinary for us, but it feels different this time. This time it's someone I care about—someone I love.

"I just wanted to make sure she has the right intentions."

Eden's response is so straightforward and nothing I didn't expect, but it still catches me off guard as I take the seat next to her, drink in hand.

"She does," I reply with confidence. "And you realize I'm not a child and I don't need my mother to vet the women I date."

Eden laughs, leaning her head on my shoulder. "But I'm a good mother. I just get a little possessive. Okay?"

"I know," I reply, throwing an arm around her shoulder to hold her closer.

"But hey, so is she."

I lift my head. "She was possessive?"

With a laugh, Eden grins. "Oh, she nearly bit my head off when I implied that *I* cared about you more. She even said, 'If Ronan didn't have a dime to his name, I'd still love him,' which is a little sappy if you ask me, but sweet."

The hairs on the back of my neck stand up as my brows pinch inward. "She said that?"

Eden slaps a hand over her mouth. "Fuck. I wasn't supposed to tell you that, was I?"

"It's okay. I figured that's how she felt."

"So what's the problem?" she asks, reading my tense expression.

"The problem is that I've heard that before."

"I know you have, and I really don't want to see you get hurt again," she says, touching my shoulder.

"Thank you, Mommy," I reply with a laugh.

"If I don't look out for you, who will?"

"I really need you to protect me from beautiful twenty-one-year-olds," I joke.

After we laugh for a second, it grows silent, and I practically feel her concern radiating off her. "She is really young, Ronan."

"I know," I reply.

"Just be careful letting her become dependent. Shit never works out well when that happens."

I force a smile as I turn toward my friend. I see the sweet

woman under the tough exterior that no one else sees. As tough as she is, Eden has a soft side too, and when she does love, she does it fiercely.

I can still remember the young woman I found nearly seven years ago, battered and afraid but not broken. And not alone. Even when she was twenty-seven, she seemed wise beyond her years. And she's come a long way since then.

"Thanks for watching out for me," I reply, kissing her forehead.

"What else did you want to talk about?" she asks, taking my wine and sipping from the glass.

When I let out a sigh without responding, she picks up the hint.

"Oh…" Clearly rousing her interest, she turns toward me. "Your girl wants to play?"

"She feels safe with me. Safe enough to ask for things that I don't know if I can give her."

"Sure you can," Eden replies with sincerity.

"I need your help. It's just hard for me. You know that."

With a nod, the corners of her lips lift in a tight smile. "I know. You know I'll help you give her whatever she wants, but is it what *you* want?"

"I want what she wants," I reply plainly, and I can already see Eden's expression hardening.

"Ronan…"

"Do I sound too desperate?" I ask with a forced smile.

"You sound scared. Are you afraid of losing her if you can't give her what she wants?"

"Yes," I reply with a nod. "I'm afraid of a lot of things, Eden."

"Like what?"

"Like what if she's using kink to mask the pain of something bigger? What if she's only with me because I make life easy for her? What if she heals…and doesn't need me anymore?"

Tears well in Eden's eyes as she stares at me. It feels as if I've shredded a hole in my chest and everything I'm afraid of coming out is ceaselessly spilling from my heart.

"Oh, Ronan," she whispers, a tear spilling over her cheek. I lift a hand and quickly wipe it away. "You are such a nurturer, and it's something everyone loves about you, but it's far from the only thing. I don't need you anymore, and I still love you. She will too. If she's got any brains in that pretty head of hers."

A smile cracks on my hardened face. "Thanks."

"You need to talk to her. Your heads both need to be in the right place for this."

"I know," I reply sternly.

"And if you decide this is what you want, you know I'm there."

I drag a heavy breath into my lungs and letting it out feels like shedding a layer of something that was weighing me down. I feel lighter.

Eden wipes at her face and quickly composes herself before standing. I rise up from the couch and stare down at her.

"Thanks, Eden," I say, pulling her to my chest.

She wraps her arms around my torso and squeezes hard. I almost forget how small she is for such a dominating woman.

"Where is your girl now?" she asks after pulling away.

I nod toward the door. "They put her back in the VIP area."

"The VIP area?" Eden says with a smile. With her lips around the rim of the wineglass she stole from me, she adds, "They grow up so fast."

"Very funny," I reply, giving her a gentle nudge.

"I think I'll go find her. Are you busy tomorrow night?"

She gives a shrug. "Nope. I'm all yours."

"Okay. I'll talk to her then."

Eden waves her fingers at me as I slip out the door of her room. I'm feeling restless as I march down the hall toward the VIP bar. As I reach the open area, I spot her immediately. She doesn't see me. She's too busy talking to a table of women, the bright smile on her face like sunshine.

Just staring at her, the weight of the conversation I just had heavy on my mind, I realize that I'm in love with Daisy. Helplessly. Hopelessly. Foolishly.

I've fallen for women this fast before, but it was never quite this hard.

Without letting her see me, I pass through the crowd around the VIP bar and slip through the curtain to the large private room. The open display of sex doesn't even faze me anymore. If anything, it almost calms my nerves. It seems strange, but the sounds of pleasure drown out the noises in my head.

But the only reason I'm going in now is because I want her to find me. I need to see her in this environment. And when her shift is over, I'm going to take her to my room. Tomorrow night, she'll have it her way, but tonight, she's going to have it mine.

There's an empty table near the center of the room, so I take a seat and watch the door, waiting for her.

It doesn't take long before a beautiful woman with dark eyes and black hair approaches me. She's in nothing but a pair of thin panties, and her tits are in my face as she leans over, placing her hands on the back of my chair.

"Hey there, need some company?" she asks.

She's beautiful. Two weeks ago, I'd have let her sit down. I'd have let my hands roam her body, exploring the way she responds to my touch. I'd have let her kneel by my feet, and if I was in the mood, I'd have taken her to my room and have some fun with her.

But there's not a single part of me that wants to do that anymore. She's beautiful, but she's not the delicate blond with pretty pink lips that I want.

"Not tonight, sweetheart," I reply with a smile.

She shrugs, looking momentarily disappointed. "Bummer."

I laugh as she stands upright. Light from the bar shines through the open curtain as I look up and watch Daisy walk into the room. She spots the half-naked woman standing near me, and her eyes widen.

The dark-haired woman leaves, and I lick my lips, staring at Daisy. There are drinks on her tray, and she swiftly takes them to another table. Then a moment later, she's standing in front of me.

"What are you doing in here?" she asks.

Needing my hands on her body, I pull her into my lap, both legs hanging off one side. Without answering, I slide my fingers up the front of her tight black skirt, running my thumb along the soft fabric covering her warm cunt.

She hums, and I take the opportunity to kiss the soft pulsing surface of her throat.

"I'm working, Ronan."

"I couldn't wait," I mumble. Shifting her panties to the side, I rub my finger through her sweet, warm core, making her gasp.

"Ronan!" she argues, but she doesn't move to get up. Instead, she spreads her legs a little farther for me.

"People are watching you," I whisper in her ear. "Does that bother you?"

"No," she mumbles.

I can't get the thought of her acting so weird this week out of my head. I know this isn't a solution, but I want to pretend it is. If I can make her body feel good, I can ease whatever is plaguing her mind. I can make *us* good.

Her drink tray falls to the floor with a clang as I slip my middle finger inside her, thrusting hard because I know that's how she likes it.

"Oh my God, Ronan," she cries out. "I'm going to get fired."

"No, you won't," I reply, sliding out and back in. "You're not leaving my lap until you come."

"Fuck it," she mutters as she twists her upper body and grabs my face, kissing me hard on the lips. "It'll be worth it if I do."

I smile against her lips, holding her tight to my body. She's writhing against me, searching for her own pleasure, when I add friction to her clit with my thumb. The deep groan she lets out is breathtaking.

"Listen to everyone fucking around us. Does it turn you on, baby girl?"

"Yes, Daddy," she cries out.

"That's my girl," I mumble against her ear.

She lets me rub and thrust and massage between her legs until her spine straightens and her legs tense. When she reaches her climax, going breathless for a moment, I soak up every second of it. I love the way she looks as she reaches her peak, the delicate features of her face tensing and creating a cute little wrinkle between her brows.

"You are so fucking perfect, Daisy. Tell me you're all mine."

"I'm all yours," she says, after opening her eyes and gazing up at me with adoration.

"After your shift, I'm taking you to my room and then I want you to be truly mine. Understand, Daisy?"

She blinks. Then nods.

"You'll submit to me. Let me do whatever I'd like to you?"

Another blink. Then another nod. "Yes, Daddy."

I can't hold back. I pull her mouth to mine, kissing her hard. If I had my way, I'd make her mine forever. I'd never let this one go.

But I feel her pulling away already. Maybe it's the age thing that's getting to her. Maybe seeing men like Clay makes her realize that she could have any man she wants, especially one her own age. There's no reason for her to settle for a man thirty-five years older than her.

Or maybe there is something else that's bothering her.

Whatever it is, I plan to make her forget all about it tonight.

Rule #31: Even pleasure can feel like torture.

Daisy

THE CLUB IS QUIET WHEN I CREEP DOWN THE HALL. I'M UPSTAIRS where Ronan has his private room, right next to Eden's, and he's already in there…waiting for me.

I have no idea why I'm nervous, but tonight feels important. Tonight is the first night I'm going to truly…submit to him. So yes, I'm nervous. What if I don't like it? What if I'm bad at it?

What if it's perfect, and I fall even more in love with him? Somehow that feels worse.

At some point, I have to come clean and sooner rather than later feels appropriate.

Tomorrow. I'll be off work and it will just be us for the day. I'll tell him everything and beg him not to hate me for keeping this secret. He'll be a little upset, maybe even spank me for it. Then, we'll talk it through and I'll do whatever I have to, to make it up to him.

Then, the rest of our lives can start.

When I reach the door to his room, I pull the key card he gave me last night out of my back pocket. After swiping it, I open the door and notice the room is different from before.

The lights are dim, and there are black restraints attached to each post of the bed. Ronan is sitting in the chair across the room. I freeze under his potent gaze, unsure if I'm supposed to be submissive already or if he's going to go over some rules or something first. He already made me talk about my limits and he explained the safe word system to me—red, yellow, green. Seems easy enough.

I'm just so afraid I'm going to mess this up somehow.

He crosses the room and pulls me in gently, kissing me as a greeting. The moment his lips are pressed softly to mine, my anxiety dissipates. Ronan has this ability to calm me with his presence.

And I realize that, even if I do somehow mess this up, he'll be there to help me. He won't hurt me, or humiliate me, or patronize me. He said he will always protect me, and I believe that.

I melt into his arms, suddenly feeling a little more excited than nervous.

"I bought you something," he whispers against my lips.

My eyebrows perk up at that. "What is it?"

When he lifts his hand, I look down to see a small gift bag, my heart hammering in my chest at the sight. "If you don't like it, you don't have to wear it."

I take the bag from his hands and smile up at him. "Can I open it?"

"Go into the bathroom to try it on. Then let me see you in it."

"Okay," I reply with a bite of my lip.

When I reach the bathroom, I close myself in and pull the tissue paper out of the bag. Inside I see black, but not very much. Pulling it out, I stare at what can't be more than a handful of black silk in the shape of a nightie. Gentle sable straps and delicate silky fabric. It's beautiful while looking fierce, and I tense for a moment when I realize…this isn't me at all.

I don't want to disappoint him, so I shed my clothes and slip the lingerie on, and I'm pleasantly surprised by how I look in it. With my pale blond braid and porcelain skin, I'm practically glowing in contrast with the dark silk.

I stare at myself in the mirror for a few moments. Pulling my hair out of the single braid, I let the waves cascade over my shoulder, and I let myself imagine that I'm not Daisy, the grief-stricken, practically homeless lost cause in need of guidance. I'm Daisy, the sexually confident, world-traveling, fearless vixen.

It's laughable. But it helps me not feel so out of my element.

When I step out of the bathroom, Ronan is standing near the bar not wearing a shirt. I'm staring at him in much the same way he's staring at me. I can't wait to get my hands on him, to touch him and soak in the warmth of his body like it's comforting heat on a cold night.

"Daisy," he whispers. "Come here."

I move across the room, feeling a wave of nerves again. When I'm within arm's reach of him, he slides a hand into my hair and drags my mouth toward him for a burning kiss. His tongue glides against mine and I marvel at how his kisses can feel so raw and passionate, yet so tender and loving at the same time. He kisses me like he wants to savor me. Like he wants me to *feel* him.

He kisses me with his whole soul.

Oh, that would be a great lyric. God, I hope I don't forget that line before I have a chance to write it down. Not that I could ever forget how Ronan Kade's kisses feel. They are burned into my memory forever.

Although I hope I never get a chance to forget them. After tomorrow, I just don't know.

"Do you like it?" he asks as he pulls away.

I press my lips together before looking down. "I do," I say, but he's lifting my face with his fingers under my chin.

"But?"

"Is this really me? Black and sexy," I reply with a laugh.

"This is how I see you." Then he spins me, so I'm facing the mirror, with him standing behind me. "I might treat you like my baby girl, but this is how you look to me, Daisy. I don't want a girl who bends easily. I want to know I brought a woman to her knees for me. And every time you call me Daddy, that's how I feel."

My brow furrows. "Really?"

With his lips against my neck, he mumbles, "Really."

This whole time I thought Ronan viewed me as nothing more than a grown woman in need of guidance. Not a child, but not an adult either. But this woman standing in front of the mirror is what he's seen this whole time? How have I missed this?

I replay every moment of our relationship up until now, trying to see myself through his eyes. Sleeping in my van, nearly fighting him off when he tried to force me to his apartment. Playing piano on the street. Coming in his lap in front of the Eiffel Tower.

Suddenly, the idea of submitting to him, with this new perspective, sends a shot of arousal to my core. Especially when I realize it's the same for me. Ronan Kade is the richest man in town. He could have anyone he wants, but I'm the one who brings him to his knees.

I spin to face him as I pull his lips down to mine. This kiss is hungrier, more passionate, making me grow wet between my thighs.

"I want this," I whisper to him, after pulling my lips away from his. "I want you to do whatever you want with me."

"You want to be mine. Truly mine?"

"Yes," I gasp with zero hesitation. "All yours, Ronan."

Using his name instead of Daddy feels significant. We're not playing and I'm not taking this lightly. I'm serious when I say I want nothing and no one else. I am all his for as long as I can be. Without hesitation.

"I'm going to strap you to the bed. You won't be in any pain, but I'm going to blindfold you. And then I'm going to play with your body, Daisy." His voice is warm yet authoritative, and I find it comforting. "I'll make you feel good, but at some point, you will beg me to stop, and I won't. Not unless you use the safe word.

I want to see how far I can take you, and I promise it will be nothing like anything you've felt before."

My hands are trembling with anticipation as I slide them over his chest, feeling the beat of his heart under my palm. "You'll get off too, right? We'll…have sex, right?"

He smiles down at me. "Don't you worry about me, Daisy. This isn't about sex, but if I want to fuck you, I will."

I swallow, loving the way those words sound on his lips. A little harshness and coldness on his usually kind and warm demeanor.

God, I hope he does. The idea of coming so much I beg for mercy sounds nice, but what I really want is him. For him to lose control and not be able to help himself anymore.

With that, I set my shoulders and smile. "I'm ready."

"Get on the bed," he says in a cool command.

Taking a deep breath, I walk over to the bed. Unlike the last time I was in here, the pillows and duvet are gone, leaving only black sheets. I climb up and turn to face him, waiting for further instruction.

"Lie down," he says.

I do. He takes each hand and binds it in the Velcro strap, before moving to my legs. Then he picks up the blindfold from the mattress and situates it over my eyes. My heart is beating so hard in my chest. I am completely at his mercy, and even though I know Ronan would never hurt me, it's still unsettling and a little scary.

His hands glide over the top of one leg and down the other, as if he's just letting me feel his touch. Connecting us.

"You look so beautiful like this, Daisy. I'm committing the sight of you to memory."

I want to tell him he doesn't have to commit it to memory. I'll be like this for him whenever he wants. Forever.

But I don't speak. I just focus on his touch and the sound of his voice.

"This is just a stimulant. It's going to feel cold."

I jump when his fingers skim through my folds, rubbing something cool over my clit. Immediately, the skin between my legs pulses, and I'm hyperaware of even the air touching my most sensitive spot.

"Uh…" I gasp, starting to squirm.

"Does that feel good, baby girl?"

"Yes," I whisper.

Then his fingers are gone from my skin and I wait. It's silent, which is why I nearly jump when I feel something soft against my chest. It's a feathery light touch, but not knowing what it is makes me panic.

"Relax, Daisy. Trust me."

The softness is drifting upward to my neck and then my cheek. He's skimming it over my neck when I feel his fingers sliding up the inside of my thigh.

But just when I expect him to reach the apex and slide over my exceedingly sensitive sex, he moves away. Again and again, he does that, as if he's rubbing my muscles instead of making me come.

Suddenly, I catch the scent of something aromatic and put it all together. He's rubbing oil over my skin. He's literally massaging me. And the anticipation of his touch is killing me.

I should be so relaxed and enjoying this, but instead, I'm a ball of nerves, waiting for the other shoe to drop. All of my fears and anxiety are hanging in the air, blocking me from really connecting to this the way he wants.

"You're tense," he says, and I swallow back tears.

Let it go, Daisy. It's okay to feel good. It's okay to be happy.

I do my best to quiet my mind, focusing only on his touch, the sound of his breathing, his nearness. The tingle of warmth between my legs. That intoxicating scent of lavender and sandalwood. It's invigorating and sexy and I chant to myself in my mind that there is nothing else but this. *Nothing else but this. Nothing else but this.*

I've nearly silenced the voices when something starts buzzing quietly near my head and I swallow.

It's a low vibration and he drifts it up the inside of my legs in the same pattern as his hands a moment ago. And just like his hands, he detours the vibrator before putting it where I really want it.

I let out a groan as I lift my hips, trying to chase the thing in his hands with my body. But he only chuckles quietly to himself before teasing me again.

"My girl is so eager," he whispers darkly. "You want this, don't you, baby girl?"

"Yes," I breathe out.

"Yes, what?"

"Yes, Daddy," I say in a sweet plea.

On the next round up my legs, he inches closer, but not quite where I want it. I'm writhing and begging for him to touch me, and I almost can't believe how badly I want to come already. Just from his fingers all over my body and whatever he rubbed on my clit. I'm craving a climax so much I could cry.

When he finally presses the vibrator against my clit, I let out a squeal, my body fighting against the restraints. I come fast and hard, the pleasure ending as quickly as it came. All too soon, I'm left panting and wondering what happens next.

The bed dips and I feel Ronan settle his weight between my bound legs. "You have no idea how beautiful you are when you come, Daisy. I could watch it over and over again."

I need his touch more than anything. His hands skate up my legs, and then I feel his lips trace the path his hands just drew. He's kissing his way up until I feel something warm and wet, wiping my folds clean. There's a residual burn from whatever he put there, but it's quickly replaced with his lips. A high-pitched hum bubbles out of me as he licks my tender clit. He has me desperate and needy, so it doesn't take long with him sucking on the sensitive spot and I'm already coming again.

The restraints are keeping me from fully indulging in the pleasure, which means the orgasm comes and goes too fast again. My legs flex and fight against the binds.

Then the vibrator is back and I'm starting to sweat. He teases me for a while, pressing it to my nipples, my stomach, my thighs, before trailing it to my clit. Then, I'm coming again.

And again.

And again.

Until pleasure starts to feel like torture.

I start to lose sense of time, never quite knowing when one orgasm ends and another begins. I sink further into myself until I'm nothing but sensation, and I can no longer define what feels *good* and what feels *bad*. There is just his voice, his touch, his mouth. It's like Ronan has become my god and I can do nothing but obey.

Somewhere in this abyss of pleasure, I lose sense of myself entirely.

Rule #32: A good Dom doesn't lose control.

Ronan

SHE IS EXQUISITE. JUST AS I KNEW SHE WOULD BE.

My stubborn girl, full of passion and fire. Watching her writhe and scream is everything I wanted and more.

Although I have no intention of pushing her past her limit today, I'm enthralled by the idea that she simply does not have one. Or at least she thinks she doesn't.

Everyone has a limit. It's getting them to find it that's the fun part.

Some Doms use pain. Degradation. Humiliation.

I use pleasure.

By the time she leaves here, I want her to feel things she didn't know she was capable of feeling. Sensations her body was capable of but never came close to experiencing.

There's a pleasant little notion in the back of my mind as I make Daisy climax for the tenth—or is it eleventh?—time. The notion is a reminder that she and I have time. I don't need to rush things or break her right away. We can delicately creep our way through this process, one session at a time, until she says we're done or we find new ways to play—including *her* way.

Daisy is as curious as she is innocent. She's not afraid to tell me what she likes or doesn't like, which means we can have all the fun we want. I trust her to speak up when she's reached her breaking point, which means I can really have fun without having to worry. With one major added bonus on top of it all.

I'm in love with her.

Absolutely out of my mind, twisted up, and drunk on this thing between us. This relationship that didn't exist a month ago but has single-handedly breathed new life back into this old man. This bond is nothing like what I felt before—ever. My heart has been through a lot, but it's never met its match like it has with Daisy.

"You're doing so well, baby girl," I murmur against her cheek, leaning down to kiss her sweat-soaked skin. "How are you doing? Give Daddy a color."

"Green," she says breathlessly.

"That's my girl."

She whimpers as I kiss her mouth, licking a line across her lips before taking her mouth to taste her desperation.

"You've soaked the bed, Daisy," I say after pulling away. "I think you can give me one more."

She whimpers again. "No, I can't. No more, please."

I run my fingers through her folds, spreading her wide before rubbing her swollen clit just to watch her writhe. "You're not done yet, baby girl."

"Fuck me," she cries out. "Please, Daddy."

I pause, my mouth halfway down to her throbbing core. My cock aches in my boxer briefs, desperate to give her what she wants. Desperate for a release of my own. This was never about getting myself off. Her pleasure is my pleasure. But knowing that fucking her is what she wants makes everything that much more potent and surreal.

A good Dom doesn't lose control. I shouldn't be letting her make demands like this when she's supposed to be the submissive one, but I'm a weak man where she is concerned. After ripping my boxer briefs off, I situate myself between her legs. My protruding cock is pointed right at her glistening cunt, wet and ready for me.

I grip her thighs tightly as I hold her down and mutter, "Say it again, Daisy. Tell me what you want."

Her lips part as she sucks in a delicate gasp. "Fuck me, Daddy."

Reaching behind me, I yank off one Velcro strap, releasing her left leg.

"Again," I say in a quick command.

"Fuck me, Daddy, please." This time, it comes out in more of a whine, and I know she's leaning into the role. I know it's going to feel so fucking good when I finally sink into her. My cock is already leaking at the tip with anticipation.

I quickly tear off the other strap, freeing her other leg, then both of them are instantly wrapped around my hips, trying to pull me to her.

"You have a filthy fucking mouth, Daisy. You know that?"

"Yes," she replies, then lets out a gasp when she feels the head of my cock teasing her.

"My dirty girl," I say with a raspy inflection as I thrust inside her. She lets out a cry as soon as I'm buried deep. Her cunt is like heaven, warm and throbbing. And once I'm in, I can't stop. Hovering over her, I pound her into the mattress, her thighs clenching tightly around my hips. I can hardly breathe from the tightness in my chest as I lose control.

"You make me crazy, baby girl. Look what you do to me." I grunt breathlessly.

When I notice her arms pulling against the restraints, I quickly undo each one, and her hands find my face, pulling me down for a kiss.

For a moment, we are breathing the same air. Our hearts pounding in unison. And we feel like one. We come at the exact same moment, both of us moaning and shivering together.

Neither of us moves for a long time. Our hands are clasped and our chests are fused. I don't ever want to leave this spot.

But I realize that she needs aftercare. And I might have gotten a little rough toward the end there. So I pull out, lifting myself from her body as I notice that her cheeks are flushed red and she's still wearing the blindfold.

With a smile, I pull it from her eyes, and she squints up at me. Her makeup is smeared, but she's never looked more beautiful.

"How are you feeling?"

With a sweet, gentle sigh, she smiles. "Good."

I kiss her nose. "Good."

Reluctantly, I climb from the bed, going to grab her a bottle of water from the bar. Then I wet a washcloth in warm water and return to stretch out next to her.

"Come here, baby," I murmur, pulling her into my arms. She sits up and takes the water, gulping down almost the entire thing. Once she's done, I use the warm cloth to wipe her face and body, taking gentle care with each part.

She lies on the bed in a sleepy daze as I cover her with a blanket and pull her into my arms. We can't sleep here, but I want to let her come down for a while before I move her back to the apartment.

"How was that?" I ask, eager to know her initial reactions.

Her voice is soft and quiet when she responds. "It was great. How did I do?"

I laugh, pressing my lips to her hair. "You were perfect, baby girl. Would you like to do that again? Let me have my way with you?"

"Yes," she replies sweetly.

"I spoke to Eden today," I say. "Tomorrow, we could try what you want with her."

Her head turns as her eyes find my face. "Tomorrow?"

"If you want," I reply.

She doesn't respond, and I sense her hesitation. When she does speak, it's not what I expect.

"Ronan," she whispers, her hot cheek pressed against my chest, "I have to tell you something."

The moment grows silent and heavy as I wait, but I know what she's going to say. I can practically feel the words on her lips, but I can't stand the idea of her voicing them before I have the chance to. So before she can utter a word, I quickly blurt out, "I love you, Daisy."

She tenses in my arms, the movement of her throat as she swallows pressed against my skin.

Then she rises and looks into my eyes, tears welling between her thick lashes. Her lips part and I wait for her to speak, but I know that if she doesn't return the sentiment, that's okay. I don't love her to get love in return. Just feeling it is enough. Breathing life into the emotion coursing through my veins.

But when she blinks and a single tear spills over, sliding down her cheek and onto my arm, I quickly wipe it away.

"I love you too," she whispers with my thumb against her cheek.

The next words slip through my lips without hesitation. It's an impulse, and my rational brain knows that aftercare is *not* the time to be making emotional commitments, but I can't help it. It's not the first time I've thought about it, but it is the first time I've had the guts to speak the words out loud.

"Marry me."

Those two words land like thunder, heavy and shocking, even to me. But I don't regret them. Not at all. Instead, relief washes over me for finally having the courage to love again.

"What?" Her eyes are wide as saucers and her breath is coming out in a shaky quiver.

"I know it sounds crazy, baby girl. And maybe it is. But I want to take care of you. And I want you to be taken care of for the rest of your life. When I'm gone, you'll never want for a single thing."

"I'll want you," she replies softly and without hesitation, another tear spilling over. "Ronan, I don't care about the money or any of that."

"Is that a no?" I say, forcing in a chest full of air. It feels as if I can barely breathe at all.

She opens her mouth to respond to my question but pauses, and I'm staring at her in desperate anticipation.

"I…" She's torn, a whirlwind of thoughts swirling in that perfect head of hers. I can read every single one on her face. "Are you asking me because you want me to be taken care of financially?"

"I'm asking because I love you. Daisy, you brought the color back into my life. You with all of your poetry and music and happiness. I know I should meet your family and buy you a ring. I know this is all happening so fast, but I love you like fucking crazy. And I want to marry you."

Another tear falls over her flushed cheek. "Yes," she stammers with a small laugh. "Yes, I'll marry you."

My heart hammers in my chest as I gather her up in my arms, kissing her as she clings to my body. She lets out a squeal of excitement, and I feel the warmth of that energy surge through me like lightning.

I think somewhere in the last twenty years, I gave up on having a real life. I let go of the idea of being this happy again, experiencing the best days of my life. Daisy gave me something I thought I'd lost.

The next moment we look at each other, that feeling of excitement surges again. I can't remember ever being this elated and excited for my own future.

As Daisy and I dress and head out of the club together, every step is fueled with a newfound vigor. When we get home, I shower with her, washing her body with delicate precision. Then I feed her in the kitchen, savoring every moment.

My life could be like this every day. That would be heaven.

When she falls asleep on the couch, her head perched on my lap, I pull out my phone and start making a list of the things i need to take care of before we take our next step. Draft a new will.

Put her name on the account. Make an appointment with the jeweler for a ring.

As I pull up my email to set up a meeting with Fitz, I notice the email to my investigator I started yesterday. I thought it had been deleted, but it must have been saved in my drafts. My eyes freeze over the email, and I know, deep down, it would be the wise thing to do. Just as a precaution before either of us enter into this marriage with skeletons in our closet. I mean...I'm sure she's done a search on me too. My life is just a little more public than hers.

Asking her to marry me was impulsive, so sending this email is just my way of being careful.

Without another thought, I hit Send.

I don't feel an ounce of guilt for it. Daisy never has to know I sent it. At least when he emails me back with nothing alarming, she and I can move forward with our lives knowing we love each other unconditionally.

Pocketing my phone, I lift Daisy from the couch and carry her to bed. As she sleeps on the pillow next to me, I realize that all the heartache and ruined relationships led to this moment right here, which makes it all more than worth it.

Rule #33: It's okay to like the pain.

Daisy

I'VE BEEN PLAYING SO LONG, MY FINGERS ARE STARTING TO ACHE. The music echoes loudly through the empty apartment. It's lovely, but it's not calming my senses.

My mind is a mess, a whirlwind of elation and dread spinning around in my head, muddling all my thoughts. As soon as I woke up this morning without him next to me, I came here. I needed to get lost in the music for a while, hoping if I played the notes loud, they'd drown out my thoughts.

It hasn't worked yet. Between each chord, my mind reminds me.

Ronan proposed.

I said yes.

I have to tell him the truth.

Over and over and over in my mind.

When he finally comes back, it's late afternoon, and he finds me in the formal living room, still vainly pounding away at the keys. His touch along my arms and over my fingers finally silences everything—the music and the dreaded thoughts. So I let him continue his way down my back and over my breasts.

"I'm sorry I wasn't here when you woke up," he whispers in my ear.

"It's okay," I reply, leaning into him, craning my neck in hopes that he'll touch me some more. This time, it's his mouth that trails long, tender lines on my skin.

"How are you feeling today, baby girl?"

I hum in response as his beard scratches my throat. "Great," I lie.

His gentle hands turn my body, placing my legs on the opposite side of the bench, so I'm facing him. Then he kneels on both knees between my legs. As our eyes meet, I swallow.

I'm still full of joy and excitement from the proposal, but it's the fear and dread of having to tell him the truth that's tainting everything.

"Daisy, I'm serious. Last night was intense. If you have any regrets—"

I press my hand against his mouth to quiet his words. "Not a single regret," I reply. "Do you?"

My hand falls away from his face as he shakes his head. "No, baby girl. I don't regret a thing."

A smile creeps slowly across my face as he leans in, pressing his lips to mine. I let him engulf my body, seeking his touch for comfort. There's not a safer place in the world than in his arms.

His lips find my neck again, sinking lower as he pulls the strap of my cami to the side and kisses his way across my shoulders. When his hands skate up my bare legs, I gasp as he brushes them across my sensitive core.

"Do you still want to meet with Eden tonight? Two nights in a row might be too much. We can reschedule."

"I'm ready," I reply eagerly. I need this. If his soft touch eases my worries, I know the pain she will bring will silence it altogether.

"If you change your mind, let me know."

"I will," I say, letting my legs drift apart as he lowers himself, kissing my chest and then my stomach.

"And how is this pretty pussy feeling after last night?" he whispers.

"A little sore," I reply, biting my lip as I gaze down at him.

"Daddy's going to kiss it all better now." He looks up at me with a wicked smile, and I grin in response. Then he winks and settles himself between my legs, letting out a husky groan as his mouth sucks eagerly on my clit.

My body relaxes against the keys, both my elbows hitting off-key chords that echo through the room. And when I escape into the pleasure of his touch, it finally does what the piano couldn't—it makes me forget everything I was ever worried about.

Ronan's hand is warm in mine as we enter the club. It's my night off, so it's a little strange going in through the front, like a member. Tonight, I'm technically his guest.

After Melody, the hostess I've only spoken to a couple times, waves us in through the front curtain, she gives me a secret smile and a wink. Walking into the club on Ronan's arm makes me feel like royalty. Out of everyone in here, every beautiful, sexy, confident woman he could choose from, he wants me. I'm not one for low self-esteem, but even that feels astounding.

And maybe that's what love is—feeling unworthy and astonished that the man you think is the greatest person alive wants you. What a gift a love like that is.

Ronan doesn't stop at the bar to chat with the regulars. He doesn't take me into the open VIP area. He doesn't even take me to his own room.

We're going to a new room tonight. As we approach the room next to his, I take a long, deep breath and square my shoulders. I'm not nervous...I'm excited. I want this. I *need* this.

Ronan scans his key card against the lock, and it buzzes before he pushes it open. But he hesitates, pulling me into his arms and pressing his forehead to mine.

"I haven't told anyone the news yet. We'll tell them when we're ready."

I nod, and he takes my mouth in a quick kiss before gently pulling me into the room.

Eden is already here, setting up as we close ourselves in the room. There are things laid out on the bed, and I wince at the sight, each of them looking painful and a bit scary. Eden is dressed like I've seen her many times before. Fierce black lingerie, strappy and beautiful on her light tan skin.

She turns when she hears the door click, sending us both a menacing smile.

"There you are," she says calmly, and I look to see what she's doing, noticing a few things on the counter in front of her, quickly taking stock of it all—a jar of something that looks like cream or lotion, silver metal that I'm assuming are clamps, and a pitcher of water, condensation dripping over the glass.

She leaves what she was doing and walks toward us, her eyes on me. "How are you feeling, Daisy? Excited? Nervous?"

I square my shoulders and swallow. "Both?"

Her response is a light laugh as she brushes a loose blond curl out of my face.

"We're going to have fun. Did Ronan go over everything with you? Safe word, limits, expectations?"

"Yep," I reply with confidence.

Eden laughs again, this time sounding a little more sinister than sweet.

"Yes, Madame," she says. "I'll let that one slide, but next time you slip up, it'll cost you. Understood?"

My cheeks burn as I nod. "Yes, Madame."

Ronan's hand is on the small of my back and I resist the urge to look at him. He'll try to comfort me, and right now, I'm afraid if I tempt myself with the safety of his arms, I'll back out of this.

"Take your clothes off, Daisy," she says, her voice taking on a dominance that is much different than the woman I shared a glass of wine with in this very room just a few days ago.

"Yes, Madame," I reply. As I move away from Ronan, he crosses the room and takes a seat on the bed, loosening his tie as he watches me. I feel his eyes on me as I pull off my dress and bra. When it comes to my lace panties, I hesitate for a moment. He prepped me before we came, explaining that I could get as naked as I felt comfortable, without pressure or expectation.

But I feel safe with both of them. If he trusts her, then so do I.

As I pull down my underwear, I find his gaze with my own. He's staring at me with adoration in his eyes and it boosts my confidence as I pick up my clothes and set them on the bench against the wall.

"Come here, Daisy." When I turn toward Eden, I swallow at the sight of a paddle in her hand. As she approaches me, she jerks her head to the floor and I obediently lower to my knees. My eyes are still trained upward to her face as she runs her hands through my hair. "Your daddy told me you're a brat."

I squeak when her grip turns painful.

"I hate to hurt you. You are such a pretty little thing," she murmurs. "You're a beginner, so we're going to start slow. I know Ronan went over everything, but I need to hear you say it. What should you say if you want to slow down?"

"*Yellow*, Madame."

"Good girl. And if you want to stop?"

"*Red*, Madame."

"Good. Now, are you ready to begin?"

"Yes, Madame."

The corners of her mouth pull upward into a smile. "You're a good girl for me." Then her voice takes on a colder tone. "Now, climb onto your daddy's lap."

I crawl over to Ronan, climbing onto his lap much like I did the day he spanked me in the bedroom. Just taking the same position makes my stomach flutter with excitement. He strokes my hair with one hand, holding my arms in the other.

"We'll start with twelve. Your daddy will count."

I find myself tensing, afraid of the pain before the paddle flies. But the moment it lands against my bare backside, I remember why I wanted this. It burns and hurts like hell, but the sudden rush of adrenaline gives me something I haven't felt in a long time. And I don't even know what it is yet, but I crave it like air.

"One," Ronan grunts.

Then, Eden smacks me again, and the sting is worse this time, and a gasp slips through my lips without warning.

"Two," he says, his voice sounding strained.

On the third hit of the paddle, my body starts tensing on its own. My stomach muscles clench, my thighs tremble, and the sex between my legs pulses.

I love it.

Is there something wrong with me for loving this so much? For acknowledging that it hurts but enjoying it for that exact reason? With each harsh swing of the paddle, it feels as if I shed a layer, freeing a part of myself I've been missing. And it accomplishes so many things at once.

It's turning me on, which, by the moisture between my thighs, is obvious.

But it's also bringing me to life. Forcing a stronger, more confident, and independent person out of me that I always thought I was meant to be. It replaces the pain of grief and loss with a physical pain that manifests itself into strength. I can't face the overwhelming anguish of living without my mother, living *alone*, but I can face this. I can take this.

And last, after nine swings of the paddle, I know deep down that this is my self-inflicted punishment for what I've done to Ronan. Deceived him. Essentially stalked him. And then let him fall in love with me. I'm breaking the heart of the one man whose pain guts me worse than my own. I may never forgive myself for that, but at least punishing myself makes me feel better. I deserve this.

When I feel a soft hand circling my tender backside, I open my eyes. Realizing I zoned out for most of the hits, connecting only with the sting on my ass, I nearly forgot I'm not alone.

As Eden's hand trails between my legs, sliding through the moisture of my arousal, I let out a wanton moan.

"Oh, Ronan, she's soaked. What a dirty little girl you have."

"Yes, I do."

Then I feel his hand on my ass, and I come back to reality. He's roughly massaging my flesh before giving it a light smack.

"Let's get her up and see what else she likes," Madame Kink says with eagerness in her voice.

It's weird how much I like to hear them talking about me like I'm not here. Meticulously planning my punishment while I lie here silently waiting for what's to come.

"How are you feeling, baby girl? Give Daddy a color." With a finger under my chin, he turns my face toward him. When our eyes meet, that sense of safety washes over me.

"Green," I reply.

With a nod, he smiles.

"Now, get up, Daisy," Eden says assertively. So I do.

She leads me over to the middle of the room, where a pair of soft black cuffs are hanging from the ceiling by two silver chains. I follow the chains, which are strung through a pulley, and affixed to the wall on the opposite side by a mechanism that allows someone to adjust how high or low they are.

After my hands are bound above my head, Ronan pulls the chains, lifting my wrists higher until I'm strung tight from top to bottom. I can barely touch the floor, so I rest on the balls of my feet to keep my balance.

Eden spins me, so I'm facing away from Ronan, and with her face close to mine, she smiles. "You should see the way he stares at you when you're not looking. I've never seen him look like that before."

It takes me a moment before I realize she's breaking character. This isn't Madame Kink talking. It's Eden, his friend. *My* friend.

I gulp in a lungful of air because those words somehow hit harder than any paddle or whip. With tears in my eyes, I nod with a sad smile.

"I think with some encouragement, we can get him to do this for you. It's not easy for him, though. It's not in his nature to hurt you, but you have to make him understand how much you want it. How much the pain helps. How good it feels."

Quietly, I whisper, "Yes, Madame."

"Then you two won't need me anymore. But of course, if you do, I'll be here. Okay?" Her voice has taken on a softer, more intimate tone, and it tears at my heart. She cares for *both* of us.

As our eyes meet, I feel an overwhelming sense of connection that I never felt with her before. Suddenly, I don't feel so strange for liking this. Because I think...Eden does too.

"Yes, Madame."

"Good girl," she replies with a soft look in her eyes.

Then just like that, the warmth is gone, and I glance down to see the black leather rod in her hand. I don't know the name, and I don't know what it's going to feel like, but I have a feeling it's going to hurt.

With a wicked gleam in her eye, she smiles. "Now the fun part begins."

Rule #34: It's okay if you don't like the pain.

Ronan

I've been in this place dozens of times, watching Eden inflict pain and punishment. But it's never bothered me so much. It's hard to watch, although Daisy takes it all so beautifully. When she says *green*, I believe her. And I can tell Eden is taking it easy on her, but I can also tell Daisy could take more.

My beautiful girl wants this.

After a round with the riding crop, Daisy looks to be in agony. A sheen of sweat covers her body. Her cheeks are red and she's breathing heavy, eyes closed as she practically hangs from the ceiling.

Eden caresses her body, massaging her back where the red strike marks are starting to rise on her skin. Then her hands move to Daisy's front, fondling her breasts and pinching the already tight buds between her fingers.

My molars clench tightly as I try to rein in this sense of territorial jealousy I've never felt before. Normally it's arousing to see Eden with one of my subs, but this time feels different. Especially as she whispers in Daisy's ear and my girl responds with a smile, her body leaning toward Eden like she needs her.

Suddenly, I'm crossing the room, my hands taking Daisy's face and pulling her close to me. She instantly opens her eyes when she feels me, gazing up into my eyes with love.

"Told you," Eden says with a small laugh.

She was doing this on purpose, making me jealous, egging me on. But Daisy's eyes are still on me. "You're doing so well, baby girl." With a hum, she leans toward me as I press my lips to her forehead, trailing them down to her mouth.

When I feel something soft poking my side, I lift myself away from Daisy and stare at Eden. She's holding the black leather flogger up toward me as if she wants me to take it.

"If you want to reward her, you need to make her earn it."

What she really means is that *I* need to earn it.

My gaze travels back to Daisy and I find it laughably ironic that she's the one wearing the expression of encouragement. As if this will somehow hurt me more—maybe it will.

"Please, Daddy," she whispers, and I give her a confident nod before leaning down to kiss her head again.

"Yes, baby." Then I take her jaw in my hands, holding her face up so our eyes are locked. "I'm giving you ten, and you better let me hear it."

A filthy little smile creeps across her flushed cheeks.

"Yes, Daddy," she replies, before letting her eyes close and her head hang forward. When I move to her back, Eden brushes a hand along my arm. Then she takes my place, standing in front of Daisy. I hardly noticed the clips in her hand, but when Daisy lets out an ear-piercing scream, I know it's because of the clamps now firmly pinching each nipple.

My fist squeezes around the handle of the flogger, and I take a deep breath, quickly reminding myself that this is what Daisy needs and giving her what she needs is all I want. If I love her and if I truly am a pleasure Dom, then it's up to me to give her what feels good to her.

So with that, I land a harsh backhanded swing with a

resounding *thwap* against the flesh below her shoulder blades. Her screams of anguish fill the room, just before she starts gasping for breath.

I've felt a hit like this before and I know how shocking the first one is, like loads of little sparks stinging her skin.

"Count, Daisy," Eden barks out.

"One," Daisy cries.

I can do this.

Closing my eyes, I hit her again, this time a little lighter than before. But her scream is louder. "Two!" she belts.

My skin is growing hot and my chest is starting to ache. I just want to swallow her up in my arms, tell her how much I love her, and take all her pain away.

Why can't she need *that*? Why does she need this pain so badly?

"Three," she says breathlessly, followed by a heady moan.

"Oh, Daisy, you're so wet," Eden mutters against her ear. "Can I make you come while Daddy makes you cry?"

Daisy moans loudly again. "Yes, Madame. Please, Madame."

The fourth hit is hard, harder than I intended. Daisy's body trembles, and she tries to fight her way out of the restraints, like she can run from the long-lasting sting of the leather strips of the flogger.

"You had everyone fooled, Daisy. You're not a sweet and innocent little girl at all, are you?" Eden mutters, her fingers disappearing between Daisy's trembling thighs.

My fist clenches again. She *is* my sweet girl. With every strike of this thing in my hand, it feels like I'm losing her. That beautiful angel I found only a few weeks ago.

I zone out through the fifth, six, and seventh hits. Daisy's cries of pleasure mingle into one with her screams of agony, and when I notice that Eden is now on her knees, her face buried in the sweet, aching sex of my beautiful girl, I lose control again.

A man can only be tortured for so long before he snaps.

Grabbing a handful of her hair, I crane her neck toward me, bringing her parched lips to mine. I dominate her mouth in a bruising kiss until she melts in my hands.

Then I pull my mouth away and mutter darkly, "Let me see you come, Daisy, because the minute she's done with you, you're mine. Understand? You can come for her, but you belong to me."

She lets out a scream, her body contorting through her orgasm.

I don't even wait until she's caught her breath. In a rush, I'm reaching up to unfasten the binds around her hands. She falls like putty, so I quickly hoist her into my arms, her legs wrapped around me as I carry her to the large chair in the corner. Then I take her mouth again, relieved to feel her kissing me back with as much passion and need as I'm kissing her.

All we need is each other.

All I need is her.

She's writhing against me, drenching my pants when I pull my mouth away, holding her face in my hands when I say in a rough command, "Unbutton my pants and take Daddy's cock out, Daisy."

With the nipple clamps still dangling from her chest, she reaches for me. Her fingers frantically fumble with the belt and zipper of my pants. My cock is leaking inside my boxer briefs, desperate to be touched by her. She's humming with each breathless exhalation as she tries to hurry and free it.

The moment her soft hand slides along my stiff length, I shudder.

"That's it, baby girl."

She wraps her hand around me, softly stroking from base to the tip and staring down at my cock in her hand. My eyes close, letting her delicate touch tease me for only a moment longer.

Then, I pull her face closer and whisper against her mouth. "Daisy…"

"Yes, Daddy," she replies obediently, and I know she does it because of how much I fucking love it when she calls me that.

"Ride my cock like a good little girl."

She doesn't hesitate.

Lifting her hips, she settles her wet pussy over the head of my dick and only winces a little at the size as she slowly lowers herself over me.

"Atta girl," I say in a low, growling tone as I brush her sweat-soaked hair out of her face. "God, you feel so good. Does that feel good, sweetheart?"

I kiss her jaw, her cheeks, then her mouth as she latches her lips on mine, grinding her hips down on me as I lick my way into her mouth.

"Yes," she cries out, her voice thick with lust. "So good."

A part of me wishes I had more discipline. I could have taken my time with her before fucking her like this, but watching someone else lick between her legs was more than I could handle.

"You're mine now, Daisy. Understand?"

She looks into my eyes as she grinds herself down on my cock. There's more awe and adoration on her face than passion and need. This isn't part of a scene or a joke to her. This is real. "Yes," she whispers.

My cock is aching, and my balls draw up tight at that response. She's mine. She's really mine.

"I mean it, baby girl. Mine to take care of. Mine to keep. Mine to fuck. Mine to love."

"Yes," she cries out again, clearly feeling her own pleasure starting to build.

Without warning, I ease the clamps off of her nipples, and she lets out a husky yelp from the mix of pain and pleasure. The sensation has her picking up the speed of her hips.

"That's it, Daisy. Come on Daddy's cock. Then I'm going to take you home and make you come again and again and again. Because you're mine."

"I'm yours," she cries out. Her hands latch around my neck as she holds me tight, grinding her clit against me. When I feel her body tremble, I lose it.

With a harsh grip of her hips, I drive my cock even farther inside her and come so hard, I lose the ability to breathe.

"Oh fuck, Daisy," I groan, drawing out her name. She slumps against me as we come together, our hearts hammering in unison.

With her body in my hands, I softly stroke her hair as I wrap my other arm around her to hold her close.

After a few moments of heavy breathing, I hear Eden on the other side of the room. "Well, that was fucking beautiful."

Daisy smiles, letting out a tired-sounding laugh as she turns to face the woman reclining on the bed.

When I feel ready, I pull Daisy off my lap and carry her over to the bed, placing her next to Eden, who immediately starts petting Daisy's hair out of her face.

"How are you feeling?" Eden asks her.

Daisy lets out a long exhale. "I feel…great."

"Good," Eden replies. While they talk on the bed about coming down and aftercare, I pull up my pants, stuffing my spent cock inside, then button them up before grabbing the water from the counter.

With each of us on either side of Daisy, we make her drink nearly half the pitcher, before turning her over and covering her back with a soothing balm to help with the soreness.

"This is his favorite part," Eden says, and I know she's teasing me.

But she's right. Because every moment that I spend coddling and nurturing the girl I love, I'm thinking about how much I hated bringing her pain. Even if she loved it. Even if she came twice. Even if she *needs* it.

It pains me to think I can't give my girl everything she needs.

After we feel Daisy has fully come down and recovered, we urge her to get out of bed and get dressed. She hugs Eden and says her goodbyes before I tuck Daisy inside the car. Then, we're finally alone.

"Are you okay?" she asks, her head on my shoulder.

"Yes, baby girl. I'm okay. Are you okay?"

"I'm better than okay."

My mood is still tense as I stare out the window. Suddenly it's her comforting me. She pulls my face toward her. "You think there's something wrong with me, don't you? For liking that so much."

"No, baby. Of course I don't." I take her fingers in my hands, kissing her knuckles with affection.

"Then, what's wrong?"

"Daisy, I want to give you everything you need. I want to be the only thing you need."

"But you don't think you can do this?"

"I'll get there," I reply.

"If you don't like it, then I don't want you to do it."

"So, what? You'll go to Eden whenever you need...that? Do you have any idea how that makes me feel, Daisy? I'll do it."

"I'm sorry," she whispers, tucking her body closer to mine. "I didn't mean to imply that."

Petting her head as she rests against my chest, I try to shove all of my worries away. "It's okay, baby girl." Then I lift her chin, so she's gazing up at me as I whisper, "I love you."

"I love you too," she replies.

And I believe her. She does love me as much as I love her. I just hope it's enough. It has to be.

Because I don't know what I'll do if it's not.

Rule #35: Heartbreak is the worst pain of all.

Ronan

FOR THE FIRST TIME IN YEARS, I SLEEP PAST SEVEN. APPARENTLY last night took more out of me than I realized. Daisy's warm body is draped over mine like a blanket, keeping me glued to my slumber like a potent drug. When I finally peel my eyes open, I see a mess of blond, the sun shining through Daisy's hair creating a halo over her sleeping face.

My bed has never felt more inviting. And I'm half-tempted to wake her up with my mouth between her legs, but after last night, I want her to rest. When Daisy is with me, I want her to always be well rested, well fed, and well fucked.

Then I let the conversation in the car replay in my mind, the same fear and anxiety surfacing once again. Is this how it's going to be? Constant worry that I won't be enough? That I won't please her enough? That she'll need something from someone else and leave me brokenhearted?

Sooner or later, I have to relax. She loves me. I'm confident of that. So why am I still so worried?

When I finally crawl out of my bed, it's with the intention to go to my office to follow up on the email to Fitz. And I realize the desire to get married and settle our business as fast as possible is just another form of that anxiety and unease. I'm covering that up with the excuse that I just want to be sure Daisy is taken care of.

So after a rushed shower, I'm dressed and sitting in my office, opening my email. I'm halfway through typing out the message when my phone rings.

Glancing down at the caller ID on the screen, I recognize the investigator's name, and my stomach instantly fills with lead, and I'm flooded with shame. I nearly forgot about that email. The one I never should have sent.

Which is why I nearly let it go to voicemail.

But maybe it's curiosity that inspires me to pick it up. He wouldn't call if there was nothing.

"John," I say as my greeting after swiping the screen.

"Ronan," he replies coolly. And then he gets right into it. No salutations or small talk. "I ran a search on Daisy Bennett's family history. Her father, Alan Bennett, is a chiropractor in Chesapeake, Indiana. Her mother, Shannon Masters, was a real estate agent. She died of breast cancer three years ago."

As I listen to him rattle off facts, it sounds at first like nothing I didn't already know. But when I hear a name I've heard before, I freeze. "Wait, what? Say that name again."

"Shannon Masters. If it sounds familiar, it's because you wrote her a million-dollar check nine years ago. I did a scan of your finances and business history on all of these names, and Shannon's name popped up."

He's talking so fast and I'm struggling to keep up, I barely notice Daisy walking into the room. All I can picture is Shannon's face, seeing her as she stands in the doorway of my office— brokenhearted and afraid.

Much like Daisy is now.

Long blond hair, round blue eyes, full lips…

It hits like déjà vu.

"Ronan?" Daisy whispers hesitantly as I stare at her with wide, frightened eyes.

On the phone, John continues, "Shannon Masters cashed the check and deposited the funds into a savings account with your name in the memo, the beneficiary being Daisy Moon Bennett."

"What's wrong?" she mutters, gaping at me with concern.

"Thank you, John," I rasp into the phone.

"I'll email you the report. Bye, Ronan."

The phone line goes dead, and I stare at Daisy.

My mind is on a loop. No emotions or feelings building just yet. Just their faces, their names, this new revelation cycling through my brain.

Daisy is Shannon's daughter.

Shannon's daughter.

Shannon is dead.

"Ronan, what's going on?" she cries, louder this time, her voice full of desperation.

When I glance up at her face again, I see the remorse. The fear. The regret.

She knows.

She's known this entire time.

"Please talk to me," she begs, stepping toward my desk.

I glance up at her, emotions battling for control as I let everything sink in. Shame and disgust with myself for *touching* Shannon's daughter. Anger and regret for not knowing until now. Disappointment and fear in realizing that everything I've had with Daisy up until this moment has been steeped in deception.

I'm such a fool.

Normally, I'm not a spontaneous man. I make thoughtful, strategic, careful plans. My business and my success have proven that. So then why am I such a fool when I'm in love? Why do I fall so easily? Give away my heart at every opportunity?

"Daisy," I mutter, my hand covering my mouth, my scorn-filled eyes burning. She's crying. Large tears stream effortlessly over her face, an expression of worry written in the furrow of her brow.

"I assume whoever was on the phone just now told you about my mother."

"I don't understand," I mutter, and she hiccups through a sob.

"Why? I've already given you money. Did you want more?"

Her face contorts into anguish. "No. Ronan, I meant what I said. I don't want your money. It was never about that."

"Then what was it about?" My voice is a cold, emotionless void...exactly how I'm feeling inside.

"I just wanted to know who you were. She left your name on this account for me, but all I knew about you was that you spent time with her. I didn't know you loved each other...until you told me. I had no idea why you left me so much money."

Something in me cracks. A splinter in the shield around my heart.

Everything with Daisy has been...a lie.

"Why didn't you tell me? Why couldn't you just ask me?"

"I don't know. Ronan, you were all I had left of my mother. I think deep down I was afraid that if I asked you, and you didn't remember her, it would hurt. Or that she meant nothing to you."

"I loved her," I snap, my hand slamming against the table.

Daisy flinches, more tears cascading over her cheeks.

And every memory of what I've done with Daisy, what I've done with *Shannon's daughter*, comes flooding back to my mind and I keel over, my head in my hands.

"Please get out," I mutter.

Daisy sobs again. "This changes nothing for me." Her voice is so small and sad.

"It changes *everything* for me," I reply, leveling my gaze on her face. And I watch as those words hit her, their meaning heavy and harmful. The proposal. The promises. The way I felt for her...gone.

She sucks air into her shaking chest as she steps backward toward the door. Before disappearing, she pauses and wipes her face. "You promised you would never hurt me," she says with a whimper. "This hurts, Ronan."

I don't respond. I don't even look up. Staring down at the floor, my elbows on my knees and my body folded inward like I've been shot, I sit in silence as she leaves.

The sound of the front door slamming moments later rings through my ears, echoing with the same pain it inflicted nine years ago.

Rule #36: You can't appreciate happiness if you don't know pain.

Daisy

WHAT DID I EXPECT? A FAIRY TALE? I WANTED MY LIFE TO BE poetic, and I feel like an idiot now for ever dreaming that it could be anything more than cruel and lonely. Life isn't poetic. It's unfair, ruthless. Nothing more than a fight for survival in a bleak, brutal existence. It takes but never gives.

Life is nothing but a series of days in which you work, grieve, sleep, and eventually die. Alone.

I'm being dramatically morose, but considering I'm lying on my thin foam mattress, parked in the same city parking lot I was in when Ronan found me, I'm allowed to be morose right now.

I had my chance to come clean to Ronan, and maybe if I had done it early on like I was supposed to, then we'd still be together. We could have worked it out. Maybe.

Or maybe not. It's obvious he's still hung up on my mother. He clearly loved her for real. Not some short-lived fascination like it was with me. And now not only is he coming to terms with my lies, he's also grieving her death.

I've fucked up. I *am* a fuckup.

But who cares? It's better this way. With Ronan, I had something to lose. Happiness is dangerous. The more you have, the more that's at stake. The higher you feel, the further you fall. I was happy before. I should know better. Just before my mother was diagnosed, I was happy. My future felt bright. An acceptance letter to the music school of my dreams. A beautiful, poetic life like I always dreamed.

But that was ripped away too by a long, painful battle. There was nothing beautiful about that. Orange pill bottles and sterile hospital rooms and the incessant beeping of those machines. The blue vinyl chair she would sit in while they filled her bloodstream with poison, in hopes that it would kill the thing killing her. Daytime talk shows droning on in the background with people smiling and winning cars and trips, plagued with happiness that we would never feel. My mother would never feel that sort of elation ever again.

Because life is unfair.

Her last days feel closer now than they did before. The way her body withered away as fast as her mind did. Watching her organs shut down slowly, drugging her to the point where she lived her last days in an inebriated haze of confusion.

Those final moments soaked my existence, turning even the sunshine gray and filtered with sadness, so every day that existed thereafter felt tainted—until him. Until Paris and pianos. Until private jets and pleasure so palpable, I choked on it. I was blinded by that happiness. I was blinded by *him*.

But the sunshine is gray again because I was a fool who fell into life's little trap. I made the mistake of feeling an ounce of bliss, because what is joy if we don't know the opposite? If I had never felt the overwhelming rush of anguish, joy would be flat and pointless.

Fuck, I should write this down.

But who wants to listen to a song like that?

My tattered backpack sits next to me, the same backpack that's been to chemo rooms and then to France. I packed everything I had taken to Ronan's in a rush after he sent me out of his office. A pile of dirty clothes, my makeup bag, and my journal. I'm sure I left stuff behind, but some leggings and bodywash are the least of my concerns compared to what else I lost—the pieces of me I left with him.

I can't think about him. My mind won't let me go there.

His warm smile. The way his soft hands felt on my body. The comfort of his touch on my back. And the intoxicating scent of his cologne.

Him.

And just like that, I'm thinking about him. I don't even feel the first tears start to brim in my eyes before they fall. Maybe if I let my mind replay all the things about him that I love, then it will eclipse the way he looked when he told me to leave. The expression of disappointment on his face, and how all the love was gone as he stared at me with anger.

No, erase that.

Keep the good stuff.

Reaching into my backpack, I pull out my notebook and mindlessly flip through. Notes and lyrics scribbled messily onto each page. Memories unlocked on every line. I can practically smell the croissants in Paris. The aromatic espresso they served in those tiny cups.

His hand on my knee under the table.

I wish I could write that feeling into a song.

Unable to string together a coherent line of words, I flip to the next page. And there it is.

The lines he scribbled for me. The poetry he wrote...*for me*.

I gasp for breath before closing the book.

I hurl the journal across the van. Without much space to fly, it slams into the back window and falls, pages crinkling on its way down. I throw myself facedown onto my pillow, and I scream like a child. I wish I never gotten on that stage in the first place, so I would have never known what it's like to be loved by Ronan Kade.

Rule #37: A man isn't responsible for your happiness.

Daisy
Nine years ago

"Daisy," my dad calls from the bottom of the stairs, "your mom's here!"

I hear their muffled voices talking as I jump up from the spot on my bed, where I was watching an old episode of *Judge Judy*. In a rush, I grab my backpack from on top of the bed and barrel out the door of my room and down the stairs.

The moment I spot my mom standing on the welcome mat, the first time I've laid eyes on her in six weeks, I can tell something is different. She's tanner than normal, for one thing. But she's also wearing an expression of immense relief when she sees me.

I sprint through the foyer, past my dad, and slam into her, wrapping my arms around her as she engulfs me in a tight hug. She squeezes the life out of me, nearly lifting me off my feet, although I'm just as tall as her now.

"Daisy Moon, I missed you!" She squeals in my ear.

For the first time all summer, I feel at ease. I love my dad and I like spending summers with him, but I hate being away from my mom. There's no one else on earth that I can talk to so easily. I love my friends, but I doubt I'll ever meet anyone who makes things as effortless as she does.

It is always like this with us. Like we share the same soul. She can yell at me one minute and then laugh with me the next. My dad tries to be as comfortable with me as she is, but it always feels forced, so I figure she and I are just special.

"Did you have a good trip?" I ask after finally pulling away.

One of her arms remains around my shoulders, squeezing me as she nods. "California is hot, and the beach was nice, but I missed my girl."

"I missed you too." I wrap her in another hug.

"Why don't you say goodbye to your dad, and then you and I can go school shopping. We need to get you ready for middle school."

"Can we go eat at Hanson's too?" I ask with excitement. It's her favorite burger place, so I know she won't say no.

"Of course," she replies.

After I give my dad a hug and my parents say their goodbyes to each other, my mom and I pile into her old car and pull onto the main street toward the mall.

"So, why were you gone so long?" I ask, plugging my phone into the charger in her car and cueing up the playlist I've been listening to all summer.

A soft smile curls on her lips. "I made some friends, and since you were with your dad, I just decided to stay."

"What kind of friends? A *boyfriend*?" I tease her, and she lets out a loud belly laugh.

I've missed that laugh.

"That is none of your business, Daisy. Besides, what good would a boyfriend in California do?"

"I bet the boyfriends there are better than the boyfriends here," I say, turning up my nose as I think of all of my friends' dads. There's not a single man in town I could imagine with my mom. They're all old and boring.

"I'm not getting a boyfriend!" she says with a laugh.

"Okay, good," I reply, just as my favorite song comes on. I quickly turn the radio up and we sing along together.

"Did you write more songs this summer?" she asks, raising her voice over the music.

I answer with a shrug. "A couple, but they're not any good."

"Bullshit," she snaps. "I bet they're total hits."

I laugh and roll my eyes. "The only trip I've taken all summer was the two nights Dad took me to that old amusement park two hours away. I have nothing exciting to write about."

"Daisy Moon," my mother barks. "You could write a song about burgers and milkshakes, and it would be perfect."

"You're just saying that because you're my mom," I argue.

"I did not come back from California to hear you talk badly about my favorite songwriter. As soon as we get home, you're playing me those new songs."

My eyes widen as I let out a giggle. "Geez, okay."

When we pull into the parking lot at Hanson's, I glance over and notice that my mom looks happier than when she left. I can't imagine why anyone would be so happy to be back here instead of California.

Before we get out of the car, I glance over at her. "You know, if you do get a boyfriend, that's okay with me. I won't be mad."

Her eyebrows pinch together as she turns toward me. "What makes you say that?"

I shrug. "I don't know. Don't you want to get married again?"

She takes my hands in hers as she leans closer. "If I happen to meet someone, then sure. I'd get married again. But I don't need to. A man isn't responsible for making you happy, Daisy. I love my life the way it is right now. I've got you."

Then she presses her forehead to mine, and I start to feel my throat get tight.

"I missed you," I whisper.

Her eyes start to get teary as she replies, "I missed you too."

"Next time you go to California, you have to take me, though."

With a laugh, she pulls away and quickly wipes her eyes. "I don't plan on going back, but if I do, I'll definitely take you with me."

"Okay, good."

"But they don't have Hanson's in California. I couldn't find a single good burger the entire time I was there."

"Seriously?" I reply.

"Seriously. Nothing would make me happier than a big double cheeseburger with onion rings and a milkshake."

"Race you," I say as I jump out of the car. She doesn't even take the time to lock it as we both sprint toward the front door of the burger joint, laughing hysterically as we step inside.

We're still breathless as we order, my arms still wrapped around her waist. It was the longest summer ever, but at least it's over. She's home, and everything feels right again.

Rule #38: Whatever you did, chances are the bartender has heard worse.

Daisy

GEO KEEPS LOOKING AT ME. HIS CURIOUS GREEN EYES ARE TRACK-
ing me between drinks, his lips ready to ask what happened.
But I can't tell him. It's only a matter of time before Ronan tells
Emerson Grant about my secret, how I essentially stalked him all
the way to the club, and I'll lose my job. Might as well get in one
more night of tips before that happens.

As soon as I walked in, Geo could tell. There's not a touch
of makeup on my face. My hair is a disheveled mess. I finger-
combed it into a messy bun before getting out of my van behind
the club. Honestly, my appearance might be grounds for firing
anyway. No one wants to have their martinis delivered to them in
an exclusive sex club by a walking hot-mess express like me.

I don't make eye contact and I can't even force a genuine smile
as I work. My eyes are on the door every chance they get, but
Ronan never passes through that curtain. I don't know if I want
him to or not.

My eyes are craving the sight of him, but even I know that if
he comes to the club tonight, he won't be spending it with me.

Just the thought of him with another woman has me wanting to throw up.

He will, though.

A man like Ronan doesn't stay lonely. I hope for his sake that he's not torn up for long. The idea of him being even a little unhappy guts me to my core.

"Okay, what the fuck?" Geo ambushes me on my way out of the storage room, and I stare up at him with wide eyes.

"What?" I act naive as I try to move around him.

He steps in my way. "What happened with Ronan?"

"Nothing," I blurt out, sounding less than convincing.

"Did you break up? Get in a fight?"

"Geo!" I snap, but the moment I look into his eyes, my throat starts to sting and I struggle to form any words without completely losing it. So I just stare at him through moist lashes without speaking.

"Oh, Daisy." His shoulders slump and his head tilts as he pulls me into his arms, hugging me tightly.

And I lose it. Silently, I cry into his shirt, my chest shaking with my sobs. He holds me long enough to let this round of tears complete before he pulls away and wipes my hair out of my face.

"You don't have to tell me anything. Unless he hurt you," he replies, leveling his intense stare on my tear-soaked face.

I shake my head as I wipe my cheeks with my sleeve. "He didn't hurt me."

"I didn't think so, but I had to be sure."

"It was my fault. It's all my fault."

With his firm hands on my shoulders, he leans his head down, so I'm looking at him again as he says, "Everyone fucks up, Daisy. Everyone."

I force a sad smile. "I know. But not everyone fucks up as bad as I did."

"I'm a bartender. I hear it all, and trust me…yes, they do. And I don't even know what you did."

A wet laugh escapes my lips. I feel about a hundred pounds lighter, but not a whole lot better. I still have to face that floor full of customers, and I'm not ready.

"Take a few minutes to get yourself cleaned up. And after work, I'm taking you to that stupid fucking piano bar to cheer you up, okay?"

"You don't have to do that."

"I want to. Marianna will cover for me. It's slow tonight, and she'll love the extra shift."

"Okay, fine," I reply.

Geo presses his lips to my forehead before disappearing through the door and back out to the floor. I stand in the hallway for a while before heading to the bathroom to clean up and return to work.

Marianna takes the shift, and when I'm cut around midnight, Geo and I walk arm in arm down the dark streets toward the bar.

I didn't think I'd be in the mood to drink and have fun tonight, but the minute the bartender brings me my whiskey sour, I realize all I really want to do is get as drunk as possible. The bar is already packed, and I feel as if everyone is way ahead of me on their path to intoxication. So the first one goes down fast.

Geo and I find a table by some miracle, and we sit down to watch the dueling pianos onstage. The crowd is wild, singing along and dancing as the two musicians play. By the second song, I'm ordering my second drink...but the moment she delivers it to our table, I can't seem to stomach even a sip. I want to throw up already. I feel pathetic.

Geo is watching me like a hawk until his second drink is gone, and then his attention is stolen by a handsome man sitting with a table full of rowdy couples. Judging by the trucker hat and bootcut jeans, I'd say he's barking up the wrong tree, but I trust Geo to make the right call on that.

The piano bar isn't easing my pain the way I wanted it to. If I could stomach more than a few sips of this drink at a time, maybe I wouldn't feel anything. Instead, I'm doomed to suffer through this heartache sober. I'm singing along like my life depends on it and scribbling request after request on the slips of paper they leave on the table in hopes that I can savor an ounce of distraction.

Geo and I sing and laugh together. More than once I catch him texting someone on his phone and I lean over, trying to see who it is, but he pulls it away.

"Who are you texting?" I ask with a teasing smile.

His grin is tight and thin as he shrugs. "No one."

After his nonresponse, I turn back to the stage to watch the piano players, and my mind wanders on its own, trailing down memory lane without permission. It's the tip jar that does it. Seeing someone slip a bill into the jar on the piano calls back memories of Paris, playing that dirty old piano on the street and watching as someone dropped a bill on the top of it for me.

Ronan's proud grin as he watched me play.

I nearly start crying just as one of the musicians calls out my name. Then he breaks out in a rendition of "Hey Jude," one of my requests, but instead of singing along, I break out in tears.

"Are you okay?" Geo asks, and I try to focus on him, but my stomach turns instead.

"I'm fine," I reply.

"Why don't we call it a night, Daisy? It's late."

"Go home, Geo. I'll be fine," I say, my voice strained.

"Yeah right," he says with a laugh, just as the noise and music and drinks become too much.

When I bolt up from my seat, I do it too quickly and the chair falls to the floor behind me. I stumble as I try to pick it up, feeling as if I'm going to pass out again.

"I'm fine!" I shout at Geo as he tries to help me. He gives me a shocked expression.

The music of the pianos is still blaring around us, the room still happy and energetic, although I feel as if I'm dying inside. When the fainting turns into an urge to throw up, I tear myself away from Geo and sprint to the bathroom.

It's crowded, girls gathering around the mirrors and talking loudly. I rush straight into the stall and the moment I see the toilet, I fall to my knees and throw up everything in my stomach. By the time I'm done, I'm sobbing and struggling to keep myself off the floor.

I've been in here for a while. I don't want to leave. Time melts and morphs until it doesn't exist, and I'm resting my head against the bathroom stall, wishing I could just close my eyes and not have to face reality anymore.

Then a deep voice calls me back to life.

"Sorry, ladies, excuse me," he bellows, and my eyes pop open. "Daisy, where are you?"

There must have been something in that one drink because Geo sounds a hell of a lot like Ronan right now.

"Ronan?" I mutter.

The stall door shakes.

"Open it, Daisy. Now." That authoritative command sends a chill down my spine and I nearly start sobbing as I reach up to flip the lock on the door.

A moment later, it's open, and I'm staring up from the grimy bathroom floor at the sexiest man in all of Briar Point.

Of course he looks gorgeous in the dive bar bathroom lighting.

"Jesus," he mutters angrily. Then I'm being lifted into the air by two strong arms, and I find myself melting against his chest. I swallow down the taste of shame on my tongue. He sounds so disappointed, and I try to shield myself from it.

The room is still spinning, while the scenery around me changes from bathroom to bar to cool night air. Then the inside of Ronan's car.

And just like that, everything feels right again.

Rule #39: Sometimes what you need isn't what you want.

Ronan

WHEN I COULDN'T SLEEP, I CAME INTO THE CLUB WITH NO OTHER intention than to see her. I'm still angry, and I'm not ready to forgive her, but I just needed to see her. I craved the sight of her so badly, I couldn't stand another moment in that empty apartment.

When she wasn't at the club, I asked Marianna if she had been sent home, and she informed me that she left with Geo.

A few texts with Geo—just to check on her and make sure she was safe—led me to learn that they were at the piano bar down the street and she was so sick she wouldn't come out of the bathroom.

Which led me here, with her asleep on my lap in the back seat of my car as my driver takes us back to the apartment.

I had the entire day to regret sending her away. I'm mad at her, but I don't want her sleeping in her van on the street again. Especially now that I see how she's going to behave. Finding her nearly passed out on the bathroom floor of a dive bar is not at all what I expected tonight.

I should be flattered. Breaking up with me devastated her. Except, I don't want to devastate her.

My emotions are all over the place. That innate desire to take care of Daisy is still there. That craving to be her...daddy. It still exists. That sort of thing doesn't just go away. But I can't keep saving her. I can't keep licking her wounds. I can't take care of Daisy if she won't take care of herself.

When we get back to the apartment, I take her upstairs immediately to the bedroom—the *guest* bedroom. She stirs as I lay her in the bed, carefully removing her clothes down to her bra and panties, before going into the bathroom to run warm water over a washcloth. I take it back in to clean her up.

Wiping her face and hands with the cloth, my heart lurches in my chest with every delicate touch of her skin. She slowly wakes up as I run the warm cloth over her eyes, noticing just how swollen they are.

She blinks up at me. "Where am I?"

"My apartment."

Her eyes scan the room before realizing what room she's in. "Where's Geo?"

"He got home safely."

Her eyes are on my face, looking more sober than I expect. "I'm sorry I'm such a mess," she says, her voice cracking on a sob.

"Don't apologize, Daisy. Just get some sleep."

As I move to stand, she reaches for me, latching her grip on my arm. "Don't leave me."

I hesitate. Part of me wants to stay. I'm not strong enough to say no. But I need to. To protect my own heart, I need to set boundaries with her. At least until I figure out what I'm going to do.

"Sleep, Daisy. We'll talk in the morning," I reply. Then I watch as she turns over, crying into her pillow, and I leave her like that.

Even though it shreds my heart into pieces to do so.

———

I don't sleep for shit all night. In the morning, I hear the shower running and the scent of her shampoo escaping the bathroom. Two nights ago, I was going to marry her. I wanted to.

I still want to.

Even though it's wrong. So fucking wrong.

After thinking it through all night, replaying every moment of our relationship, I figured out what I need to do. I know now what Daisy truly needs from me, but I don't know if I have the strength to give it to her.

When she finally comes out of the bathroom, she's dressed in the clothes I left on the counter, a few things she left behind. She stops when she sees me standing in the kitchen, like I'm waiting for her.

Wordlessly, I open the bottle of ibuprofen on the counter and take two out. Then I take them to her with a glass of water. She stares at them with sadness in her eyes.

"Thank you," she whispers, taking them from my hand.

"You're welcome," I reply.

When her eyes find my face, I know she's searching my expression for something soft and loving, but I'm cold and frozen behind a wall to protect myself. If I bend, even a little, I will break entirely.

"I'm so sorry," she says, breaking into a sob.

In a moment of weakness, I pull her into my arms and hold her against my chest. But that's it. I'm not a monster, and it would take a monster to turn her away when she's in this emotional state.

"We can go back to the way things were. This doesn't have to change anything," she cries into my chest.

With my hands rubbing the shivering surface of her back, I wish more than anything her words were true. When I don't respond, she pulls away and stares up at me.

Here comes the hard part.

"We can't."

"What? Why? Because of my mom?" Her voice is high-pitched and riddled with pain and desperation.

"It's more than that."

"Then, what is it? Because I lied to you? Ronan, I was scared of losing you. I should have told you, and I'm sorry."

"Did you ever really want me...or did you just need me?"

Her mouth hangs open in shock as her brow furrows. The pain is etched in her features.

"Ronan," she sobs, tears streaking across her face, "I *need* you because I love you."

"Daisy, as wonderful as this past month has been, I realized something yesterday. I realized that we would never work, not like that. As long as you needed me, then I would have loved you. But I don't want you to need me anymore, Daisy. I want you to stay because you *want* to."

"I do want to," she cries.

"Listen to me, baby girl. We both have some growing to do. You need me in the same way I need to feel needed."

"I don't want to do it alone," she sobs, and it breaks my heart to hear her say it because I know it's true.

"As much as I want to take care of you, Daisy...I need you to be able to take care of yourself." My voice cracks as emotion builds in my chest.

"Please..."

My bottom lip quivers as I hold her away from me. This is the hardest thing I've ever had to do. I've lost loved ones countless times, but I've never had to push one away, and it hurts so much worse.

She fights, her face turning to anguish, and I can see her wishing this moment weren't real. That it had any other outcome than this one, and honestly, so do I.

When she turns away, holding her hand over her face as she squeezes out another round of tears, I feel the moisture pooling in my own eyes.

"So it's not even about my lies or my mother. It's because you don't want to take care of me anymore. It's because I'm a mess."

"You're *not* a mess, Daisy. You just need to figure some things out first. You never properly dealt with the loss of your mom. You were thrust into adulthood alone, and I'm afraid you clung to me and I let you. Yesterday was a wake-up call for me. I want to take care of you more than anything, baby girl. But if I do, you'll never have a chance to truly heal on your own."

She practically falls to the floor, crouching down to her knees as she sobs, and I'm racked with guilt. It's obvious to me now that Daisy never let herself feel the grief from losing her mother, and keeping that secret was just another way to keep her memory alive. Which means she has a long road ahead, and it's one I can't help her with.

If I thought for a moment that Daisy would sink, I wouldn't do this to her, but I know how strong she is. I know what she's capable of, and I know she needs me out of the way until she can do it on her own.

Before long, she rises up from the floor. And when she turns back toward me to give me one last look, I blink away my own tears.

"Goodbye, Ronan," she whispers, and I swear I don't breathe again until she's gone.

As long as she's not in my arms, I don't want to breathe at all.

Rule #40: Big risk, big reward.

Daisy
Two months later

THERE'S THIS PART OF GRIEF COUNSELING WHERE WE'RE SUPPOSED to sit in silence for a few moments. It's meant to be meditative and calming. For five minutes, we listen to nothing, and it allows us to just focus inward.

It's my least favorite part.

It feels like being shut alone in a room with someone I've been avoiding. Painful and awkward and torturous. But I do it. Because that was the promise I made myself. I'm not going to cut corners and fake recovery. I am going to do the hard things.

Big risk, big reward.

The five-minute timer beeps and everyone slowly opens their eyes. Another least favorite of mine. Staring into the grief-stricken faces of survivors like me. But it turns out convincing yourself that someone else has it worse doesn't actually make you feel better. Because sadness is just…all around. And I don't mean in just these meetings, but everywhere. No one is really immune or safe from sadness.

No one has perfect, poetic lives.

It took me having one for a split second to realize that. Even on private jets and balconies overlooking the Eiffel Tower, the grief and pain I'd been bottling up and shoving into a ratty old backpack stuck to me like static cling.

But I also learned, through these harrowing and sometimes overwhelmingly sad meetings, that while sadness does permeate the air nearly everywhere, so does joy.

Ironically, it turns out that that's sort of what makes life poetic in the first place. It's not an Instagram filter or a Pinterest board. It's gross and gritty and beautiful and stunning all at the same time.

I also had to accept that love could be just a memory, and it wouldn't make it any less perfect or significant.

My mother loved me so much, she walked away from the man of her dreams. She walked away from real love. But she came back a happy woman. It might sound sort of weird, and I don't share this part with my grief group, but knowing that I fell for the same man my mother did made me feel strangely close to her. Without thinking about the gross parts, of course. I love that her heart beat for the same person mine did, and that means something. Like she's still here.

I've let go of Ronan Kade.

I don't cry about it anymore. At least not every day, like in the beginning. I just remember the truly perfect moments and the surprising ones. Honestly, I've gotten to a point in my healing where I'm sort of astounded and shocked that it happened at all.

I fell in love with a man thirty-five years older than me. Who happens to be a billionaire.

Who also happens to be the most romantic, passionate, caring, down-to-earth, perfect man—no, perfect *person*—I've ever known.

I mean, how many girls can say they've experienced something like that by the age of twenty-two?

I'm lucky. Or at least I keep telling myself that.

When I think back on the whole experience, I try to remember the reason I came out to Briar Point at all. Why did I go to such lengths to find him? Was it really about understanding why he left me the money? Or was I somehow picking up where my mother left off?

I don't see him at the club anymore. Everyone's talking about it, and I'm starting to feel the pressure. Like all of their harsh glares are really saying, *Why don't you quit so the billionaire we love will come back?*

But I can't quit. Because I need this job. Even though I know Geo won't hound me for my half of the rent, I have to pay him or else this has all been for nothing.

"Daisy, did you want to answer today's prompt?"

I look up from the knot of wood on the floor I've been staring at since I've been lost in my own thoughts.

"I'm sorry...what was it?"

"What are you excited for? It can be anything. An event. Big or small. Or a milestone, maybe."

I look around the circle at the faces staring back at me. I can tell by the nervous, jittery energy that they're not a talkative bunch today, which is why she's asking me. I sort of like talking and starting the conversation. Even if it does usually end up in tears and grief, at least by the end we're laughing and smiling.

"Umm...I have a gig tonight at this piano bar I love. It's like...a showcase they have once a week. They're going to let me play my own songs...as long as I promise to play the classic covers too."

"Did you finish your song?" the moderator asks.

"I finished a couple actually."

A few people around the circle clap and aim their tight-lipped smiles in my direction.

"How do you think your mom would feel about your songs?" she asks in a follow-up. My chest tightens at that question.

"Umm..." I smile to myself, thinking about the fact that

some of my songs definitely make reference to the same man she was in love with nine years ago. But all of that aside… "She called me her favorite songwriter. So I know she'd be really proud."

"She *is* proud," one of the older women in the group adds, and I grin at her.

"Thanks," I reply.

From then on, someone else answers and then another, and soon, we're all talking about the things we're excited about, encouraging each other, and you almost wouldn't recognize us as a grief counseling group.

Which I guess is sort of the point.

As it turns out, healing from grief and a breakup at the same time is really exhausting. Which means when I'm not at counseling or working or writing a song, I'm sleeping. And every moment I'm not sleeping, I'm wishing I were.

"Daisy," Geo calls, tapping on my bedroom door. I roll over and check the time on my phone. "It's seven. You don't want to be late."

Actually, yes, I do.

I think I might have lied when I told the group I was looking forward to this night because I'm actually dreading it. This will be the first time I perform any of my own songs in front of a crowd that's not my mom or Ronan.

"Big risk, big reward, Daisy," I mumble to myself, imagining it's my mother's voice harping at me to get out of bed and go to the bar. I only have to tell myself the same line about ten times before I finally sit up and pull on my pants. And since I took a little too long, I now have to rush, throwing my wild hair into a long, messy braid over my shoulder. Then I slip on one of my mom's old band tees that's been ripped to make it more of a crop top.

I toss my journal into my new backpack and rush out the door. Geo is standing in the hallway waiting. He's dressed up tonight, and I pause as I take in his whole look. He looks fine as hell in those black leather pants and a pair of high-heeled boots, making his slender legs look longer than they already are. The black eyeliner brings out the green in his eyes and his shirt is so tight his toned biceps are on display. It makes me wish he'd dress up like this more at the club.

"Daaaaaamn," I drawl as I let my gaze sweep up and down his body. "Mr. Tall, Dark, and Sexy as Fuck."

"Oh, stop," he replies, and I laugh as I throw my arms around his neck.

"You got dressed up for me," I mumble into his ear, and I feel him smile against my cheek.

"Of course, I did, Daisy Moon. This is your big night. And we all know I'm your only friend."

When I pull away from the hug, I give him a shove. Then I take his hand in mine, our fingers entwined, and even I'm surprised to find I'm the one pulling him to the door.

It's a short walk from Geo's apartment to the bar, but I feel like I'm practically running all the way there. I don't want to be late, but I'm also terrified to get there, so every step feels ominous and exciting at the same time.

When we finally arrive, my hands tremble as Geo pulls open the door. It's not nearly as crowded as it normally is on the popular dueling piano nights. But there is a nice little crowd of people lingering around the tables. When I spot a familiar face standing at the bar, I freeze.

Eden St. Claire is holding a martini glass next to a grinning blond. It takes me a moment to recognize Garrett's wife, Mia. I coast their way with a look of surprise on my face.

"Oh my God, what are you doing here?" I ask as I put my arms around Eden.

"A little birdie told me," she says, glancing up at Geo standing behind me.

I glare at him with wide eyes, and he does his best to look

innocent. But I can't even be mad at him. The way it feels to have someone else here for me is…amazing. It makes me feel a little less alone.

"You're going to do great," Mia says with a beaming smile.

"Thank you."

Just then I spot the organizer waving at me from the bar, so I excuse myself and rush over. He quickly goes over the lineup and what I should do when it's my time.

I swallow down the sudden urge to vomit again. "Want a drink?" he asks when he notices my complexion turn pale.

I shake my head. The thought of alcohol only makes it worse. "No thanks. Knowing my luck, I'd forget my lyrics or something."

"Okay, break a leg, kid," he calls as the announcer takes the stage.

Hearing my name uttered through the mic feels like a dream. Slowly making my way up to the stage, all eyes on me, the moment goes by in a strange haze of slow-motion surrealism. But as I take my seat on the bench and the crowd goes quiet, I glance out to the floor again, bright overhead lights blinding my vision.

But one face stands out. Sitting at the bar, a glass of bourbon in his hands, he watches me with a warm, comforting expression. Suddenly, I remember that day on the street in Paris.

Just play for me, he said.

So that's exactly what I do. I imagine there's not another soul in the room, just his rich chestnut eyes and the proud look on his face. If I'm just playing for him, I couldn't screw this up if I tried.

"Thank you," I mumble into the mic, and the crowd quiets to a low hush. "My name is Daisy Moon. And this song…is called 'The Highest Bidder.'"

Rule #41: Know when to walk away.

Ronan

LISTENING TO DAISY PLAY FEELS LIKE MEETING FOR THE FIRST TIME and reliving every moment of our relationship together. She sings about Paris and L'Amour and the Eiffel Tower and the terrible lighting in the ER. She even sings about the fucking cheese.

Some songs are upbeat, and I recognize the melodies from when she played in my apartment. There are a couple that are slow and sad, and I know they're about her mother. She has a way of manipulating the mood in the room effortlessly, making all of us feel what she's feeling.

I'm so incredibly proud of her.

When she finishes her set, she's bombarded by people when she tries to leave the stage, and I watch with pride as they ask for her autograph and photos.

"She's pretty good," Eden says, stepping up next to me at the bar. I've stood back while she and Geo and Mia cheered Daisy on from one of the tables. I didn't want to complicate things by mingling with Daisy's friends. As much as I wish I were part of her crowd, I know that's not the case anymore.

"Pretty good?" I snap, sounding offended. "She's a fucking star."

Eden laughs as she waves down the bartender. "I know. I'm just getting you riled up."

"Very funny," I mutter.

"You're going to stick around and tell her yourself, right?"

I take a long, deep sigh as I swirl my bourbon in my glass. "I don't think that's a good idea."

"It's been two months, Ronan. She's proving to you right now that she can take care of herself. That's what you wanted, right?"

Forcing myself to swallow, I nod. "Yeah. That is exactly what I wanted."

Eden lets out a long huff. "Ugh, don't tell me you're going to try and give me that *she's better off without me* bullshit."

My only response is the clenching of my jaw. "She's doing pretty good, though. I don't need to fuck that up for her."

"What, by giving her love and support? Oh yeah, better not do that," Eden replies sarcastically.

I shake my head as I down the rest of the liquor in my glass. The thing I don't tell Eden is that Daisy might be making progress, but I'm not. She needed me, and I needed to be needed.

So what does that make us now?

It's best to just let things go. She's happy and doing well. That's all I want. If she's happy, I'm happy.

"Is that Ronan Kade?" Mia jokes as she approaches the bar on the other side of me. "I haven't seen you in a while. You're starting to freak out my fiancé, so I really need you to come back to the club."

I laugh as I greet the bubbly blond taking the seat next to me. It wasn't all that long ago that I was giving her romantic advice at the bar in Salacious. She and Garrett clearly worked things out.

"Hey…" she says with excitement as her wide eyes meet Eden's.

"What?" I ask with trepidation.

"You should be in our charity auction tomorrow night."

My brow furrows as I glance at Eden. "It was my idea. We're doing a sort of…reverse-auction type thing. Asking our VIP members to auction off something and match the bids. It's for the DV support shelter."

"Why didn't you tell me about this?" I ask, feeling a little hurt that she wouldn't think of me.

She shrugs. "You've been going through stuff. I didn't know if you were ready to come back."

I turn toward Mia with a smile. "I'll match all the bids, Mia, but I won't be getting on that stage."

"Come on," she pleads with a pout. "Everyone would love to see you. You don't have to actually go on any dates or anything. Hell, you could auction a fucking hug and people would go crazy."

"I'll think about it," I reply gently.

The next time I look up, Daisy's there. Standing behind Mia, she gives me a small smile.

"Hey," she mumbles. Her cheeks are flushed and she looks thirsty, so without responding to her greeting, I grab the bartender as he walks by.

"Ice water, please."

He gives me a nod before quickly filling a glass. As he passes it to me, I hand it directly to Daisy. She gives me a tight-lipped smile as she takes it.

"Thank you."

The first thing I notice about her is that she looks good. Her hair has gotten longer. The fringe that used to hang over her eyes has grown out to curl behind her ears, and her cheeks have taken on a fullness, which means she's eating well. That makes me feel better.

The others make small talk around us as I watch Daisy. I haven't laid my eyes on her in so long that it feels good to just look at her.

"I missed your birthday," I mutter, and she responds with a casual shrug.

"It's okay."

After a moment of awkward silence, I confidently add, "You did great tonight, Daisy. I'm proud of you."

Her smile slips before she quickly looks away. "Thank you."

I want to say something else—anything else. I want to drag out this conversation for hours, days, years. The urge to keep her in my sights is visceral, but when Geo throws his arm around her and the rest of them squeal in celebration of her, I stand from the barstool. I've already paid their tabs and I'm sure they want to party without me hanging around.

"Make sure she gets home safe," I mutter to Geo, and he gives me a reassuring expression. I trust him. "Good night," I say to the rest of them, letting my eyes stray for a moment to Daisy's face. Her lips are parted as she watches me leave.

I make it all the way to the street before I hear her voice behind me.

"Ronan," she calls, before I climb into the back of my car. When I turn, she's standing there in that cut-up T-shirt and tight pants. I have a feeling just by the look on her face that whatever she's about to say right now isn't about us or getting back together.

"I never really got any answers to my questions. And something I never understood…"

"What is it, Daisy?"

"Was it for her or for me?"

"The money?"

She nods.

I take a step toward her, my face pinching together in concentration as I remember that day and the pain I felt letting Shannon go. I remember writing that check like it was yesterday. And I recall distinctly why I wrote it.

"It was for you, baby girl."

"Why?"

I take a moment to form my response, not quite sure how to express exactly what I felt that day, writing such a big check for a little girl I had never met. A girl who should have meant nothing to me, but I wanted her to have the world regardless.

"Because I wanted to take care of you."

The moisture in her eyes glistens from the streetlamps overhead. When she doesn't respond, I take another step closer, wiping where a single tear trails over her cheek. "It's your money, Daisy. Do whatever you want with it. Go live your big, poetic, musical life. Make it fucking amazing."

When she sucks in a breath, another tear falls, but I don't wipe that one away because she doesn't need me to—not anymore.

Rule #42: Put your money where your mouth is.

Daisy

I NEVER SHOULD HAVE LET HIM LEAVE. THERE WAS SO MUCH I wanted to say. Instead, I stuck around at the bar with Geo, Eden, and Mia for another hour before my exhaustion hit again, and Geo walked me home.

The entire night, instead of replaying every moment of being on that stage and singing my songs out loud for the first time, I was replaying the few short moments with him. I wish I could give him back that million dollars and make him mine again.

When I woke up today without an ounce of energy, I laid in bed all day, trying to catch up on enough sleep to make climbing out of bed even possible before my shift at the club. It's packed today, and I'm still dragging as I try to deliver drinks to everyone here for the charity auction.

It's probably a good thing he's not here because if he knew that I skipped two meals today, he'd be very disappointed in me. But with everything going on lately, the most I can manage is a small snack here and there, without wanting to either throw up or pass out every chance I get.

Oh yeah, he'd be so pissed.

It's so busy tonight that both bartenders are behind the bar and Mia has stepped in to help me deliver drinks.

"Quite a turnout," I say as we pass each other. She beams proudly as she takes a look around the crowded room. As the event planner of the club, Mia puts a lot of work into each of these events, and I've never seen one go badly.

"If only I could get that billionaire boyfriend of yours to show up, I'd call it a real success."

I stiffen at that word. "He's not my boyfriend," I correct her with a polite smile.

She screws her face up as she quickly apologizes. "I'm sorry. I'm just flustered. I didn't mean that."

"It's okay, Mia," I reply with a laugh. "Don't worry about it."

A moment later, the auction begins, and I'm so busy rushing around the room, I barely get to watch as each VIP rich guy takes the stage. On the side of the room, there's a screen showing the bids as they grow higher and higher toward the donation goal.

It's rowdier than I'm used to, and I like the energy. Especially since they're tipping bigger than normal tonight. When I look up and see Clay standing in the middle of the stage, he and I make eye contact. He shoots me a wide-eyed, scared-looking expression, and I laugh as I drop off a tray full of drinks at a table full of women excitedly bidding for a date with him.

They bid back and forth for a while, but just when I expect him to go to a nice older woman for over six grand, a confident voice at the back of the room calls out, "Ten thousand," and we all turn to see Madame Kink herself holding up a hand with a devious grin.

When I catch him grinning back, the announcer calls it, and everyone cheers just as Clay climbs down from the stage. I make a mental note to myself to ask her about that later. I sort of assumed it was a one-time thing with them. But maybe I was wrong.

After Clay, there are a few more men to take the stage, and I start to feel more and more dizzy with each trip back and forth from the bar. I just need to keep it together for another hour and then I can ask to be cut early and go home to sleep this off.

"All right, ladies. You won't want to miss this one," the announcer says, and I'm barely paying attention until I hear his name. "Mr. Ronan Kade."

I whirl around so fast, the room keeps spinning once my eyes have met his. He's standing onstage in a black suit, the first few buttons of his shirt undone. He shoves one hand in his pocket as the other waves, shaking his head at the same time.

"Sorry," he says proudly. "Not for auction tonight."

"Awwww," the announcer says, getting the crowd to join him.

"Only here to share that I'll be matching the donation tonight—"

"Two thousand dollars!" a woman at the table nearby shouts with an excited giggle.

"Three thousand," another woman shouts. When my gaze dances her way, I notice that she's about my age, and my blood boils at the very idea of her touching him.

"Five thousand!" the first woman screams.

Pretty soon, the room erupts in bids and cheers. On the stage, Ronan looks humbled and slightly embarrassed as the announcer tries to control the crowd. But there is no controlling them. The bids are growing higher and higher, even without the announcer's encouragement.

"One million dollars!"

Suddenly the crowd goes quiet and all the eyes in the room shift to stare in shock at me, my hand held proudly in the air. I'm looking at him with a buzz of excitement under my skin as his smile grows. The room is dead silent for three long seconds.

"Um…sold," the announcer says, and the crowd breaks out in laughter. "I don't know if anyone is going to beat that."

On the screen next to the stage, the donation amount spikes, covering tonight's goal and then some. My head starts to feel heavy and out of sorts as Ronan steps down from the low stage and walks toward me.

I distantly recognize that maybe I should be nervous about spending so much or losing the money he gave me, but it's honestly the furthest thing from my mind. All I see is him coming closer. I manage a smile as he steps up to me.

"Why did you do that?"

"I couldn't just stand by and let someone else win a date with you," I reply. When I sway gently on my feet, Ronan reaches out a hand and catches my arm.

"Daisy, are you okay?"

"I'm fine," I mumble to myself, but the words barely leave my lips before the tunnel vision sets in and the room tilts completely. Then, I'm falling. At least this time, he's there to catch me.

Rule #43: Live in the moment.

Ronan

I scoop Daisy up in my arms, and she's already opening her eyes when I carry her out the front door. Garrett is quick on my heels, followed by a few others concerned about Daisy.

"Do we need to call an ambulance?"

"She just needs some air," I reply.

"Someone get her a bottle of water," another person shouts.

Once we reach the warm night air, Daisy takes in a deep breath and a bit of color returns to her cheeks. I'm already carting her to my car without a destination in mind.

In my head, I'm running through all the things she needs from me. I can feed her. Take her to the emergency room. Give her a warm bed. *My* warm bed.

"Is she okay?" Garrett asks as I set her in the back seat of my car.

"I'm fine," she mutters, sounding tired. Mia appears behind me with a bottle of cold water, passing it to Daisy.

"She does this a lot," I say through gritted teeth as I stare down at her with disappointment. I'm willing to bet she didn't eat enough today. And judging by the apologetic look on her face, my suspicions are correct.

"I'd feel better if she was seen by a doctor," Garrett replies, and I understand from a liability standpoint that he needs to be sure his employees are healthy and well taken care of medically.

"I'll take her," I answer in a rush.

"Is that okay with you, Daisy?" Garrett asks.

She's halfway done with her bottle of water before replying, "Yes. He can take me. I'm so sorry, Garrett…"

"Don't apologize. Just get some rest and feel better."

"Thank you," she mumbles.

"Thanks again for your donations, Ronan," Mia adds, pulling me in for a hug before I turn to climb in after Daisy.

"Of course."

After I shut myself in the back seat, we wave goodbye to the couple through the window as my driver takes us directly to BP Medical Center. The moment Daisy and I are alone, I turn to check on her.

"I'm okay, really," she says, but I can tell by the listless way she's leaning back on the seat that she's not feeling well.

I no longer resist the urge to hold her. Now, I just do it. Gathering her up against my body, I wrap my arms around her and breathe in a giant sigh of relief. It feels amazing to have her back for as long as she'll let me.

When I feel her body shudder like she's crying, I pull her away from me to stare down at her face.

"Baby girl, what's wrong?"

"I missed you," she sobs, her fingers clutching my suit jacket tightly in her fists.

I kiss the top of her head and hold her closer. "I missed you so much."

"I'm sorry if I was too needy and I'm sorry for not telling you about my mother. I'll do whatever you want to make it up to you." She whimpers against my chest. "I've done everything you told me to, and I'm doing so much better. I go to counseling and I pay my rent on time. I'm taking care of myself and I don't need you anymore, Ronan. But I *want* you more than anything in this world."

I tilt her face up to mine, brushing her tears away as I smile down at her. "Hush, baby girl," I whisper, kissing both of her cheeks to quiet her crying. "I'm not letting you go. Not for a second."

When she licks her lips, I close the distance and press mine firmly to hers, sucking the bottom one between my teeth, and she hums, clutching my neck tightly to hold me closer. As our tongues tangle in soft friction, I barely come up for air at all.

I'm so relieved to have her here that I never want to stop kissing her. As she starts to recline, my body follows her, draped over her small frame in my cramped back seat. My cock is growing thick in my boxer briefs and I grind between her legs, just to hear her moan against my lips.

I missed the taste of her mouth, and I'm half-tempted to take her straight home now and reacquaint myself with the taste between her legs. A growl emits from my chest at the thought.

The glass partition lowers, and I hear my driver mutter, "Mr. Kade, we're here."

It takes my mind a few lagging moments to register where *here* is—the hospital.

"Just take me home," Daisy gasps breathlessly against my lips.

"I promised Garrett we'd get you looked at. They're just worried, baby girl. As soon as we get home, I'll make it up to you, okay?"

"But I feel fine," she whines.

Lifting myself from her body, I give her a stern glare. "Daisy."

With a relenting sigh, she nods. "Okay, fine."

It takes us a moment to compose ourselves and fix our clothes—and wait for my stiff cock to soften—before Daisy and I climb out of the car and head into the ER waiting room.

Luckily, it's quiet here tonight, and we only have to wait for a few minutes before the nurse calls us back. With my jacket draped over her shoulders, Daisy explains to the triage nurse how she's been feeling lately, and I start to find myself a little concerned that it's not just one fainting episode but weeks of feeling run-down and dizzy.

I clutch her fingers in mine as they take her blood for testing and then reluctantly let go of her while she slips into the bathroom to provide them with a urine sample. This testing feels like too much, and I have to talk myself down from panicking.

I assumed they'd hear her symptoms, tell her to eat better, and send us home. But when the doctor mentions a CT scan and possibly keeping her overnight, my stomach sours with fear.

"Could this be something serious?" I say, Daisy's fingers squeezing mine tighter.

"We won't know anything until those tests come back. It shouldn't be too long."

"Thank you," I mutter, forcing myself to swallow.

When the doctor leaves us alone, I pull Daisy into my arms. Why did I have to be such an ass and let her be alone for two months? How stupid would I have been to let her go for longer? I hate myself for wasting that much time as it is.

"I'm sure it's nothing," she whispers against my neck. It sounds as if she's comforting *me*. "Maybe low iron or low blood sugar or something like that."

"Yeah," I mumble with my lips in her hair. "Tell Geo you're moving out," I say.

She lets out a laugh and pulls away. "Are you asking me to move in with you?"

"Well, you just spent all the money you had saved up."

Her laugh is louder this time. "It was worth every penny."

When the doctor returns a few moments later, I quickly pull away from Daisy but remain positioned next to where she sits on the paper-covered examination table. He's looking down at the chart in his hands, and I wait with bated breath for whatever those results are about to tell us. In my mind, I just keep praying it's going to be something like she said—blood sugar, iron, anything that could be easily remedied so my girl can be healthy again.

"Well," he says, drawing out the tension. Then his eyes scan upward, landing on *my* face, and I furrow my brow at him. It's as if he's trying to discern if I should be here, if I'm her family, worthy of standing next to her to hear whatever he's about to deliver.

"What is it?" Daisy asks. When she pulls our clasped hands into her lap, he glances at her.

"Your pregnancy test was positive."

The blood drains from my face as his words penetrate my ears, and at first, they don't make any sense. He's confused. He has the wrong results or something. We didn't ask for a pregnancy test. Then, I turn toward Daisy and she's staring at me with her mouth hanging open, tears brimming in her wide eyes, and it all feels...*right*.

"Judging by the HCG in your urine test, I'd say you're well over eight weeks along."

"I thought..." The words die on my lips. It seems so trivial now, whether or not Daisy was on birth control or whether or not she took it.

She's *pregnant*.

At the exact moment that a smile starts to stretch across my face, Daisy slaps her hands over her face and starts sobbing. Ignoring the doctor behind me, I gather her up in my arms and hold her tight against me.

"I'm sorry, Ronan," she cries.

"Why are you sorry, baby girl?"

"I forgot to take it for a few days. We were in Paris, and I-I'm so stupid—"

Taking her face in my hands, I pull her away from my chest and let her see the solemn look on my face. "You are not stupid, Daisy."

"Are you mad at me?" she asks through her tears.

The ridiculous grin returns to my face. "Mad? Are you kidding me? I can't remember the last time I was this fucking happy."

"But...what are we going to do?" Her voice is tight and trembles with fear. I hate to see her so terrified.

I force my smile away as I stare into her eyes. I suddenly realize that Daisy is so young and this might not be what she had planned for her future—no matter how I feel about it. "Baby girl, we're going to do whatever you want to do, and no matter what, I'll be here. Okay?"

Teary-eyed, she nods. When she finally smiles in return, it's a beautiful, wide-eyed look of joy and excitement and I can't help but kiss her right then and there.

Thoughts are running rampant in my head until our lips touch, and then everything goes silent. No worries or fears. It's just us, and a long, beautiful future together full of the unknown.

Who knows what the fuck is going to happen from here, but in this moment, everything is perfect.

Rule #44: Everything is going to be okay.

Daisy

I'VE FELT LIKE I'M FLOATING, FROM THE MOMENT THE DOCTOR uttered those words to this moment now, as I sit at the table in Ronan's apartment, finishing the dinner Agatha prepared for us.

I'm...*pregnant.*

Suddenly everything just clicks. With the way I've been feeling lately—the nausea, exhaustion, dizziness—it all makes perfect sense. I almost feel like an idiot for not connecting those dots sooner.

And now, here I sit in this penthouse suite. Even though I know I shouldn't feel the least bit nervous or worried, I still can't help but wonder what exactly this means for my future, for *our* future.

We have options—I know that—but in my heart, I know how much I want this.

But does he?

Ronan said he was happy, but is he really considering what sort of change this will mean for him? He's fifty-six...about to turn fifty-seven. Does he really want to start a family *now*? Will bringing home a child bring back too many harsh memories of the one he lost?

Has he truly forgiven me enough to want a commitment this serious?

Nine years ago, my mother chose me over him. If I choose to keep this baby, will I lose him?

My mind is a mess, like a ping-pong ball moving back and forth from pure exhilaration to profound dread.

Moments after I hear the front door close as Agatha leaves, I know Ronan and I are alone. His hands caress my shoulders as he leans down to press his lips to my head.

"You look deep in thought. Are you okay?" he asks.

"I'm going to keep the baby," I say in a confident whisper. His hand strokes my back, but he stays silent. Inside, my stomach turns. I feel as if I'm channeling my mother, suddenly understanding what it must have felt like to choose me over him. Except, I don't have half the strength she did. Right now, I'm terrified.

"Ronan, say something, please," I stammer nervously.

As I pull away, I stare up into his eyes and let out a short gasp. There are tears brimming in his eyes and a look of joy in his expression. "I don't know what the fuck to say, Daisy."

"I need to know you're sure about this," I whisper.

He pulls me from the chair and wraps his arms around me as he gazes into my eyes. "I'm sure, Daisy. Are you?"

"I'm terrified," I reply, my voice breaking on a sob.

When his face falls into a somber expression, I realize that what he's holding on to more than anything right now is *hope*. Ronan has every reason to be as terrified as me, if not more. He's already been through the worst parenthood could give him. But he's still holding me and our unborn child together, as if he would willingly walk into that fire again with the *hope* that it will all work out.

"It's going to be okay, Daisy."

It's funny how those words, spoken by someone you trust, can mean so much. How it somehow quiets all of those worries and makes breathing a little easier.

I don't respond, but I do give him a gentle nod.

"I could tell you exactly how this is going to go, and we could map out the rest of our lives to ensure that every single moment is perfect, but the only guarantee in life is that it won't happen the way you think it will, baby girl. All we can do is enjoy this moment right now."

The breath that comes out of me is heavy with relief. I wrap my arms around his waist and bury myself in his chest. I feel his heart pound against my cheek as we hold each other, and slowly, the terror I felt a moment ago starts to melt away.

"Join me in the shower," he whispers, and my stomach flutters with excitement. Two months without his touch and now it's all I want.

He takes me by the hand, leading me to the bathroom, and I let him peel off every layer of my clothing until I'm standing in front of him naked. As his hands drift down my body, his lips follow the trail, from my shoulders, over my breasts, and then pausing as his hand rests over my belly.

As he holds it there, the emotion barrels over me again. The moment his eyes meet mine, my heart swells in my chest. This is a moment I'll remember for as long as I live.

Then, he drops to his knees in front of me, pressing his lips to my stomach, and I run my fingers through his hair. We stay like that for a while, both of us absorbing this new reality that came barreling into our lives without warning. It may have been a surprise, but it feels right.

When he rises from his knees, I pull his mouth to mine. His kiss feels like home. I want to enjoy every second of this moment right now, savoring the intimacy between us.

The world feels so much safer when I'm in his embrace and not because he'll protect me from everything that could happen to me, but because I know that no matter what happens, he'll be there.

Our kiss grows more heated by the moment. Without pulling my mouth away, I undo each button of his white shirt, tearing it off his body before reaching for his pants. Our fingers fumble together to get them down, and when his boxer briefs slide out of my way, I reach for his stiffening length, eliciting a moan from his body as I wrap my hand around him.

After a couple soft strokes, he hoists me up, so I wrap my legs around him as he carries me into the steaming shower. Then my back is against the wall and he's grinding his erection between us, hard against my clit.

We are in a frenzy of desire as our mouths and hands devour each other, and when Ronan aligns his cock with my aching core, I nearly yank him into me.

"Fuck me, please." I groan before finding his eyes with my own and adding the one word I've been dying to say over the past two months. "Daddy."

With a guttural moan, he thrusts inside me and holds himself there, so we can both savor this feeling. Our bodies are bonded as one, as he slowly withdraws and slides back in, finding a slow rhythm together.

It's like the moment in the bathtub all over again. The years between us don't matter. Our ages mean nothing. In this small space, our connection outweighs all of that.

As he thrusts harder, slamming into me at a quicker pace, I let out a breathless moan. My body starts to tighten with pleasure, so I reach between us, finding my clit and rubbing in tight, fast circles.

"That's my girl," he mutters between the forceful drives of his hips. My legs squeeze tightly around him as I'm nearly blinded by the sensation of my orgasm.

"Come on Daddy's cock, Daisy." His voice is strained as he slides in one last time before shuddering his own climax inside me.

We're both gasping for air as he releases my legs and eases out of me. Light-headed from the steam and exertion, we cling tightly to each other as we slowly catch our breaths.

"I love you," I whisper into the crook of his neck.

As he strokes my head, peppering my face with kisses, he whispers against my cheek, "I love you more than anything in this world, baby girl."

My heart swells in my chest as he brings our lips together. And as he washes every inch of my body, from my head to my feet, I feel every ounce of that love.

Deep down, I know that Ronan and I were always meant to find each other. The odds may have been stacked against us, but there was something far more powerful bringing us together. In some strange way, I think my mother would be relieved to know we found each other. It may seem unconventional, but this is what she wanted—for both of us to find the kind of love that makes life worth living.

And no matter what this cruel, poetic life brings us, I know he'll be there to take care of me. And I'll be there to take care of him.

Rule #45: You can't knock up an already pregnant woman… but it doesn't hurt to try.

Ronan's Epilogue

THE CROWD TONIGHT IS THE LARGEST I'VE SEEN. I HOPE TO GOD they're here to see my beautiful wife playing her newest songs and not marvel at the way her very pregnant belly protrudes between her body and the keys of the piano.

Daisy has picked up a regular spot at the piano bar, and it's no wonder why. The crowd loves her. It's generally a mix of her originals and some classic covers, and she nails each and every one.

I watch from the bar, a single bourbon in my hand as she sings, the people at the tables joining in. Every few moments, her eyes find mine, and I give her a quick, comforting smile.

I couldn't be more proud.

I also couldn't be more nervous. Daisy is two days past her due date, and the doctor is using terms like *dropped, dilated,* and *induction.* As hard as I tried to talk her out of performing tonight, she convinced me that she feels fine and that a little excitement might help nudge things along.

All I know is that she's not leaving my sight for a moment.

When her set comes to an end, she waddles off the stage and

meets with the same regular group of listeners who show up every week. After conversing with them for a while, she comes over and gulps down two large glasses of ice water. Hugged close to my side, she leans against me, swaying where she stands.

"How are you feeling, baby girl?"

"My back is a little sore from sitting on that bench, but otherwise good. No contractions."

My hand roams the hard surface of her round stomach. My little boy kicks against my hand as I do, my heart practically flipping in my chest.

"I swear he has a foot in my rib cage." She arches her back, trying to make more room in her body for the baby growing inside.

"Let's get you home," I whisper against the side of her head. After she says goodbye to the bar owner and the new friends gathered around her, I walk with her hand in hand out to the car waiting by the door.

As soon as we get home, she goes straight to the shower, shedding her clothes until she's standing in the bathroom naked from head to toe. As I take in the sight of her in the mirror, I let out a husky growl, making her grin from ear to ear.

I'm always attracted to Daisy, but seeing her like this brings out that wild inner caveman in me. There's not a moment in the day now that I don't want to fuck her senseless and fill her up, although she's clearly already bursting with my child.

But fucking in the shower isn't as easy as it used to be, so I let her step under the spray alone, watching her shower through the glass and waiting patiently with a fresh towel for when she climbs out.

When I catch her wincing as she arches her back, I ask for the hundredth time today, "How are you feeling?"

She rolls her eyes with a menacing smirk. "I'm fine, Ronan. I promise I'll tell you when the contractions start. Besides," she says, pulling me against her, "you know what Eden said is supposed to induce labor?"

God, I love her like this. Makes me want to keep her pregnant forever.

"I know exactly what she said," I mutter, tilting her chin up to face me.

"And she would know…"

With a smirk, I kiss her on the lips. "Get on the bed right now, baby girl."

"Yes, Daddy," she replies, waltzing straight into our bedroom and lying on her side. Then she watches me with a hungry gaze as I pull off my clothes, slipping my belt off with a quick swipe.

"You know as soon as that baby is out, I'm going to fuck another one into you," I say as my gaze roams her naked body.

She bites her lip as her fingers roam down to her clit, rubbing herself as she stares at me in anticipation. As I crawl onto the bed, I swat her hand away, holding her wrist in my hand as I drag her closer.

"That's my job," I mutter, lowering my face to the warmth of her moist cunt. With a long swipe of my tongue, I draw a sweet, mewling sound out of her. Lowering myself to my stomach, I take my time devouring her just to make her feel good. She writhes and moans until her cries turn breathless and needy. Sucking hard on her clit, I slip two fingers in and thrust with the rhythm of my tongue until she's clutching my hair and her thighs are trembling around my head.

"Yes, Daddy. I'm coming," she cries.

My cock is throbbing between my body and the bed. Letting out a growl, I flip her over, carefully moving her to her hands and knees. Her pussy is still pulsing as I thrust my way in, slamming my hips against her backside.

With her fists clenching the sheets, she shoves herself back against me, meeting my thrusts slam for slam.

"You drive your daddy fucking crazy, baby girl. You're gonna take every drop, aren't you?"

"Yes, Daddy," she squeals into the mattress.

"That's my girl," I reply. "Tell me you want it."

"Fill me up, Daddy. Come inside me." Her voice is practically a scream at this point, and it drives me over the edge. With the sound of her pleas echoing in my ears, I lose control, coming so hard I stop breathing. My cock pulses inside her as I groan out my release.

When I open my eyes, I stare down at her. Sweat covers her back in a thin layer as her chest swells and deflates with her heavy breathing. I can hardly see her face through the mess of blond waves fanned out around her head, so I cascade my hand along the length of her spine until I reach her head, brushing her hair out of the way.

"How are you feeling, baby girl?"

She laughs. "I'm fine. Great now."

"Good," I reply, leaning over to press my lips between her shoulder blades.

After pulling out, I keep my eyes on her to watch as the cum drips out of her. It's so fucking hot to watch—I don't think I'll ever get sick of that. Climbing from the bed, I go to the bathroom and grab a washcloth, running it under warm water before taking it back to the bed and delicately wiping her body with it, kissing her skin as I go.

Every inch of her body is as perfect now as it was before. Thin lines are scattered over her hips and breasts, and my fingers dance over each one.

Soon, we'll have a son.

I have days when I worry that I'm not ready. Because I know the way it's going to feel the moment I see him. The overwhelming swell of my heart and the way our lives will be completely rearranged to make room for the biggest and greatest thing that we could receive.

Our lives will never be the same. Instead of just having her to take care of, I'll have both of them.

I never stopped being Miles's father, but there are days when I worry that I've forgotten how to be a father at all. Then I remember that I had no clue the first time either. It'll come to me as naturally as it will come to her. And if it doesn't, then we'll struggle together.

Daisy seems to have fallen asleep, curled up on her side with the giant pregnancy pillow shoved between her legs. So I turn off the light and crawl into bed behind her, pulling the blankets over her still naked body.

I know I won't fall asleep nearly as easily, but I try anyway. Holding her warm body in my arms, I press my hand against her round stomach, waiting to feel my son squirming around inside.

Sleep takes me as I wait. But I don't know how long I'm out before I wake to the sound of Daisy moaning. My hand is on her stomach, but instead of feeling the baby kick, I notice how incredibly hard it is.

"Daisy…how are you feeling?"

"My back hurts," she complains, trying to reposition herself to escape the pain. With my hand on her rock-hard stomach, I wait for it to subside before I start to panic. It could be just another round of those Braxton Hicks contractions. After a few moments, she relaxes again, this time facing me.

Minutes pass by before she moans again—*six* minutes to be exact. A smile stretches across my face as I kiss Daisy on the forehead.

"Baby girl, I think he's coming."

She blinks her eyes open. "I think so too."

"Are you ready?" I ask in the quiet space between us on the pillow.

"No," she replies.

With that, I kiss her forehead again and grip her hand tightly in mine. "It's gonna be okay, Daisy."

"I know," she mumbles, her body tensing a little more this time.

After a moment, when I think another contraction has subsided, she looks up at me with that beaming smile as she says, "Okay. Let's go."

Rule #46: Life is a messy dream.

Daisy's Epilogue
Three Years Later

JULIAN SMILES SHYLY AS RONAN KNEELS BY HIS SIDE, HANDING him the remote for the little toy sailboat that dances across the water of the giant fountain in the middle of the park. I laugh at the sight, and when he looks over at where I'm nursing his baby sister on the bench, I give him an excited expression.

"Good job, buddy!" I say with a smile.

Amelia is snoozing in my arms as I carefully pull her off my breast and lay her against my shoulder to burp her. She's almost one and still nursing like crazy. By this age, Julian was already on the move, ready to explore everything he could get his hands on with no time for nursing. But my sweet girl likes to take her time. She's perfectly content cuddling with her mama.

While the baby naps and the boys play, I relax on the bench, jotting down lyrics in the notepad app on my phone. It's funny to see how differently my songs turn out now, since becoming a mother. The way I see life compared to how I saw it before. Not better or worse—just different.

For one, I understand on an entirely new level why my mother made the decision she did. How choosing me over Ronan was never a sacrifice but a choice that ended in love either way.

I've also learned to embrace the mess like I couldn't before. I dreamt of a life that looked more like a vision board or a magazine spread instead of reality. There are days when I struggle to find anything poetic—when the kids are screaming or the house is a mess or my music just won't come. Nights when I feel like the least sexy person on the planet, sure that my husband will never want to touch me again. Moments when I feel like a failure.

Those moments are perfectly balanced with the ones that feel like a fantasy—when I can watch the man I love cuddling our daughter or laughing with our son. When the lyrics flow or when he pulls me into his arms at night, spoiling me with pleasure and love like it's the first time.

Without the mess, those beautiful moments would feel flat and meaningless. So I've learned to embrace it all.

I hear Julian's cry across the park and I look up to see him lying flat on the ground, his little glasses slipped off his nose, and his tear-soaked face contorted in pain. He must have tripped on his way over to me, but Ronan is there in a heartbeat, pulling him up to his feet and brushing off his scraped knees.

My heart swells in my chest as I watch him pick up our son, running a soothing hand over his back as he kisses the side of his head. Julian clings to his neck as he cries.

"Is he okay?" I ask when the two of them reach the bench where I'm sitting.

"Yeah. He's okay," Ronan replies, but Julian shows no signs of letting go of his daddy.

"We should head back to the house for lunch," I say as I carefully maneuver Amelia into her stroller. She stays asleep when I lay her down. Standing up, I notice Ronan's eyes drifting down to my chest.

"You might want to put that away," he says with a smile, and I glance down to find my breast still hanging out the top of my blouse.

"Oops," I reply as I tuck it away and fix my shirt. It hardly fazes me anymore. I guess it's a good thing we're in Paris, where no one bats an eye at a nursing mother's breasts.

Yet another reason why I'm glad we moved here.

We decided to make Paris our full-time home before Amelia was born. We loved Briar Point, but it never felt like *us*. This city is where our relationship was born, where we both feel most at home, and where we want to raise our children.

So we sold the apartment in the Latin Quarter and bought a bigger house on the outskirts of the city. It's a dream come true.

Ronan stepped back from his role with his company, but I couldn't get him to fully retire. Instead, he helps Matis with L'Amour, something I can't really complain about. Three nights a week, we leave the kids with the au pair and go into the club together—sometimes to work and sometimes to play.

He's really started to expand his horizons, if only to indulge me in the things *I* enjoy, and when he's open to it, we invite others to join us.

Just thinking about it has me anxious to take the kids home and get ready for another night out. As we walk across the park, Julian still in Ronan's arms, I think about how Ronan and I met.

"Why don't we do an auction at L'Amour?" I ask.

He puts his hand at the small of my back as he considers my question. "I can bring it up to Matis. I'm not sure why I haven't thought about that."

"It might be a great draw for membership. Not to mention, they're very fun."

He smiles. "And you can meet the love of your life in an auction."

"I don't think that's common," I reply.

"No, but it happens."

"What's an auction?" Julian asks, lifting his head from Ronan's shoulder.

"Um…" I say, letting my voice trail off.

"It's where people can buy very valuable things."

"Like a shop?" he asks.

"Sort of," Ronan replies, looking more confused than Julian.

"Does Daddy have lots of money for the shop?"

"Yes, Daddy has money for the shop," I say, brushing his brown hair away from his eyes.

"Because Daddy is rich?" Julian mumbles, making both of us laugh.

Ronan flips him around and hoists him up until Julian is sitting on his shoulders, keeping a tight hold of one of his legs. "Yes, buddy. Daddy is the richest man in the *whole* world," he jokes in a booming voice.

"In the *whole* world?" Julian asks in amazement.

Then, Ronan brings his free hand around my shoulder, squeezing me tight as we slowly stroll down the pathway of the park. With his lips against my head, he softly replies, "Yes, Daddy is the richest man in the whole world."

And I know he's not talking about money.

Rule #47: Be everything she needs.

Bonus Epilogue
Ronan

"Ready?" Daisy stands in the doorway of our bedroom. Her long blond hair cascades over one shoulder in soft waves. She's wearing a tight, black, velvet dress with a plunging neckline. It hugs her breasts and hips, and I let out a surly growl at the sight.

"It's a good thing I'm taking you to the club, baby girl. Because what I want to do to you in that dress isn't fit for anywhere else."

She smiles wickedly, biting her bottom lip. "Then let's get going."

We wave goodbye to the au pair who is washing baby bottles in the kitchen. She gives us a sweet smile as we disappear out the front door. Both kids are asleep, so I know Daisy can relax.

"God, I love her," Daisy says as she takes my hand out front. The car is waiting for us, and I open it for my wife, ushering her inside before I follow.

"She loves our kids and that's what really matters to me," I reply.

As soon as the door closes and we take off toward the club—a short twenty minute drive from our house—Daisy rests her head on my shoulder. She hums a song as we go, a new tune I've been hearing her rehearse over and over the past few months. I don't pry much when it comes to her music. She likes to share them with me when she's ready.

But God, I love to hear her work. She's full of more magic and creativity than I ever truly knew before we married. I've never met a mind more captivating than Daisy's.

My beautiful, perfect Daisy.

When we pull up to the club, the driver opens Daisy's door first. She steps out and waits for me. After I've laced my fingers with hers, we walk into L'Amour hand in hand.

Matis is there in the lobby and gives us a dashing smile as he holds out his arms for a hug. "I didn't know you two were coming in tonight!" he says with an enthusiastic greeting.

"It was her idea," I reply with a grin.

Matis gives Daisy a mischievous expression. "It always is."

"How are things tonight?" I ask, keeping the business conversation casual and light.

"Quiet," he replies plainly.

"A good quiet or a bad quiet?" Daisy asks.

Matis shrugs. "I'm not sure. Hopefully good."

"Well, Daisy had a great idea for the club. We could hold an auction," I say, touching my wife's lower back.

Matis's eyebrows shoot up. "An auction?"

Daisy cuts in excitedly. "Yeah, we had them at our last club. I think they would pull in some members and get everyone excited."

"I love this idea. And you'll help us plan it?" he asks.

Daisy looks at me with a soft laugh. "Ronan will."

Just then, someone pulls Matis's attention away and he excuses himself. I tug Daisy to my side and press my lips to her ear. "What is my girl in the mood for tonight?"

I can tell by the way she practically melts into my arms

that Daisy is bone-tired and in desperate need of some delicate pampering.

Turning toward me, she presses her hands to my cheeks. "I just want you."

"I'll do whatever you want," I reply, kissing her softly on the nose. "Do you want your Daddy to make you feel good?"

She lets out a sigh of pleasure. "Yes, please."

"I know just the thing." Smiling, I kiss her again, this time on the forehead. With my wife tucked under my arm, I walk her to our room at the back of the club. Once we get there, I use my key to open the door. The lights are already dim for us and it smells heavenly, like lavender and rose.

I remove my jacket and hang it on the hook. "Come here, baby girl," I say to her.

Daisy buries herself against my chest, wrapping her arms around me as she breathes me in. To this day, nothing makes me happier than being her rock. Daisy has proven to me that she can do anything, but the fact that she still lets me take care of her means more than she'll ever know. I want to support her and love her and protect her until the day I die.

And long after if I can.

"Take everything off. Lay face down on the bed." I kiss her on the head again.

"Yes, Daddy," she whispers before tilting her head back and letting me plant my lips on hers. She hums as I deepen the kiss. Her fingers dig into the hair at the back of my head as she grinds her needy body against mine.

It pains me to pull away, but I don't want this to get too heated before I've had a chance to pamper my girl. "Go ahead now," I say softly.

She turns her back to me, moving her hair out of the way so I can unzip her dress.

As she undresses, I pour myself a small drink and watch her with interest. I will never tire of just watching her. And I will never, for one second, take what I have for granted. Daisy is perfect, and she's given me two perfect children. I may never feel worthy.

Once she's lying on the bed, her naked body stretched out before me, I set my drink down and gather some things from the cabinets.

Oil. Blindfold. Feather duster. Pinwheel.

I set all of these things on the bed next to her. Then I take off my clothes, one piece at a time, stopping when I've reached my boxer briefs. Picking up the blindfold first, I gently tie it around her eyes. She lets out a high-pitched hum, letting me know she's excited for what's to come.

As I climb onto the bed behind Daisy, I straddle her thighs and pour a generous amount of oil in my hands. After warming them, I start at her shoulders and slowly massage every muscle and joint.

She lets out one moan after another. I gently rub out the tension in her shoulders and neck, taking my time with her. Careful not to apply too much pressure, I softly rub every inch of her back and arms until she's like soft putty on the bed.

"That feels so good," she mumbles into the mattress.

Moving myself down her legs, I massage more oil into each cheek of her ass and the tops of her thighs. When I ease my fingers in between, rubbing through the wet folds of her pussy, she moans louder, pressing her ass in the air.

"You like that, baby girl?"

"Yes, Daddy. More."

"You'll get more. Be patient."

My cock is aching now. It's straining against my boxer briefs. Just the thought of sinking deep inside her has me leaking cum at the tip.

I tease her opening a little more before pulling my fingers from between her legs. I finish my massage, working my way down her legs, but I can feel how restless she is now. She wants more.

I'm not ready to fuck her yet.

Grabbing the feather duster next, I ease Daisy onto her back. She holds her arms over her head, resting them on the pillows as she waits for what's coming. When the feathers touch her skin, she gasps. It's the anticipation and mystery that is really arousing. Her nipples pebble with her arousal, and I continue to lightly tease every inch of her body.

Her breasts, her belly, her clit.

She's trembling with need by the time I'm done.

As I set the feather aside, she squirms, anxious for my touch. Because I know my girl likes a touch of pain mixed in with her pleasure, I gently press the pinwheel to her thigh first. She gasps, her back arching off the mattress, as I roll it upward. It glides over her hip and gently to the side of her breast, pricking her with every spin of the metal pinwheel.

When I lift it from her skin, she cries out. "More."

I roll it gently over the skin of her arm, across her belly, and finally, up the inside of her thigh. As I delicately roll the metal closer and closer to her aching cunt, I gently slide a finger inside her. That really gets her squirming.

"Please, Daddy. I need you," she cries.

My thumb circles her clit as I fuck her softly with my two middle fingers. The pleasure mixed with pain drives her wild.

"Does that feel good, baby girl?"

She lets out a feral groan. "Yes. Please, Ronan. I need more."

"More what, Daisy?"

Her hands reach blindly for me as I continue to torture her by holding what she really wants just out of her reach. Her skin is covered with tiny red spots from the pinwheel moist with a sheen of sweat.

"Fuck me, Daddy. Please." Her cries are desperate now, and I can't stand the sound of her pain.

Dropping the metal toy on the mattress, I ease my boxers down and toss Daisy's legs over my shoulders. Lining my cock with her soaking core, I drive inside of her with force, savoring the sound of her cry of relief.

"Yes!" she wails.

With her legs against my chest, I thrust in as deep as I can go. Her back arches and she moans loudly again. Her body is my home, and every moment I'm inside her, I am the luckiest man on earth. Nothing could possibly be better than this.

I keep my strokes slow and deep, letting her enjoy the buildup before she breaks. Because once I start moving, I won't be able to stop.

My thumb finds her clit again, and I rub her in tight circles as I watch her body tighten with pleasure. She won't last long like this.

"Faster," she pleads. "Harder!"

Nearly folding her in half, I pound into her with force. My hips piston as I watch her slowly start to slip over the edge. First, her body stills. Then her breathing quickens. And last, it's like an explosion inside her body. She lets out a high-pitched sound as she comes.

Her nails dig into my arms as if she's holding onto me for dear life.

A moment later, I lose control and my orgasm collides into me like a freight train. A groan shudders through my chest while I unload inside her.

It's perfect. And when it's all over, we collapse together on the mattress.

Her arms cling to me. Still wearing the blindfold, she finds my face and kisses me deeply. I gently pull it from her eyes and smile down at my wife.

"That was amazing," she whispers.

"Yes, it was," I reply.

Daisy can never seem to understand how I can get just as much, if not more, enjoyment out of making her feel good. That massage was just as pleasurable to me as it was to her. She may never get it and that's okay.

If I was put on this earth to be everything she ever wants, I'm perfectly happy with that. I've spent so much of my life twisted in grief and running from the feeling of loss. Daisy has renewed my life with purpose. I no longer care about money or success.

Making her happy makes me happy. And as long as I have that, I have everything I'll ever need.

Keep reading for an excerpt of
Madame, the final book in the red-hot
Salacious Players' Club series by *USA
Today* bestselling author Sara Cate

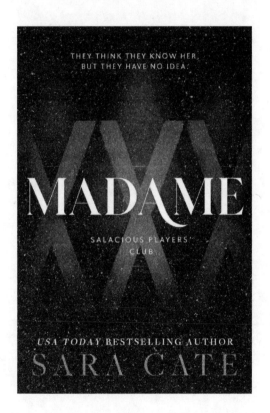

THEY THINK THEY KNOW HER,
BUT THEY HAVE NO IDEA.

MADAME

SALACIOUS PLAYERS'
CLUB

USA TODAY BESTSELLING AUTHOR
SARA CATE

Rule #1: Love is just another form of control.

Eden

"You've been a very bad boy."

The whip flies with a crack, and the man currently bound to the cross hollers around the ball gag in his mouth. In his right hand, the red silk handkerchief is still safely clutched in his fist. This is our nonverbal sign to communicate since his mouth is a little stuffed at the moment. The second that piece of fabric falls, I stop.

Once every sixty days or so, he comes in and pays me to take him to the extreme, pain-wise, and he loves a lot of degradation while we're at it.

For all I know, the guy is guilty of something and he needs someone like me to punish him for it. Some people go to confession or say their Hail Marys—and some people come to me. It's not my business to know all the details. It's just my business to be his Domme for the night.

After our third round of six hits, I give him another break, letting him breathe, sweat, and cry.

"Pathetic," I murmur against his ear as he moans in agony. "A good boy would take the pain, but you're not a good boy, are you?"

He shakes his head.

"Are you going to be a good boy now?"

He nods. His eyes are clenched shut while tears, drool, and sweat cover his bare chest. And as gross as it is, I love seeing people like this. It's like a cleansing ritual or an exorcism. They come to me carrying baggage, guilt, pain, worry, and stress, but within a few hours—whether it be from pain or some time in subspace—they leave feeling refreshed and renewed.

I unclasp the ball gag at the back of his head. He groans again when he's finally able to close his mouth with an ache in his jaw.

"Say it, Marcus. Promise your Madame that you'll be a good boy from now on."

"I promise," he croaks. "Madame."

"I don't believe you," I reply in a cold, emotionless tone.

He whimpers because he knows what this means. I take another glance at the silk handkerchief again, but he's still holding it tight.

"I think you need six more to be sure. What do you think, Marcus?"

His chest is heaving with each breath, and he looks like he's about to cry again. Then he nods. "Yes, Madame."

I'm not too concerned. He always gets like this at the end, looking like he really wants to stop, but he never does. I trust Marcus to tell me if he's at his limit.

"Give me a color, then."

"Green, Madame."

I lean closer, grabbing him by the hair and craning his neck until he cries out in pain. "You really deserve this, you know."

"I deserve this, Madame." His voice is strained and raspy.

"After these last six swings, you're going to be my good boy again, aren't you?"

"Yes, Madame."

"Good. No gag this time. I want to hear you count them out. And don't forget to thank me after each one."

He whines when I let him go and step away, and his first shout of pain nearly shakes the walls. The sound of it is beautiful. Doing this gives me purpose and control. Even when my arm tires and aches, I love it.

An hour later, after some much needed aftercare, I spot Marcus coming out of the changing room, looking refreshed and lighter than he did when he first arrived. His shoulders are no longer hunched by his ears, and he's wearing a lazy smile. I'm unwinding with sparkling water at the bar as he leaves the club, waving to me as he goes.

Even though he's a regular and accustomed to the routine, he will still receive the automated email with instructions on caring for his welts, bruises, and feelings. Not everyone who leaves my sessions is hunky-dory happy and I just like them to be prepared. Getting your ass flogged and spanked—literally and metaphorically—tends to bring up a lot of thoughts and emotions not everyone is ready to deal with.

All that to say, I haven't had any complaints yet.

As I sip my drink, I make a list on my napkin of the things I need to do at some point tomorrow, or rather, today, considering it's already two in the morning.

1. Pick up cupcakes
2. Order movie tickets
3. Write the sponsored sex toy review post
4. Make waxing appointment

Lost in my thoughts as I try to think of what else needs to get done, I look up from my list and see a man walk by in a dark blue suit. He has longish brown hair swept back and a narrow, athletic build.

For a moment, I pause, waiting for him to turn around.

From the back, it looks like *him*. Although I'm not sure why I expect it to be *him*. *He* hasn't been here in months.

A beautiful woman scurries over to the man, who puts his arm around her, angling his face toward me. I feel a wave of relief *and* disappointment when I realize it's definitely not *him*.

With a mixture of unidentified emotions coursing through me, I turn back to my list. But now I can't focus. All I can do is reminisce on that night when I opened my door at the club to find Clay waiting for me. The night everything ended between us. When he uttered those earth-shattering words—*I just want you.*

Anxiety burrows its way into my chest at the memory. Not a night goes by that I don't wonder if I did the right thing. I keep reliving that moment, telling myself over and over that it was for the best.

But I'm never fully convinced.

In an effort to distract my brain from having the same conversation again, I wad up the napkin and shove it into my purse. Then I climb off the barstool and wave goodbye to the bartender before heading for the exit of the club.

I toss my workbag into the trunk of my car and climb into the front seat, mentally planning the order of events for the morning. The entire drive home, my brain is making a schedule. If I make it home by three, I can get six hours of sleep before I'll have to get ready for the day. If I order the tickets by noon, we should be able to squeeze in cupcakes and presents with Ronan and Daisy before Jack and I go to a seven o'clock show tonight. If I keep him out any later than that, he'll be a major grump tomorrow.

I pull into the garage at exactly two thirty-seven. Being as quiet as possible, I sneak inside. There's a kitchen light on, which means my nocturnal nanny is still up. Sure enough, she's sitting at the island typing away on her laptop. When she sees me come in, she pulls the AirPods from her ears.

"Hey," she whispers with a sweet smile.

"Hey, you're up late. How's that paper coming?"

She rolls her eyes. "If I never have to write the words child welfare again, it will be too soon."

I laugh as I drop my purse on the counter. "Well, you might have to if you're going to be a social worker someday."

She slams her laptop shut. "Don't remind me."

"How was he?" I ask, changing the subject.

"Perfect, as always," she replies. "We ate the leftover spaghetti for dinner and read four books before bed. He was out like a light by eight."

"Awesome. Thank you again, Madison."

"Of course. I love hanging out with him, plus it gives me somewhere quiet to work on this stupid paper."

She packs up her laptop and rubs her eyes as she yawns. I walk her to the door, grateful she lives with her parents just one neighborhood over, so I don't have to worry about her driving too far this late at night.

"You're almost there. Just stick with it," I say with encouragement as I pat her on the back.

"Thanks, Eden. Tell Jack happy birthday for me," she adds. "See you on Thursday."

"See you on Thursday," I reply. I wait for her to get into her car and start driving away before I close the door.

I hired Madison three years ago when the club opened, and it's been working great. She's a college student who needs extra cash and time away from her parents. She doesn't mind the late nights and *adores* Jack.

The best part about Madison is that she knows exactly what I do for a living and thinks it's *badass*—her words exactly. But for propriety's sake, we keep that information to ourselves. I'm not ashamed of my work, but I have enough awareness to know that not everyone is so accepting, and plenty of people would be happy to make my life harder with that piece of information—especially where Jack is concerned.

After Madison leaves, I tiptoe down the hall and peek into the first room on the right. The shark night-light glows in blue and green against the walls and ceiling, and I have to creep over the scattered toys on the floor to reach his bed. He's sprawled face up on top of the covers in his blue-striped pj's, so I take a moment to be sentimental and stare at him.

Messy dark brown curls fan out over his pillow. I reach down carefully and brush them out of his face before leaning in and pressing a kiss to his forehead. He's a deep sleeper like me, so he doesn't stir at all.

Then I take another moment to stare at him. As of today, he's officially seven.

His birthday has me reminiscing on the day he was born. Living in the guest room of Ronan's apartment in the city, I thought I had another couple of weeks before I'd have to make room for a baby. Ronan was out on business and my water broke without warning as I was reading an internet article about the right and wrong ways to use a spanking bench. To this day, I can't even see one without remembering the pain that followed that moment.

I labored for hours completely alone, without a single person to hold my hand. By the time Ronan arrived at the hospital, Jack was sleeping peacefully in his bassinet.

A couple of days later, I brought home a seven-and-a-half-pound baby that changed my world forever. By the time he started crawling, we had the keys to this house, and I was running my blog full time.

On that day, I made a promise to myself that I would always put Jack first. It was just us, and it would always be just us. I would die before bringing home another man who could do to Jack what his father had done to me. No matter how charming or rich, I refuse to fall for that trick again.

Love is nothing more than a form of control.

And from here on out, I will be the only one in control.

Rule #2: Forbidden fruit always tastes the sweetest.

Clay

"Fuuuuuuck." I groan. "I'm gonna come."

Immediately, Jade pulls those beautiful lips from around my cock and gives me a playful, wide-eyed stare. "You're gonna get us caught," she whispers.

"I'll be good," I reply in a breathy mumble.

As her perfect mouth engulfs my cock again, I nearly break that promise. With my teeth clenched around the knuckles of my right hand, I keep it quiet as she sucks the life out of me through my dick.

Staying silent as pleasure radiates through every extremity of my body is damn near impossible. Especially when I open my eyes to find her swallowing with a mischievous grin on her face.

God, I love this woman.

Of course, I haven't told her that yet. That would be insane. Jade and I have only been seeing each other for a little over five months, and half of that was spent with me in a major post-breakup depression.

But she is amazing. Every single day, I see how easy it is to love her.

Then again, I thought that about someone else recently too, and look how that turned out for me.

Besides, Jade and I have a major hurdle to overcome.

"I'm going to miss sneaking around," she whispers as she rises to stand from under my desk. With her hands perched on either side of my chair, she leans toward me, and I reach for her mouth with mine for a kiss.

"We should really tell him," I reply as I tuck my shirt back into my pants and zip them up.

She pulls away. "Should we, though?"

I laugh, shaking my head. "The longer we keep it a secret, the more likely I'll end up dead when he does find out."

"I'll avenge you," she replies. Then her nose wrinkles up in that adorable way it always does.

Wrapping my hands around her waist, I hoist her onto my lap. "Baby, if you're really not ready, then I understand. You know I'll do anything you tell me."

"I do love that about you," she replies, finally pressing her lips to mine.

I'm caught on the fact that she said *love* when my watch buzzes on my wrist.

"His meeting is almost over. You better go."

She groans. "Fine."

"Make sure to look both ways before leaving."

"I will," she whispers. Once she's standing, she fixes her knee-length floral skirt and white tank top. Using my framed college diploma as a mirror, she brushes her chin-length brown hair and blunt bangs back into place with her fingers. Then she grabs her purse from on top of my desk and catches me gawking at her. "What?"

"You're just...perfect," I reply. Which is true, but it's not what I was thinking.

What I was thinking is that Jade isn't like any other woman I've dated. She's young, sweet, and funny as hell. She might as well be the polar opposite of the last woman I dated.

Maybe this is my way of protecting myself. Date a woman so different that I lessen the risk of fucking things up again.

But the weird thing is, as different as she and Eden are, my feelings for them are strangely similar.

With a quirky smile, Jade peels open my office door and looks both ways before slipping down the hall toward the exit. I'm lucky to have an office near the back door, so I can easily sneak her in and out undetected.

This is a good thing because a moment later, the boss's door opens at the opposite end. I hear Will Penner's footsteps, like ominous stomps nearing my door. Every time he makes that trek down the hall, my blood spikes with paranoia. But as he peeks his head in, he's wearing a smile, and I let out a sigh of relief.

"Hey, Bradley, you hungry?" he says, using my last name as he often does.

"Hell yeah. Where are we ordering from today?" I ask, swiveling back and forth in my office chair.

"I'll have Jade pick something up for us. How do you feel about sushi?"

"Sounds great," I reply.

My boss leans against the doorframe as he pulls out his phone and, I assume, composes a text to the girl who just snuck out of my office.

"Dragon roll?" he asks, and I nod in return.

"Sounds good."

I like my boss a lot. He's lenient enough to make the environment enjoyable but tough enough to make me a better analyst. I've been like a protégé to him in his financial management company for the past five years, and I'm hoping that sometime this year, I'll have a promotion to look forward to.

Will needs me as a partner in this firm if we're going to take it to the next level like he wants to. He's a great financial planner, but he's impulsive and, at times, messy. We balance each other out well, and if I get that promotion, we'll be unstoppable.

His eyes lift from his phone just as the door to the office opens, and my skin pales as a familiar sweet voice calls from the end of the hall.

"Hey, Daddy!" Jade says as she approaches Will.

"Hey, Cupcake. I was just texting you. How does sushi sound for lunch?"

She steps into the doorway and glances at me for only a second. With an awkward wave, she sends me a casual greeting. "Hi, Clay."

Acknowledgments

Thank you for reading *Highest Bidder*. It was so great to be back at Salacious, wasn't it? I missed it. Who knew a sex club could feel so comforting, like *coming* home.

I can't possibly express how grateful I am for all of you who have read, loved, and shared this series with the world. One minute I'm writing a smutty story about a man and his son's ex-girlfriend, and the next minute I'm connecting with people all over the world who feel as deeply about some fictional characters as I do.

I hope you connected with Daisy and Ronan the same.

When you connect with them, it's like you're connecting with me. And suddenly, we're all connected.

I love that about books.

This book would have never reached your hands without an amazing team who keep this Salacious train on its tracks.

My agent—Savannah Greenwell.

My team, my good girls—Lori Alexander, Amanda Anderson, and Misty Frey.

The immensely talented daddy himself, Wander Aguiar—photographer and cover model.

My editor—Rebecca at Fairest Reviews Editing Services.

My proofreader—Rumi Khan.

My graphics designer—Kate Farlow.

My beta readers—Adrian, Jill, Janine, Tits, Claudia, and Heather. Thank you for both bullying and hyping me up until the book was perfect.

My Shucky crew—the greatest friend group in the whole world.

My Salacious Sluts, who give me a safe space on the big scary internet.

My husband for the unending love and support.

And last, to every single ARC reader, blogger, Bookstagrammer, Booktuber, and BookTokker who helped bring the world to Salacious Players' Club.

Thank you. Thank you. Thank you.

About the Author

Sara Cate is a *USA Today* bestselling author of contemporary forbidden romance. Her stories are known for their heart-wrenching plots and toe-curling heat. Living in Arizona with her husband and kids, Sara spends most of her time working in her office with her goldendoodle by her side.

Website: saracatebooks.com
Facebook: SaraCateBooks
Instagram: @saracatebooks
TikTok: @SaraCatebooks

Also by Sara Cate